VILLAGE FATE

In Somerset, in Bately-sub-Mendip, Pargeter's doll factory burns down and a man's body is discovered inside. When the missing, elderly factory owner, Edith Pargeter is found drowned in a ditch, village librarian Rosie Redman suspects that Edith's brother, Edgar, was responsible for both Edith's death and that of her sister Edna six months earlier. So Rosie enlists the help of the local reporter, Charlie Walters, to investigate privately. However, her involvement antagonises the police who want them to stop interfering. But would-be-sleuth Rosie continues to throw suspicion on Edgar — despite Charlie's warning that she could be playing a very dangerous game . . .

Books by Jean Saunders
Published by The House of Ulverscroft:

LADY OF THE MANOR
GOLDEN DESTINY
WITH THIS RING
DEADLY SUSPICIONS
A PERFECT MARRIAGE
UNFORGETTABLE

JEAN SAUNDERS

VILLAGE FATE

Complete and Unabridged

ULVERSCROFT
Leicester

First published in Great Britain in 2011

First Large Print Edition
published 2011

The moral right of the author has been asserted

British Library CIP Data

Saunders, Jean, *1932* –
    Village fate.
    1. Women private investigators- -Fiction.
    2. Detective and mystery stories.
    3. Large type books.
    I. Title
    823.9'14–dc22

    ISBN 978–1–4448–0863–6

Published by
F. A. Thorpe (Publishing)
Anstey, Leicestershire

Set by Words & Graphics Ltd.
Anstey, Leicestershire
Printed and bound in Great Britain by
T. J. International Ltd., Padstow, Cornwall

This book is printed on acid-free paper

1

Rosie Redman changed into a slim pair of jeans, cotton shirt and short jacket, brushed her long brown hair over her shoulders and slapped on a bit of lipstick and eye liner. She hardly knew why she bothered. Her relationship with Damien Hall was going nowhere. They both knew it, and she had a sure feeling that this evening was going to be their swan-song. If the small village of Bately-sub-Mendip had thought it charming that the librarian and the local copper were walking out, they could forget it.

She left the house where she lived with her aunt and uncle on the outskirts of Bately and drove her small car towards the pub in the village that sat in a pocket of the Mendip Hills. Lights were already twinkling in the hotch potch of cottages in the lanes, and autumn fires were being lit, from the look of the many curls of smoke reaching up into the evening sky.

With heavy clouds overhead, it was getting dark early tonight. Then Rosie blinked, wondering if she was seeing things, because it wasn't just the lazy smoke of cottage fires that was ascending, but something far bigger. The smell of smoke was suddenly strong in her nostrils, even with the car windows closed.

She was suddenly aware that she could hear crackling too. Where was it coming from? Maybe it was just a farmer burning old stubble, she thought hopefully but it was a bit late in the day for that. Besides, she had left the farming land behind her now, and there was only the valley with the tight-knit huddle of buildings, the church and the pub and the village square ahead.

Even as another possibility entered her mind, Rosie saw a larger surge of smoke, followed by the roar of flames, and then the sound of explosions as the acrid smells became stronger. She pulled her car into the side of the road and scrabbled for her mobile phone. Fire always made her feel sick, reminding her too vividly that it had ended her parents' lives. But she knew what she had to do.

'Damien?' she almost yelled into the phone. 'I'm halfway to the village, and there's a fire somewhere ahead.'

He was at once the brisk, efficient copper. 'I'm on to it. I've called the fire service and it looks as though the old doll factory has gone up. Call your uncle, Rosie, and ask him to get over here in case we need him.'

He had hung up before she could say anything else, and she called her uncle with shaking hands. As the village doctor he might well be needed, she thought sickly. Her heart was beating very fast, seeing how quickly the fire was taking hold. The old doll factory was beyond the village and was little more than a small wooden warehouse that an enterprising businessman had bought for his two elderly spinster sisters whose pride and joy was in the dolls they made. It had begun as a cottage industry, until the brother had seen the potential in it.

Rosie stopped her wittering thoughts as she heard her uncle's voice and she quickly relayed Damien's message.

'I'm going to see if I can help,' she finished.

'No, don't go anywhere near it, Rosie. It could be dangerous,' he said urgently.

She closed her mobile without giving him an answer. Nothing was going to keep her away from the action. She might be able to help, or she might be a firsthand witness and find out what had caused the fire. The regional newspaper would be glad of a story, especially if she sent in photos on her mobile. Her addiction to crime and mystery novels had already set her nerves jumping with anticipation.

As long as there were no bodies . . . her

heart gave a sickening jolt at the thought, not only because of the two elderly ladies who had always loved their doll-making, but because of the terrible personal memories it evoked of anyone being burned to death. Unavoidably, her mind flew back to another horrific time.

She had always admired her parents' guts, even if even now, she could still remember how prickly and resentful and abandoned she had felt when they had upped and gone to Africa to be missionaries when she was only eleven years old. She had been cheated of most of her childhood with them, and as the only child in the doctor's house, she had spent much of her early years avidly reading their letters while absorbing Tarzan books and creating her own imaginary life for her parents.

On bad days she had seen them being eaten by cannibals; then sometimes seeing her beautiful mother whisked away by some handsome African chief and making her his captive slave, with her father being incredibly brave and rescuing her from her jungle prison. And on really good days she would imagine them coming home very rich after saving some other African chief from certain death, and Rosie would want for nothing.

The images frequently got mixed up in her fertile mind, until the day when the cruel telegram came to tell her they were never coming home, and she would be living at the doctor's house in Bately-sub-Mendip permanently.

She forced the memories away, because that was then, and this was now, and something terrible was happening here. Her sense of community duty made her squash her fears, and she drove on through the village to where she could see that the doll factory was completely ablaze.

She was so stunned at the sight that she couldn't get out of the car for a moment, and she sat with her hands gripping the steering-wheel. Even from here the heat was intense, and the noise was deafening. There would have been many tins of paint and glue, and other inflammable and combustible materials inside, Rosie realised, and it had gone up like a tinder-box.

It was a dreadful accident . . . if it *was* an accident. The thought was in her head before she could stop it.

There had been talk of it being taken over by some outsiders, but why any big firm would want such a tin-pot little operation was beyond Rosie. But what if the fire wasn't an accident? What if it was deliberate? Sabotage,

5

perhaps? But who would ever do such a thing?

It was Edith who had once confided in Rosie that her brother wanted her and Edna to agree to a takeover, which would bring them in a profit and leave them free to enjoy the leisure time they deserved at their age. The sisters had become so upset at the thought that he had never mentioned it again, and Edith had said indignantly that no man could understand the satisfaction they got both from making their dolls and still feeling useful.

Rosie quickly dismissed the idea of a crime being involved here, not wanting to think of anything so awful. Instead, as she heard the sound of the fire engine siren from somewhere in the distance, she continued to sit as if frozen, thinking about the last time she had seen one of the doll ladies.

It was only yesterday, Edith Pargeter's usual Friday visit to the library for her weekly fix of romances. She and her sister had always come together until poor old Edna had died from a heart attack some months ago. Rosie liked both of them enormously, despite the fact that half the village thought them weird and wacky, and without ever meaning to, she had become something of a confidante, especially since on Fridays the library remained open until seven in the evening, and there always seemed more time to chat.

Once, when the sisters both had 'flu, Rosie had taken a stack of library books to their cottage for them, and it was like stepping back in time. In between spluttering and coughing, they had kept Rosie there for ages, telling her about their dolls and the personal names they had given them, as if they were their babies, and adding that nobody listened to their nonsense the way Rosie did.

They were never going to compete with Barbie or suchlike, and nor did they try, but they had a small clientele who liked their old-fashioned style. It had hit Edith hard when Edna died, but the brother, Edgar, much younger than them and a hard-headed businessman, had taken charge and tried to persuade Edith then to sell the factory. But how could she? Rosie had thought indignantly, when it was her life?

Edgar had been so kind then, caring for Edith and seeing to everything that needed to be done after Edna's death. Edith had clung to him pathetically, and the whole village had had new respect for the brother who seemed such an unlikely relative for the two gentle sisters.

Rosie had often wondered what weirdo parents had given their offspring the names of

Edgar, Edith and Edna? It sounded like a music-hall act . . . although any trio less like a music-hall act it was hard to imagine.

She heard a car draw up alongside her, and her uncle Bernard leaned out of the driving-side window.

'Keep out of the way, Rosie, and leave this to the professionals,' he shouted, having to do so because of the pandemonium going on ahead of her now, as people came rushing out of their homes and alleyways to take in the horrific scene ahead.

'No, I'm going to see what's happening,' she said.

Before he could say anything more, she had scrambled out of the car and raced to where she could see Damien Hall ordering people to stay back. Bernard gave an oath and drove past her to get as near as he could without endangering anyone. Rosie saw him stride up to the firemen who had arrived remarkably quickly on the scene, and were vainly trying to stop the blaze. As soon as she reached Damien, she clutched his arm.

'Was anyone in there?' she gasped. 'Has anyone checked on Edith?'

'I knocked on her door earlier, but there was no answer. It doesn't mean anything, Rosie. You know how deaf she is, so she's probably out for the count, and everybody knows she never answers the door at night.'

'I know that she and Edna often liked to go the factory in the evenings to work on their dolls, so I hope that's not what happened tonight. I'll try the cottage again if you like.' Rosie stuttered, resisting the comment that they also liked to talk to their 'babies', knowing how daft it sounded, and not wanting to reveal any more of the sisters' eccentricities. It might be endearing to some, totally barmy to others.

As she twisted away from him, he let her go, knowing he couldn't stop her, and she ran all the way to Edith's cottage in Butcher's Lane. It was never locked. The sisters themselves always said that nobody would want to steal anything from two quaint old ducks like them.

Rosie went inside, wrinkling her nose for a moment at the sweet, musty smell of an old person's house. She was familiar with the downstairs rooms from the one time she had been here with the library books, and urged to drink a concoction of herbal tea that was supposed to be curing them of the 'flu. The sisters had been wrapped up in blankets then, curled up on their armchairs and refusing to give in by taking to their beds, but still ready to make her some tea, she remembered, with a catch in her throat.

There were knick knacks everywhere, with hardly a surface uncovered, and the thought flashed through Rosie's head that whoever had to clear this out eventually would have a hell of a time. On the mantelpiece above the fireplace there were photos of Edna and Edith themselves, and also many photos of their dolls in their old-fashioned, Laura Ashley-print dresses.

Rosie shook off a mild sense of hysteria and made a mental note to keep any future home of her own as uncluttered as possible. And then she forgot such emotive things as she called Edith's name as loudly as she could. There was no answer, so maybe she had gone to bed early, Rosie thought desperately. In any case, as Damien said, she was so very deaf that she needed people to really shout in her ear to make themselves heard.

Tentatively, Rosie went up the stairs, her heart in her mouth, praying that she would find Edith snoring away happily. She knocked on each of the bedroom doors, but when there was still no reply, she gingerly opened each one and looked inside. Neither of them had been occupied. Well, Edna's wouldn't have been, she thought, her jitters coming thick and fast now, and it was obvious that Edith's bed hadn't been slept in.

The presence of several dolls on each bed,

gazing up from their inanimate faces and wide eyes, made her feel slightly nauseous, and she ran downstairs again to where some of the neighbours were gathering outside, anxious and speculating wildly.

'Is she in there?' one of them shouted to Rosie.

She shook her head, her heart still pounding as the implications flooded in.

'The brother will need to know what's happened,' another one put in. 'He'll be cut up if old Edith's gone as well.'

'Wonder what he'll do with the cottage.'

As the mumbling and discussion continued, it got ever more ghoulish in Rosie's opinion, but she didn't stay around to hear any more. The brother was not high on her list of priorities right now. The fire was lighting up the night sky, and she could see the firefighters illuminated against it as they made a valiant effort to put out the flames, but with an old timber building that had seen better days, it seemed like a hopeless task.

Damien was suddenly at her side as she stood, mesmerised with horror, hardly registering the various comments of people all around her. He grabbed her arm and pulled her aside.

'She's not at home, so do you have any news of her?' she blurted out, her heart sinking at the sight of his drawn face.

'They've found something. It looks like old Miss Pargeter was in there, but they can't be sure.'

'Why not?'

But even as she said it, she knew why not. The fire had been so fierce it would have been difficult to get near it at all at first. There would surely have been little left of anybody caught up in such an inferno, especially a bewildered old lady who never moved very fast, and probably wouldn't have heard that anything was wrong until it was too late. With mounting horror she tried not to imagine Edith's reaction when she realised what was happening, and yet somehow she knew.

She would have tried to save her babies, those pudgy-faced little dolls in their crinoline frocks that had become her life, and even more so since Edna had died and she had become the sole supporter of her make-believe family.

As the crazy thoughts swept through Rosie's head she wondered if she was going as batty as Edith. But Edith hadn't been mad. Like her sister, she was just a lovably eccentric, old-fashioned woman with a passion and a skill for her craft, despite her years. The fact that it had brought a certain

12

amount of fame and fortune in the latter part of both their lives had been a bewildering bonus neither sister had ever expected — nor really wanted.

She shook herself, recalling what one of the neighbours had said.

'Her brother must be told, Damien,' she urged him.

'Nobody knows where he lives, except that it's Bristol, do they?'

'No, but I think Edith kept a little book of phone numbers by the side of the telephone,' Rosie said. 'It's sure to be in there.'

'It'll be the quickest way to contact him, rather than searching through the phone book. Can you bear to go back and see if you can find it?' he said.

Rosie's heart jumped. It had been one thing to go to the cottage hoping to find Edith asleep in her bed. It was something else to be looking for the phone number of a relative, believing the owner of the cottage to be dead.

'God, I can't speak to him,' she said in a panic.

Damien spoke shortly. 'That's not your job. Just get me the phone number and leave it to us, Rosie. Your uncle will be here for a while yet, I imagine, and he'll be able to tell you whatever news there is, so once you've got that number for me, you might as well go home. Too many onlookers only make it more difficult for us to do our job.'

Well, there was no chance of that! She had no intention of being sent home. Their date that evening was obviously abandoned, and she didn't know why she even thought about it — or cared.

She fled back to the cottage before she could fall to pieces completely. Damien had sounded so efficient and cold and professional. It was how such people had to be, of course, no matter what awful jobs they had to do or whatever they found in the course of their work. It was how *she* should be now.

How would she behave if she was a detective on the trail of a missing relative? In this case, Edgar Pargeter. She would be sharply efficient too, putting all other emotions aside. Not that Edith was strictly missing, just not available at the scene of the crime. If there even *was* a crime, she amended hastily. But if there was, a relative was often the first suspect and had to be found.

However bizarre and unreal it sounded, it made it easier on Rosie's nerves if she could think that way. Pretend that none of this night's event was actually happening, and that she was a private eye in a mystery novel, checking out all the available facts. She took a deep breath, steadied her racing heartbeats and went back to Edith's cottage to look for the little notebook by the telephone.

2

Edgar Pargeter was spending an evening in a noisy Bristol restaurant with some contemporaries, although lording it over them as usual might be a better description. He was a small, stocky man, but like many small men, he took refuge in having a booming voice and what he considered a personality to match. When his mobile phone rang the polite thing to do would be to leave the table and take the call in private, but Edgar had never been politically correct, and he barked his name into the phone at once.

'What's that you're saying? You'll have to speak up. I can't make out head or tail of it, man.'

He held up his hand, and the three other people around the table stopped talking. They saw his face change as he listened to the voice on the other end, and glanced at one another. Pargeter could be ruthless and uncompromising when anything got in his way, and rarely got phased by anything, but something had obviously got to the wily old bugger now.

'You think it must have started some time ago,' he repeated, as if momentarily dazed, and needing to say it again to let the words sink in. 'So is it completely burnt out or can it be salvaged? Has my sister been informed?'

One of the men at the table smothered a small snigger. Although they had never met them, they all knew about Pargeter's crazy sisters and the hobby that had turned out to be moderately successful. Some thought that the fact that he continued to indulge them was about the one saving grace about the man.

Then they saw him close down his phone and that his face had blanched.

'What's happened?' he was asked quickly.

His voice was hoarse with shock. 'It's the effing doll factory. It's been burnt to the ground, and they think my sister was in it.'

'Bloody hell, Pargeter. What are you going to do?'

He got to his feet, visibly trying not to sway. 'What do you think I'm going to do?' he almost snarled. 'I'm going to Bateley-sub-Mendip to find out the bloody truth of it, that's what. And if somebody was responsible for this, I'm going to kill the bugger.'

They watched him blunder out of the restaurant, almost knocking a waiter out of the way without apology, and muttered among themselves.

'If he drives down there in that state, he'll

probably end up killing himself,' one of his dinner acquaintances commented half-heartedly

'One of us should offer to drive him.'

'Or get him a taxi.'

'Or order another bottle of wine on his expenses and let the almighty Pargeter deal with it in his own freaking control freaking way.'

★　★　★

While Rosie was finding the notebook in Edith's cottage, her eyes were starting to blur. There was no way she could continue thinking of herself as a character in a mystery novel when this was all too real. She was still fumbling with the book when she heard the door open. Her heart jumped violently and then flooded with a tiny feeling of hope.

It had to be Edith! May be she hadn't been in the factory this evening. If there had been a body there, maybe it hadn't been hers but an intruder who had got what he deserved . . . not that anybody deserved to die such a horrible death.

'Uncle Bernard.' She almost wept as she saw the figure come inside.

He strode across to her and took her shaking hands in his.

'Damien shouldn't have sent you here,' he said roughly. 'I know what an ordeal all this must have been to you, and you should go home, Rosie. Aunt Laura will be anxious to know what's going on if she hasn't heard already, and you can tell her I'll be here for a while yet.'

'I can't. I just feel so sad for poor Miss Pargeter. It was her, wasn't it?'

'We don't know yet, but I'm afraid everything points to it being her. There will have to be a formal identification at some stage, even though there probably won't be much left to identify, but forensics can work wonders these days.'

He caught the look of horror on her face and went on quickly. 'Did you find that phone number?'

She handed over the notebook silently. There were very few numbers, indicating how few people the sisters ever contacted, and Bernard quickly dialled Edgar's number on his mobile. The old ladies didn't go in for such new-fangled things as mobile phones, Rosie thought distractedly. Theirs was an old black phone that must have seen service for years.

Well, if it ain't broke, don't fix it . . . She could almost hear Edith saying quaintly in one of her rare down-to-earth moments that

19

had always got Edna chuckling with laughter. She found herself staring at the photos on the mantelpiece, as if willing Edith to come walking through that door right now.

'Did you get hold of him?' she asked her uncle huskily when he finally finished speaking. She hadn't heard a word he said, still bemused by all that had happened and how she had somehow got caught up in it.

'Yes, and it sounded as though he'd either had a lot to drink or he was out at some party or other. I think he understood what I was saying, so I daresay he'll turn up eventually. I met the fellow once and never had much time for him.'

'He was still Edith's brother, though, and I spoke to him a few times when I called to see Edith and Edna. I thought he was all right, and certainly very attentive to them,' Rosie said in his defence, seeing that her uncle seemed infuriated by the call.

'He didn't bother too much about that when he wanted to get the pair of them sectioned a couple of years ago. And you never heard me say that, Rosie, so just forget it.'

Her mouth had dropped open in shock at his words. Her uncle was normally so strict about patient confidentiality, but since Edgar Pargeter wasn't his patient she presumed it didn't count.

'He wanted to get them sectioned?' she squeaked.

She was glad when he started to leave, and she followed him quickly. The cottage was very small, and the heavy furniture crowded it even more, and she was thankful to get out of the oppressive atmosphere and go outside. Her uncle went on talking briefly.

'It was for their own good, Pargeter said, because he was worried that they were going a bit doolally. And before you start reading anything into that, Rosie, I was satisfied that it was no more than a concerned query. We all know they weren't daft, just a bit vague, but to the rest of the village they'd always been the same so it was nothing new. Pargeter said he was afraid they'd taken on more than they could cope with when they got more orders for their dolls, and it made him feel guilty that he'd set them up in the factory in the first place.'

'Well, that shows that he had their interests at heart, doesn't it?'

Bernard shrugged. 'Maybe. I suppose he didn't like the thought of two elderly ladies still working or that some unscrupulous people might take advantage of them and steal their ideas. He thought they'd be better off out of it.'

'Their dolls were unique, so what would be

the point of that? He could always have got a lawyer involved if that ever happened.'

And this was a pointless conversation, she thought wildly. Nor did she want to think of anything so awful as the two Misses Pargeter being put away or other people taking over their business. She shuddered.

'I think I will go home after all.'

'Good. Tell your aunt that I'll be back when I can. Things will need to be sorted out here first, though it's possible we won't be able to move the remains until morning. It's far too hot to get near anything as yet, and the firefighters have still got a hell of a job to do.'

Rosie felt sick at the thought. Any idea that this might have been more than a tragic accident was farthest from her mind now. In fact, all she wanted was to go home and do something very ordinary — maybe turn on the TV and watch some crappy game show — anything to take her mind off what had happened here tonight. As she and her uncle left Butcher's Lane she walked back quickly to the side of the road where she had parked her car.

She didn't want to talk to anybody, least of all to Damien who would be full of his own importance by now. She kept her head down low, and had almost reached her car when she heard somebody called her name. She recognised it at once as her boss, Norman Youde, and knew she wouldn't get away that easily.

'Rosie, hang on a minute. People are saying that old Miss Pargeter was in the factory tonight. Is it true?'

He was such an old woman, she thought. His voice was part hushed, part excited. If ever there was such a thing as a male village gossip — and why not? — then Norman was it.

'It's probably true,' she said briefly. 'At least as far as anybody can tell. Her brother will have to identify her.'

'Poor devil. I wouldn't want to be in his shoes, losing both his sisters in a matter of months. I suppose the factory belongs to him now, but it always did, didn't it? The old girls made no secret of the fact that he bought it for them, and thought he was wonderful to do it, but I daresay it always had his name on the deeds. I hope he had it well insured.'

'I should think that's the last thing on his mind right now,' Rosie snapped. 'He'll be too upset and shocked.'

'All the same, you've got to be practical, haven't you? No, he'll be thinking of insurance money as well as grieving, you mark my words. I bet he had his sisters

23

insured as well, them being so much older than he was. He'll have copped a packet when poor old Edna died, and I suppose they'll pay out for Edith as well as the factory.'

'I don't want to listen to any more of this. The poor lady's died a horrible death and all you can think about is insurance money!'

She wrenched open the door of her car and slid inside, pulling it shut behind her. She switched on the engine while Norman was still talking, and backed away from him, leaving him standing in the middle of the road. Boss or no boss, she'd had enough of hearing him speculating on insurance money and picking over the facts like some goddamned ghoul.

Her eyes were still blurred, but with anger and distress now. She had really liked the Pargeter sisters. With their old-fashioned style, and their refusal to keep up with modern-day trends, they were the epitome of what English life used to be like, and now they were both gone.

She drove around aimlessly for half an hour before she could compose herself enough to go back to the house and relay all that she knew to her aunt. She had no doubt that Laura would be waiting for her return, having heard the news briefly when she phoned her uncle earlier. But she was shocked to realise it was nearly midnight, and that the entire evening had somehow disappeared. Her aunt greeted her anxiously.

'What's the news, Rosie?'

She opened her mouth to speak, and to her horror she simply burst into tears. Some private eye she'd be, the inane thought skidded through her head, if she couldn't cope with her first case of losing a client . . . She dragged her thoughts together and spoke in a shaky voice.

'The factory is completely burnt out, and they've found something inside, though they can't be sure who or what it is yet, since the heat is too intense to recover it.' She recited some of the words Damien had told her without even registering that she had heard them. 'It seems that Miss Pargeter was probably at the factory tonight though, since her bed hasn't been slept in.'

'Oh, that's really worrying. It'll be a tragedy if its true, but it'll certainly put Bately on the map, and not for any good reason.'

'I know,' Rosie said quickly. 'We may even get a TV crew down here. It would be local news, whether it was simply a tragic accident or something more. It may not be as simple as it looks — if you can call a fire and a death simple.'

'Like a murder, you mean,' her aunt

commented. 'I know the way your mind works, so don't start thinking of anything more sinister, Rosie.'

'No, I mean I hope the publicity doesn't happen. The last thing Miss Pargeter and her sister would want is for their way of life to be splashed all over the TV and mocked. They were very private people, and the way they lived was nobody's business but their own.'

'To the outside world they would be a novelty,' her aunt pointed out, trying to calm her. 'They were very close to one another, always together, and they never seemed interested in men. People will find their quaintness interesting, I'm afraid.'

Rosie was angry now. 'I don't want to even think along those lines. Have you tried the local radio?' she said. 'They might have got wind of it by now.'

A brief report on local radio wouldn't be too bad, but apart from the Pargeter sisters, most people in Bateley would hate to have their lives disrupted by the invasion of TV crews and the like. It wasn't their style. The annual village summer fete was their style.

Laura turned on the radio and they had to wait for a pause in the usual music and chat transmission before the local announcer gave a brief mention to what had happened here tonight.

'Fire engines were called out when Pargeter's doll factory in the small village of Bately-sub-Mendip went up in flames tonight from an as yet unknown cause,' said the dispassionate voice. 'It is feared there may have been one casualty, but no other news will be available until it has been further investigated. And now for some late football results.'

Rosie bit her lip: Just like that. It was Saturday night, of course. A woman's death was reported and dismissed, and then came the football results with hardly a change in the announcer's tone. Not that they had mentioned a death, nor Edith's name. They were being cautious, and rightly so.

'Look, Rosie,' Laura said, turning the radio off again. 'Why don't you go to bed? There's nothing we can do, and I'm sure Edith will probably turn up safe and sound tomorrow.'

Rosie's voice was stubborn. 'All the evidence says that she won't, and I'm not going to bed until uncle Bernard gets back with some news. I'd never sleep anyway. I know Edith often went to the factory at night, because she liked the solitude. Since losing Edna she hated being in the cottage on her own though, and she had her dolls at the factory. It had to be her.'

She bit her lip, knowing she had almost

called them Edith's babies, but she didn't want to see her aunt's raised eyebrows at the word, thinking she was as dippy as Edith. She went on determinedly.

'She wasn't at home, so where else could she have been? If it *was* her inside the factory, I hope that since she was so deaf, unless somebody was speaking directly in front of her, that she was unaware of anything until it was too late. I hope she was overcome by smoke long before the fire reached her.'

'And I think you need a drink to steady your nerves,' her aunt said.

Rosie shook her head, realising she was starting to sound hysterical.

'Just coffee would be fine, thanks. I'll make it. It will keep my hands occupied. I know I wouldn't be so upset if it hadn't brought everything back to me about Africa, even if it was ten years ago now. You understand that, don't you, aunt Laura?'

'Of course I do. You were barely sixteen, and a very vulnerable age to have to cope with such a tragedy, my love. Of course I understand. It was our tragedy too, love. Losing his brother and sister-in-law in that awful way was very hard for Bernard to deal with as well.'

'I know. I'm sorry. Of course it was hard for you two as well.'

She gave her aunt a hug, wondering what the hell was wrong with her tonight. Had she become so blinkered by this factory business tonight that she couldn't untangle the two tragedies in her mind?

'I'll make that coffee,' she said in a choked voice.

★ ★ ★

Damien Hall was taking charge of proceedings now and urging the villagers to return to their own homes and let the firefighters get on with their job. It was taking a long time to damp down the flames and to be sure there was no chance of anything re-igniting.

'As soon as there's anything definite to know, you'll be the first to hear of it,' he said in answer to the clamour of enquiries.

Norman Youde was one of those still lingering. 'You're sure it's her, though, aren't you, Constable Hall?'

Damien shrugged. 'As sure as anybody could be, considering it's her factory and she's nowhere else to be seen. How much more proof do you want?'

'Has the brother turned up yet? A big car went through the village a while ago. That was him, wasn't it? What's he got to say?'

Damien glared at him. 'Mr Youde, I know

you consider the library to be the fount of all knowledge, but you'll just have to wait like everybody else for it to be investigated thoroughly.'

'Oh well, I daresay we'll soon be seeing SOCOs and insurance companies and forensics and those kind of people down here then,' Norman persisted,

'Good God man, you're as bad as Rosie. Stick to your books and leave the rest to the professionals,' Damien snapped, finally losing patience.

Truth to tell, his feathers were getting ruffled. This was the biggest thing that had happened in Bateley and he knew his superiors would be arriving at any minute. Youde's mentions of SOCOs and forensics wasn't so far off the mark — if it *was* a crime — which nobody knew as yet. If it was, which he personally doubted, then they would certainly get involved, and he'd just be the village copper who was of little importance. Privately, he thought the dotty old girl had probably got too close to her electric fire, knocked it over and set the place alight and herself with it.

The brother had certainly turned up and was in a right old state. Damien felt sorry for him, having lost both his sisters now, and the factory as well, even though that had probably just been a sideline to him, from the look of his flash car and his expensive clothes and cigars. Having recently given up smoking, Damien had had to grit teeth as the aromatic scent reached his nostrils.

But after some distracted and frantic discussion with the brother, and the news from the firefighters that they would probably be here for most of the night, he and Doctor Redman had finally persuaded Pargeter to go back to the cottage and wait there until they knew anything definite.

What he meant, and what he didn't say, was that when they knew anything definite would be when the body was taken to the morgue and he would be called on to identify it — if he could. It promised to be a gruesome task, and Damien didn't envy him the job. The poor sod had definitely looked broken up.

★　★　★

Edgar had already drunk more than he should have done that night. He knew that, but all the same, as he closed the cottage door behind the doctor he reached in his overcoat pocket for the flask of whiskey he always carried, and took a long draught. Edith and Edna never kept spirits in the house except

31

for a small bottle of brandy at Christmas, and he guessed there would be nothing here worth drinking, anyway. He certainly needed something to steady his nerves. It had been a bugger of an evening so far, and it was far from over yet.

He looked around the room distractedly as if he was seeing it for the first time. The muddle of magazines his sisters never liked to throw out; the dozens of ornaments on every surface; the photos on the mantelpiece alongside the photos of some of their precious dolls, staring back at him with their wide, unblinking eyes.

His own red-rimmed eyes watered. His old girls, as he often referred to them, were like two peas in a pod, and he had sometimes thought that some of their effing dolls resembled them in a far too weird and creepy way.

He knew very well that they had thought of the dolls as their babies, and although he had indulged them in their odd little ways, he had privately scoffed to himself about that. But his girls had been the last of his family, and in their own wacky way, he supposed the dolls had been his family too . . .

Christ Almighty, that was the last way he wanted his thoughts to go! He shook himself, telling himself not to be so bloody stupid. If

Edith was gone, the last thing he needed was to seem as if he had gone off his rocker and sent off to the funny farm. He needed to keep his head straight. There was work to be done.

Once the formalities were over there would be things to organise. He remembered how hysterical Edith had become when they had found Edna, and he had been the one to calm her and to try to organise things.

No matter how bad the grief, the mechanics of death had to swing into operation as soon as possible. In a horrible way it helped, because you couldn't just walk away and pretend nothing had happened. Rituals had to be observed, and so they did now. His churning brain ran through the list of necessities just as it had done after Edna's death. A funeral. A will reading. Insurance claims.

The small bureau. That was where his sisters had kept all their important papers. Everything would be in there, no matter how chaotic. Somewhere there would be a Will and the Insurance policies. Edith had found Edna's with no trouble, but then, their minds worked in similar ways, however jumbled they might all seem to outsiders, while his was allegedly more businesslike. Right now, he felt anything but capable, and as he yanked down the bureau door the clutter of envelopes and papers and old newspaper cuttings burst out and onto the floor. He cursed aloud, and found himself apologising just as loudly to his girls, who disapproved of bad language.

'Christ, I really am going mad,' he muttered, glancing half-fearfully around the room as though he expected the two sisters to be sitting there tut-tutting.

'You can't get at me now,' he said more loudly, glaring at their photos on the mantelpiece. 'I'm not your little brother any more, you silly bitches.'

He hadn't meant to call them that, but the silence in the cottage was starting to get to him now. He took another deep swig from his whiskey bottle and felt the room sway. This was no good. He needed to hold himself together for what was to come. His thoughts swerved in another direction. He'd only ever seen one dead body, and that was Edna's, and he and Edith had coped with that together. Edna hadn't looked too good when she'd had the heart attack, of course, alone in her bed and unable to reach her pills.

Edith was so deaf she hadn't even heard her gasping and calling, but she'd been pathetically glad he had been staying with them for a few days when it happened even if he'd just popped out to the pub for a couple of hours.

And later, when Edna had been laid out in the coffin in her bedroom, wearing one of her favourite flowery dresses, he had indulged Edith's comment that she had looked just like one of their babies, and had insisted on putting several of them in the coffin with her to accompany her to the other side.

'*Creepy little sods,*' he said almost savagely, unsure whether he meant the dolls or his sisters.

He bent to pick up the majority of the papers and envelopes that had fallen to the floor and knew he'd need to spend some time going through them. Grief was a funny thing, he conceded. It hit you like a bucket of concrete at first, and then you got used to it. Accepted it. Almost revelled in it. And finally got what you could out of it. Both Edna and Edith had thought the sun shone out of his backside if they'd ever been undignified enough to say so. They wouldn't want him to suffer unduly at their loss. They'd want him to recover, get on with his life, benefit in any way that he felt able. Which meant the insurance money on Edith, the factory and the sale of the cottage.

Bloody hell, he'd soon get rid of this place, he thought with a shudder. It reeked of his old girls, not in a bad way, but in every effing corner. Everywhere he looked he could see them. Every creak in the old floorboards made him imagine he could turn around and one of them would be offering him herbal tea or their home-made onion soup that always gave him the squits.

If he glanced towards the stairs, he could imagine Edna walking downstairs, holding on to the banister while she clumped down with her gammy leg. If he looked back at the door he could imagine he saw the handle turning slowly, and that at any minute now Edith would be walking inside and asking him accusingly what had happened to her babies . . . as if he could have had anything to do with it . . .

His heart was suddenly pounding hard with an excruciating physical pain. Perhaps he was the next one to be having a heart attack. Sod's law. For a minute he thought he was going to vomit. It wasn't an illusion. It was an effing nightmare. The door handle *was* starting to turn and somebody was coming inside the cottage. Oh God, *Edith* . . .

The next thing he knew somebody was holding a glass of water to his lips and urging him to drink slowly. Bloody water! He didn't want bloody water. He just wanted to get up off the floor where he had hit his head and get the hell out of there before any more ghosts came to haunt him.

'Take your time,' he heard the voice say again.

He slowly registered that it wasn't Edith's voice. It was a man's voice. He'd heard it before. He opened his eyes fearfully.

'You've had a shock,' Doctor Redman said. 'Well, more than one tonight, of course. But when you fell you took a nasty knock on your head and you've suffered a slight concussion. There's no way you can drive home tonight, Mr Pargeter, especially since you've obviously had quite a bit to drink. I strongly advise you to stay here until morning.'

'I can't!' Edgar said in panic. 'My sisters!'

'That's what I came to tell you. At least there's one small piece of good news tonight, although it's far from good news for somebody.'

'I don't understand,' Edgar said, feeling more befuddled than ever.

The bloody doctor was still holding his wrist and taking his pulse, no matter how he tried to shake him off. What good news was this? That Edith had somehow crawled out of the factory and survived? The idea was so impossibly ludicrous he almost felt like laughing. Almost.

'It's fairly certain that the body in the factory is that of a man, Mr Pargeter,' he heard the doctor say, and then he tasted the bile gurgling up in his throat before he passed out again.

3

Charlie Walters heard the tail end of the announcement on his car radio about Pargeters' doll factory going up in flames. His reporter's ear immediately sensed a story, and even though he really needed to get a good night's sleep, he swerved away from the main road at once and headed across country towards Bately-sub-Mendip. He knew vaguely where it was, and he could have found it easily enough in daylight, but in the dark the narrow roads criss-crossing the Mendips could easily confuse, and in the end he pulled into the side and alerted his sat nav, praying that the ruddy thing wouldn't send him halfway around the county before it got him there.

As it happened, he hadn't needed it. The sky was lit up with a fierce orange glow long before he arrived, and he could hear the sound of fire engines and sirens. By the time he got there it seemed as though the entire village had turned out, and he pushed his way through to where a middle-aged guy was holding court to a small group.

'Bad business,' he said casually, knowing that a brash announcement that he was a reporter could make them clam up. 'What's the latest?'

Norman Youde turned at once, sensing a fresh audience.

'Nobody knows what happened yet, but they say there's a body in there all right. Probably the old lady who owns the place since she's not been seen all day. You new around here?'

'I heard something on the radio and saw the flames,' Charlie said non-committally. 'A doll factory, it said. Did you know the old lady then?'

Norman warmed to his task. 'Everybody knew Miss Pargeter. Knew her sister too before she died — well, as much as anybody really knew them,' he amended. 'They didn't mix much and they should have retired long ago. It's said the factory was really owned by their brother, but the sisters worked there and made their dolls together until the first one died. Funny little things they were.'

'The sisters or the dolls?' Charlie said.

Norman hooted, then quickly stopped. 'Sorry, not the time to be laughing, but you could say it applied to both. They were an old-fashioned pair and none would deny it, but I meant the dolls, of course. Still, they seemed to sell a few so some people must have liked them.'

Charlie decided it was time to come clean. He fished out his card and handed it over. 'Look, whatever the outcome here, I'd be interested in knowing more about these ladies, and I know my readers would too — from the human interest angle, you understand.'

Norman's eyes narrowed. A reporter, eh? He might have guessed, not that they got many of them down here where nothing of any interest happened. But he looked a decent enough young man and if it took something like this to put Bately on the map, well, all was fair in love and death, hee hee. He sniggered to himself at his own pun, then sobered.

'You want to talk to my assistant, Rosie Redman, if you want to know more about the Pargeter sisters,' he said at last. 'I'm the chief librarian here, and she was very fond of the old girls, and they always liked a chinwag with her. I think she's gone home now, but the house is outside the village at the other end. You can't miss it. She's the doctor's niece and the doc's around somewhere. So's the Pargeter brother, but I haven't seen either of them for a while.'

'Thanks. You've been a great help.'

He got away from the man before he launched into another long spiel, sensing that he'd be the village gossip. In his job it helped to memorise people by labelling them in his mind. He registered the name of Rosie Redman, who'd probably be as much of an old gossip as her boss, but he needed to see what was happening at the scene of the fire before he did anything else. There was plenty of activity, and he spoke to a tall chap he guessed could be the village copper from the way he was organising keeping people well back.

'Any news?' he asked. 'Charlie Walters, *West Gazette*.'

Damien scowled, and ignored the card he was being handed. Bloody reporters sniffing around and getting in the way. He hated the sods.

'Nothing yet.'

There was, but he wasn't telling. It wasn't definite, anyway, and the doc had been very cagey when he'd gone off to speak with Edgar Pargeter. There was a body, but the identity was still to be confirmed, and until it was, he wasn't telling any snot-nosed reporter. In his opinion it had to be Edith Pargeter. Who else could it have been? He turned back to the reporter to make some sharp remark, but he had already disappeared. Good riddance too.

Charlie approached the firefighters, keeping well away from the direction of the flames. The heat was searing, and he felt a sharp pity for whoever had been in the middle of that inferno. It was a small place as factories went, but presumably it had contained a lot of inflammable stuff. Nobody made any attempt to speak to him, and in any case it would have been hard to start a conversation in the midst of so much noise.

He decided to abandon this line of enquiry, and until there was any definite information about the identity of the dead person, he decided to follow up his one bit of information and go for the human interest angle. Rosie Redman had known the Pargeter sisters, and he had already gleaned from the librarian's words that they were an odd pair, so he would gen up on them first. Harsh as it sounded, a dead body was a dead body, but it was what had gone on in their lives previously that usually made the most newsworthy story, and *Gazette* readers relished human interest stories.

But before all that, he was going to find the local pub and see if they had a room for the night. There was no way he was driving back to his flat tonight while all this was hot news. The story could be cold by morning, and in any case other hacks would probably be on the scene by then. It could be hours before they got the body out and then it would be taken off to the morgue to be examined and try to decide on the cause of death. He guessed it would be pretty obvious. Death by smoke inhalation and burning. He'd seen one or two in his time and it wasn't pretty. He didn't envy those people their jobs. Some might say that his was an intrusive and objectionable one, but people liked to know the facts and somebody had to provide them.

He booked his room and then drove off to find the doctor's house. He'd had a heavy night and he was dog-tired, and he was starting to feel dubious about coming to question the doctor's niece now. It was well past midnight and the occupants may have gone to bed, but with all the excitement in the village he doubted it. If the house was all in darkness he'd give it up, but light was streaming out from the downstairs rooms, so before he could change his mind he strode up to the front door and rang the bell.

★　★　★

A slender vision with long dark hair and huge blue eyes answered the door. She was wearing jeans and a white shirt so she hadn't gone to bed yet. He hadn't known what to expect. After his brief chat with the bloke in the village he just knew it hadn't been somebody who looked more like a model than a librarian. And that was bloody stereotypical if anything was. Charlie cleared his throat.

'Are you Rosie Redman?' he said, annoyed to find his voice was thick.

'Yes. Who are you? Has Damien sent you — or my uncle? What's happened? Have they found Miss Pargeter?' He heard her voice flutter at the mention of the name.

'Who is it, Rosie?'

As an older woman appeared behind her, Charlie felt ridiculously nonplussed. For somebody always on top of any situation the feeling was unreal and more than annoying. It made him sharper than he intended.

'Look, I'm really sorry to bother you at this time of night, and I don't know anything more than you do about Miss Pargeter, I'm afraid. I'm a reporter on the *West Gazette*, and I've driven down here from Bristol after hearing the item on the radio.' Another card was thrust towards them. 'I was told by the librarian in the village that Miss Rosie Redman might be able to tell me more about the Pargeter sisters as I'd really like to do a human interest story on them. But I can see this is a bad time, so perhaps I could come back tomorrow. I'm staying at the pub tonight.'

He had begun to feel hellishly bad and

more than stupid, standing on the doorstep like this with two faces looking at him so accusingly. He could see the words *bad taste* written all over them, and it probably was.

'You'd better come in, Mr Walters,' Laura said after a quick glance at his card. 'If you've driven all that way you could probably do with some coffee.'

'*Aunt Laura*,' Rosie hissed, but she had no option but to let him inside. Her aunt was too nice for her own good, and would open her door to anybody, she thought in annoyance.

'We've had a coffee pot on the go all night, so my niece will fetch you a cup while you get your breath back, Mr Walters,' Laura went on. 'Come and sit down. It's a cold night.'

'Not in the village, it isn't,' he said before he could stop to think, and then chewed his lip. What a bloody insensitive thing to say. In a tight-knit community like this one, everybody probably knew everybody else, and they would all be upset over what had happened. He should have stayed at the pub and got some info from the landlady. But Rosie Redman had apparently known the Pargeter woman better than most, and one more look at her heart-shaped face and he knew he wasn't sorry he had come.

He swallowed hard, looking down at his shoes and wondering what in God's name was happening to him. Too many beers with his mates tonight, and then the radio news item and rushing down here on a whim was making him light-headed. It was a hell of a long time since he'd had any food to soak up the beer too. And now there was this vision who was glaring at him with dislike written all over her as she handed him a cup of coffee.

'This isn't a good time, Mr Walters,' Rosie said in an icy voice.

'Please call me Charlie.'

'Miss Pargeter was a very private person, Mr Walters, and I know she wouldn't want her private life scattered all over the newspapers for people to gawp over. *Nobody* with any integrity would,' she added pointedly.

'You know the *West Gazette*, do you? We're not a national paper nor a scandal rag, Miss Redman, and nor do we do kiss and tell stories. We're local, we're interested in local people, and whatever we say about them we say it sympathetically.'

Laura broke in, seeing the sudden clash of personalities. Rosie could be hot-tempered sometimes, and she was also very upset. But this young man didn't seem to be one to suffer fools gladly either, and he was only doing his job.

'It might be best if you came back

tomorrow, Mr Walters,' she said.

'No, it's all right, and I'm sorry,' Rosie said, capitulating. 'I didn't expect anyone to come asking me about Miss Pargeter, that's all. And of course we know the *Gazette*. We read it every week.'

'That's why your face is familiar!' her aunt said. 'You have your photo in it sometimes, don't you?'

'My one small claim to fame, Mrs Redman,' Charlie said with a wry smile, wishing it didn't sound so ruddy fatuous. 'But tomorrow might be better for me too. Can I call back in the morning?'

'Actually, no,' Rosie said quickly, daring him to disagree. 'I'll come down to the pub. I'll want to get the latest news, anyway.'

Before anything else could be said, the front door opened and Bernard Redman came inside. His face was gaunt and strained, and he slumped down on an armchair, blowing out his cheeks as if he had been running.

'Is it as bad as we feared?' his wife asked quickly, seeing that Rosie seemed unable to speak at all now.

He shook his head. 'They've found a body and it's being taken away to the morgue and Damien Hall's already had his nose put out of joint as the big boys take over. But it's not

47

Miss Pargeter. It's a man's body. I've been at the cottage for ages, having a hell of a time calming down the Pargeter brother. Once he heard, he went to pieces, and in the end I've had to sedate him. He'll be out of it for twenty-four hours.'

Rosie was wild with relief, hardly taking in anything but the news she wanted to hear. 'It's not Edith? That's wonderful news, isn't it? I'm sorry for the man, of course, whoever he is, but at least it's not her!'

Bernard didn't look at her. 'Yes, it's good news of a sort, but it opens up all kinds of questions now, and Damien's getting in a right old stew in having the glory taken away from him.'

'What questions?' Rosie said, feeling particularly dense, and dismissing Damien's feelings as being of little consequence compared with everything else. It had been a long night, and all she could think about was that Edith hadn't been burnt to death in her factory with her babies.

'What he means, Rosie,' Charlie Walters suddenly put in, leaning towards her, 'is that if it wasn't your Miss Pargeter, and if she's nowhere to be seen in the village, then where is she? What's happened to her?'

Bernard looked at him sharply. 'I don't know who you are or what you're doing here, young man, but you're right. This appeared to have been a straightforward tragedy, and now it's anything but. Not only have we got an unidentified dead body in the burnt out factory, but we're also having to face the fact that a woman has disappeared.'

Horrified by the truth of his words, Rosie felt the hot tears on her face and blinked them away, not wanting to break down in front of a stranger. Why didn't he leave, anyway? This was becoming a personal tragedy to her, and if poor Edith had disappeared, then where was she? Every mystery novel she had ever read seemed to fizzle into insignificance now, because this was no fictional story. It was real. And she was in the middle of it, because she had known the central figure so well.

Her voice faltered as she tried to think sensibly.

'What was a man doing in the factory?' she said, frowning.

'That's what the police will have to find out,' Bernard told her.

Charlie Walters knew he was getting in the way. He took a quick swig of the cup of coffee he had been given and got to his feet in embarrassment.

'Sorry, but I'm obviously intruding here. I'll see you tomorrow then, Miss Redman, about eleven, if that's convenient.' He addressed Rosie formally, not wanting to antagonise her more.

'At the pub,' she reiterated firmly, and then she remembered her manners and showed him out.

'I'm really sorry,' he said, and pressed his hand over hers for a moment.

Rosie closed the door behind him, not knowing what he had to be sorry for. Edith hadn't been his friend. She hadn't exactly been Rosie's either, except that Rosie had probably been the nearest thing to a friend that Edith had in the village, perhaps in the world.

She took a deep and shuddering breath, knowing she was thinking of her in the past tense. Until her uncle had come home, that had certainly been the way she had been thinking, like everybody else, but now there was hope. Edith hadn't died in the fire, so she had to be somewhere.

And once Edith was found, safe and well . . . but even if she wasn't, there had been an unexplained death at the factory, and presumably the place would be swarming with police and forensic officers, and there were many unanswered questions. In fact, the visit of one lone reporter that evening was going to be the least of their worries. Bately might not have been a metropolis before, and never would be, but it was certainly going to be noticed from now on, and not in a good way, especially if a camera crew was sent down in the interest of a local news story. Poor little Edith, Rosie thought, who never wanted to be exposed as a celebrity, but was likely to be one from now on.

★ ★ ★

Charlie drove back to the pub and coaxed the landlady into making him a plate of sandwiches to settle his gnawing stomach. It seemed that nobody in the village was willing to go to bed yet, and a few diehards were still in the bar. His journalist instinct told him to go and talk to them, but he was so damn tired he wondered if he could make sense of anything they said. Tomorrow would be a better time, but even as he thought it, an old boy with rheumy eyes came sidling up to him as he sat in one corner, and plonked himself down on the opposite chair with a belch and a sniff.

'You a newspaperman? I can smell 'em a mile off. Bert Smith, general repair man and dogsbody. If your sink's blocked I can fix it. If your garden needs weeding, I'm your man. If your old woman's giving you grief, I'll sort

51

her out for you.' He gave a wheezy chuckle as he rattled off his accomplishments.

Charlie decided this was too good a chance to miss.

'You guessed right. Charlie Walters, *West Gazette*. So you knew the Pargeter sisters then.'

Bert snorted. 'Knew 'em, cleared out their attic for 'em, changed light bulbs for 'em, drank their herbal tea with 'em and ran a mile from their lethal onion soup.'

As Bert chuckled again, Charlie doubted that he could run anywhere.

'Tell me about them, Bert.'

'Why? You payin' for this?'

'I might swing to a pint or two. It depends what you've got to tell me. Did you like them?'

'Oh ah, I liked 'em well enough. What's not to like in a coupla old birds who didn't take to everybody but seemed to take to me. I reckon I could have wed one of 'em if I'd been the marryin' kind.'

'Really?'

Bert gave a belly laugh this time. 'Not on your nelly, mate. Them two were like the vestal virgins, if you know your bible.'

'Not intimately. So they didn't like men?'

'Oh, I wouldn't say they didn't like 'em. Just never needed them. The only ones they tolerated were the ones who could do odd jobs for 'em, like yours truly, and their brother. They thought he was the bees' knees all right.' He snorted derisively. 'Nasty piece of work, if you ask me.'

'Oh?' Charlie said, perking up. This was the most pertinent piece of information he had heard yet. But half the time his job consisted of sorting out the gems from the dross.

'How about that pint then?' Bert said. 'It's thirsty work, talking.'

Charlie waved to the landlady who delivered Bert's pint without delay. He was surprised they kept to twenty-four hours opening in a sleepy little place like this, but maybe it wasn't always necessary to stay open all night so they made the most of the custom when circumstances demanded it. Like now.

'Why do you think the brother's a nasty piece of work?' Charlie prompted while Bert made the most of his pint, savouring it slowly.

'He didn't like nobody interfering with his sisters, nor coming into the cottage. I was there fixing some shelves for 'em one time when he turned up, and another time I was clearing out some old junk for 'em, and he always followed me round like a dog sniffing a bone, as if he thought I was going to pinch stuff.'

'I suppose he was only looking out for

them,' Charlie said, wondering if he was wasting his time here after all. So Pargeter didn't like to see Bert in his sisters' cottage. It wasn't much of a crime, and he said as much.

Bert suddenly sniffed louder. 'What's a bloody crime is if somebody got rid of them two old souls, who never did no harm to nobody.'

'There's no evidence to say what's happened to the Miss Pargeter at the factory tonight yet, Bert, so what did the other one die of?'

Bert took another swig of beer, followed by a heftier belch than before.

'Heart attack. She'd had a dicky heart for years and had pills to ward it off, but apparently she'd forgotten to take them to bed with her that night. T'other one's deaf as a post so she didn't hear nothing. Nor did the brother who was staying with 'em — and in any case he was here at the pub for an hour or so, a bit more chatty than usual, so he wasn't even in the cottage when it happened. He went to check on 'em both when he got back and Edna was already dead. It all came out at the inquest.'

'You sound doubtful.'

Bert shrugged. 'Who'd ever listen to me? I didn't like the slimy bloke. He never wanted me fixin' up a small electric fire for them to use in the factory on a cold night, and then he fussed and farted over checking that I'd got the wirin' right. Me, who's always been a dab hand with electrics,' he finished indignantly.

He waggled his beer mug again, and although he'd seemed to be drinking slowly, Charlie was amazed to see how quickly it had been emptied. But he wasn't having any. He'd got enough to think about for one evening anyway, and all he'd really wanted was some information on two eccentric old ladies, not a litany of the brother's faults. But he was becoming interested in the whole set-up here in Bately-sub-Mendip now, and after he'd bade Bert goodnight he spoke to the landlady again.

By now he knew what he was going to do. Since he hadn't been expecting to stay he didn't have a change of clothes or anything else with him, and he didn't fancy meeting Miss Rosie Redman in the morning looking unshaven and smelling of sleep. Not that she was his main concern, he thought swiftly. But she'd looked wholesome and fastidious, even at such a late hour, and he knew he'd feel a slob unless he did something about it.

Besides, this whole situation was more intriguing than it had seemed at first, he thought again. Edith Pargeter was still missing, and he wanted to see things through to the end.

By the time he went to bed he'd arranged to keep the room at the pub for as long as he needed, and he set the alarm on his mobile to wake him up at six-thirty in the morning. Once out of the village, there wouldn't be much traffic about on a Sunday morning across the Mendip roads. It would take him just over an hour to drive back to his flat, have a quick shower and change of clothes, collect everything he needed, including his laptop, and he could be back here well before eleven. He lay down in the unfamiliar bed and forced himself to think of nothing, knowing that if his brain was too active he'd never get even the few hours sleep that he needed, but the last image in his mind was Rosie Redman.

It seemed hardly a moment before his alarm woke him, and he struggled out of bed and back into his clothes, wanting to be back on the road as soon as possible. He could grab a bite to eat and some coffee back at his flat. By now, he was alert to everything he had heard last night, and as he drove away from the village where the smell of burning and ashes was pungent and strong on the air, and a heavy pall hung over the whole area, he was starting to put bits and pieces together.

Nobody had a bad word to say about the Pargeter sisters, so why should Bert Smith have implied that there might have been more to the first death than a simple heart attack? To Charlie's alert ear, that was definitely what he'd been hinting. Why had he been so against the brother, who had apparently had his sisters' care at heart? Most of all, where was the missing sister now, and who was the man who had gone up in smoke in the factory?

Sometimes Charlie wished he'd been a detective instead of a journalist, though there was much that was comparable in the two professions, he always thought. You were always digging and delving into mysteries.

He had a gut feeling that Rosie Redman wasn't going to be satisfied until this particular mystery had been solved either, and he was keen to hear what she had to say later that morning. It spurred him on to drive as fast as he could, so that he could get back to Bately all the quicker.

4

Apart from the usual whiffs of cow dung and other unmentionables, country air was allegedly far healthier than the stuffiness of crowded towns and cities, with the result that there were far more old people than other age-groups in Bately-sub-Mendip.

As soon as the local children were old enough and independent enough, they were off to find pastures new with more job opportunities and more life. The aging population certainly kept Doctor Redman busy.

But today was different. With the discovery of a man's body in the factory and the suspicious circumstances of how it had got there, the police were taking over, and the last thing he saw before coming home was the police wagon and forensic officers and pathologist arriving in preparation for taking the body away. It was out of his hands now and he could get a couple of hours' kip before finding out more.

* * *

Rosie awoke with a throbbing headache of major proportions. She'd hardly been able to

58

sleep at all, worrying over Edith's disappearance, and praying that there would be some
simple explanation. For the life of her, she
couldn't think of one, since Edith never went
anywhere.

For a brief moment she'd thought she
might have been dreaming, but of course she
hadn't. It was no dream, more like a horrible
nightmare, but one that was really happening,
and even from here with her bedroom
window just open, she could smell the acrid
stench of smoke.

She knew she shouldn't take it so much to
heart, but Edith had been such a sweet old
dear, and to think of her dying in that awful
way . . . she shuddered, and then remembered that it hadn't been Edith at all, but
some other poor devil who'd perished in the
fire. It was the only thought to give her a
sliver of hope that Edith might be somewhere
safe after all, but it still kept drumming in her
head that she never ventured far from home
except to the factory.

She catalogued the facts in her mind.
Edith's main sojourn out of her cottage was
to the library every Friday. It was the last
time Rosie had seen her. With a sinking
feeling she realised she could even be the last
person to have seen her, and the thought
made her heart beat uneasily, trying to

remember if there had been any hint in Edith's manner that she might be going somewhere, but there hadn't been anything unusual. As always, she was just full of chat about her dolls and their trademark blue daisy print frocks.

Rosie jumped out of bed, ignoring her rocking head, showered and dressed, and went downstairs for some toast and coffee. Even though it was already well past nine o'clock, only her aunt was up, thanks to the late night they had all had. As memory returned properly, Rosie groaned, remembering that she'd agreed to meet some reporter in the pub.

'How are you feeling?' Laura asked sympathetically.

'Don't ask. Horrible,' she contradicted.

'I'm sure Miss Pargeter will be home by now.'

'You're more sure than I am then! You know she never went anywhere but the factory. No, I'm just praying that nothing bad has happened to her.'

Laura looked at her uneasily. 'You really shouldn't let your imagination get the better of you, Rosie.'

'I call it being logical. If she's not in the cottage and she wasn't in the factory, then she must be somewhere else. But where?'

She was desperate to know that Edith was all right, knowing too how devastated she would be over what had happened to her factory and her babies that had perished inside it.

And if she wasn't careful she'd be going as loopy as Edith, she thought severely. But as long as she kept persuading herself that Edith was going to return to face her burnt-out factory, the more she felt able to cope with it.

Although she hadn't really relished meeting Charlie Walters again, she was glad to leave the house just before eleven o'clock and go to the pub to meet him. She parked in the small car park, to find him already inside, wearing different clothes than last night, and looking fresh and eager for information, which only antagonised her more.

He stood up as soon as he saw her, shook her hand, and offered her a drink.

'Coffee, thank you,' she said pointedly. 'It's a bit early for anything else.'

'Just what I was thinking,' Charlie said with a smile and raised his hand to the landlady who appeared at once with a coffee jug and cups on a tray.

'Thanks, Mrs Gentry,' Rosie said, knowing she was being unnecessarily aloof. She'd agreed to come, so why be so prickly?

''Tis a bad business, my dear, and you'll be

feeling it more than some, I daresay. Terrible to go like that, burnt to a crisp. Fond of old Miss Pargeter, weren't you?'

'I was — I *am*. She's not dead, Mrs Gentry.'

'Well, not as far as we know,' the woman said, moving away.

'We know it wasn't her in the factory,' Rosie said.

But the woman was out of earshot now, and Rosie poured the coffee with less than steady hands.

'There's going to be plenty of speculation from now on, and you'll have to accept that,' Charlie said evenly. Before she could bristle, he went on: 'So why don't we try to forget the trauma of last night for now, while you tell me what you know about these ladies and their doll factory?'

Rosie looked into her coffee cup. She didn't think she'd ever forget the shock of last night, but he seemed genuinely interested, and if it resulted in a feature about the best side of the Pargeters, instead of presenting them as somewhat weird and out of this world, then so much the better.

She had to admit a little later that he was a good journalist. He got the best out of people without seeming to do so. He admired the old ladies for continuing to produce their dolls when most would have retired long ago.

'They called them their babies,' Rosie said without thinking, and then looked at him sharply. 'I shouldn't have told you that, and I'd rather you didn't mention it or people will really think them odd.'

Charlie shrugged. 'Then I won't, even though I think it's rather poignant. Replacing the children they never had, I suppose.'

'I guess so, though I didn't expect you to suss that out.'

'Because I'm a mere man, you mean?' Charlie said with a wry smile. 'Men have feelings too, Rosie.'

'Are you married then?' she said abruptly wondering if this had a more personal meaning.

'Not guilty, m'lud,' his grin was ever wider now. 'Not that I rule it out when I find the right girl.'

She knew when somebody was flirting with her, and this certainly wasn't the time. Nor was she quite sure how she might have replied to that if they hadn't been interrupted. They both looked up as the pub door opened and two suited men walked in, followed by a frowning Damien Hall. He ignored Charlie.

'Rosie, this is Detective Inspector Forster and Sergeant Locke. I told them you knew

Miss Pargeter and they want to interview you.'

'Thank you, Constable,' the DI said firmly. 'We can take it from here.'

Rosie was annoyed to know how nervous she felt as Damien was coolly dismissed. The two police officers sat down beside her and Charlie.

'Don't be alarmed, Miss Redman.' Forster said. 'We just need to ask a few questions. Didn't take you long to get wind of it, Walters,' he said, nodding towards Charlie without expression.

'Do you want me to go?'

'*I* want you to stay,' Rosie heard herself say, and the sergeant gave a slight smile. She sat up straighter and looked at the officers unblinkingly and forced herself to relax. 'What do you want to know, Detective Inspector?'

'Firstly, how well did you know the missing woman?'

'Well, mainly as somebody who visited the library regularly. I know her taste in books, but I doubt that you really want to know how many Barbara Cartlands she's read.'

'This is not a facetious matter, Miss Redman.'

'You don't need to tell me that. Miss Pargeter was a sweet and harmless old lady, and it would be dreadful if anything's happened to her,' she said more passionately.

'Why did you use the word harmless?'

'I don't know what you mean.'

'A man has been found dead in her premises. Her factory has burnt to the ground and she's missing.'

The outrageous assumption that Edith could have had anything to do with the man's death left Rosie gasping. In fact, it was so ludicrous that the next minute she burst out laughing.

'You must be mad to think she had anything to with it!'

'I'm not mad, and it's my job to look at all possibilities,' he said calmly. 'So tell me, did Miss Pargeter have any men friends?'

Rosie closed her eyes in despair for a moment, and then she felt Charlie's hand cover hers.

'It's a reasonable question, Rosie,' he said.

'It's not a reasonable way to ask it,' she snapped. 'It's bullying tactics, and anyone who knew Miss Pargeter would know that neither she nor her sister were involved with men, other than Bert Smith who did odd repairs for them, and their brother. Please don't sully her name by implying anything else.'

Forster's manner changed abruptly. When he smiled he became instantly more human, if only when he chose to be so.

'I'm sorry. I didn't mean to upset you, and I can see that I have. I'm sure their brother's upset too. Were they very close to him?'

'Of course they were.'

'You mention two sisters, so where's the other one?'

Rosie swallowed. 'Edna died from a heart attack some months ago It was very sad, and Edith took it very hard at the time. In fact,' she looked down at her hands, trying to gauge the effect of her words.

'Yes? In fact what?' the DI prompted.

'Well, if it wasn't for her brother and her dolls, I don't think she would ever have got over it. Her brother couldn't be here all the time, but she had her work, and that kept her going.'

She almost said it kept her sane, but she didn't want to put that kind of implication into his head. She was beginning to realise how glad she was of Charlie's warning that words could be easily misconstrued.

Sergeant Locke suddenly looked up from his notebook. 'Wasn't she a bit old to keep on working? An elderly lady like that should have been at home with her cats and her knitting, shouldn't she?'

Rosie's eyes flashed and she heard Charlie give a discreet cough.

'And how sexist is that, Sergeant? Didn't

you ever hear of the Suffragettes? Women do have the right to vote now, you know, and keeping busy with her dolls kept Miss Pargeter's brain alive.'

'Thank you, Miss Redman,' the DI said. 'So we understand that the lady was still a busy and active person. Active enough, perhaps, to strike an intruder who threatened her?'

Charlie spoke sharply. 'How do you expect Miss Redman to answer that? How could she possibly know?'

'I can speak for myself, thank you, Charlie,' she said furiously. 'I know what you're implying now, Inspector, and I won't even answer such a thing. Miss Pargeter was a sweet old lady. I admired and respected her, and that's all you're going to get out of me. If you want to know anything more, you need to ask her brother.'

'I intend to, and of course I'm not implying anything. So tell me what you know about him,' he said, switching the questioning smoothly.

'I can't tell you anything much. He comes down fairly often to see his sisters, well, just Edith since Edna died,' she amended. 'I've met him a few times, and he always seemed very solicitous towards them, and a bit possessive too, I suppose.'

'What do you mean by possessive?'

'Well, Edith used to say he didn't like other people coming to the cottage and bothering them. Not even Bert Smith who I mentioned before, who used to do odd jobs for them, and he's a nice enough old boy.'

'Yes, we'll get around to him later. Do you know what business Mr Pargeter is in?'

'No. It never came up, and I had no reason to ask.'

'Just one more question. It seems you were probably the last person to see and talk to the lady before she disappeared, so what frame of mind was she in?'

'The same as always. She was keen to choose her library books and she always stopped to chat and to ask me what I was going to do at the weekend. Just general chit-chat, that's all. She didn't seem any different from the way she always was.'

'This is all for now then, so thank you for your time, Miss Redman. If I need to speak to you again, I'll know where to find you.'

To her great relief the two men stood up to leave, giving no more than a brief nod to Charlie, but Rosie was shaking after they had gone.

'You did all right, Rosie. Don't let them get to you,' Charlie said.

Her eyes were bright and close to tears as

she spoke. 'It's not that — even though I feel as though I've been interrogated. But didn't you notice that I started to refer to Edith in the past tense? It's as if I've already written her off, and I don't want to believe it. That's what's upset me.'

'You need another strong cup of coffee,' he decided, and he went to the bar to call for the landlady.

She appeared so quickly, Charlie knew she must have overheard what went on. Village gossip again, he thought. It would soon get around that the police had questioned Rosie. She wasn't a ruddy suspect, for God's sake, but he guessed that was how she would be feeling.

'Let's have this coffee and then get out of here. We'll go and see what's happening at the factory site, unless you'd rather not.'

'No. I want to see what's happening,' she muttered. She looked at him, and began to relax a little. 'I'm glad you're here, Charlie. I don't think I'd have wanted to face that alone.'

'Any time.'

She realised the landlady was still hovering when she suddenly spoke up.

'I don't know that old Bert will be pleased if he has to answer any questions, Rosie.'

'I didn't say anything against him, Mrs Gentry.'

'I know you didn't, my dear, but he don't care for bobbies in suits except for them on the telly. Your Damien's one of us, but those other two are enough to put the wind up anybody.'

She left them to their coffee and Rosie took a long draught, glad of the caffeine shot.

'Is that right what she said?' Charlie asked her. 'About the village copper being your Damien, I mean?'

She could have been annoyed by his question, but at least it took her mind off everything else for the moment. She gave a forced laugh.

'We've been seeing one another a few times recently, and to the village that's as good as an engagement.'

'And is it?'

She spread her hands. 'Do you see a ring on my finger?'

'I'll take that as a no then. So I'm not treading on anybody's toes if I say I'd like to see you again after all this is over.'

She hardly knew him, but there were far more serious matters to think about than romance. Even as the word entered her head, she knew how Edith's romantic heart would have been charmed by the thought that a dashing young reporter was interested in courting her favourite librarian. Edith's word, not hers.

'I can't think about any of that now,' she said hurriedly. 'I just want to know that Edith's safe and well, though how she's going to face seeing the end of her factory and all her dolls gone up in smoke, I can't imagine.'

'That's the ticket,' Charlie said, to her surprise. 'You're thinking positively again now. So let's get out of here and get some fresh air before any of the locals come in for their morning pint.'

By the time they left the pub the smoke still hung like a pall over the remains of the factory, where there continued to be plenty of activity going on. Because of all the materials that had been inside, the smell was corrosive and pungent, and people were curious to get as near as was allowed by the police presence. Rosie's heart sank as she saw a small TV crew and camera team just outside the police tape.

From the direction of the church on the far side of the village behind them, they could hear the faint sound of hymn singing, which was creepy and incongruous, considering what had happened here. Although Rosie's parents had been missionaries, she wasn't particularly religious herself, and she couldn't equate with a God who had let this terrible thing happen. Unexpectedly the resentment surfaced that she had felt all those years ago when her parents had gone off to save the children of Africa instead of staying home to look after her.

Charlie heard her draw in her breath and looked at her sharply. 'We don't have to stay if this is too much for you,' he said.

'No, I want to hear what that TV woman is saying,' she replied, pushing the memories away.

A slick woman interviewer was speaking earnestly to camera about the fire, and saying that the cause of it was probably due to a faulty electric fire. She went on to mention the reclusive Pargeter sisters and the dolls in this quaint little village where time seemed to have stood still. As Rosie caught the words she felt herself seethe on the Pargeters' behalf.

'Just listen to what she's saying! She's mocking Edna and Edith, and thank God she didn't know what they called their dolls, or that would have been even worse.'

'Why? What did they call them? Apart from them being their babies, which you already told me. Did they have names for them all as well?'

Rosie suddenly became wary. Charlie was a reporter after all, and part of his stock-in-trade was to charm his way into somebody's confidence so that they gave away more than they should.

'They all had names, that's how they sold them. But I don't like the way that woman is mocking them. I should go and put her right,'

'God, no. That's the last thing you should do, unless you're desperate to get your face on TV.'

'No, thanks very much. Anyway, I think I've had enough for one morning. I'm going home.'

'Have dinner with me tonight,' he said next. 'I'm sure we can find some nice little pub away from prying eyes around here.'

'I don't think so, but thank you all the same.'

'Then I'll see you tomorrow. I want to get some copy on to my laptop tonight anyway. Did I mention that I'm staying in the village for a few days?'

She started to laugh. 'You didn't, but why doesn't that surprise me?'

★　★　★

By the time she reached home she felt like a wrung out rag. She had been unnerved by the police questioning, especially since she hadn't expected it. She supposed she probably *had* been the last person to see Edith, since Edith always used the back lanes to go home from the library. As far as she could remember,

Edith had been perfectly happy and her usual self.

She stifled a sob and went into the kitchen where the succulent smells of her aunt's Sunday lunch preparations were in full swing. Roast beef and Yorkshire pudding and all the trimmings, yummy — and as her uncle frequently said, none of this curry nonsense that half the world seemed addicted to now.

It all looked so normal, and so far removed from the distressing happenings a couple of miles away that without warning Rosie burst into tears in front of Laura's astonished eyes.

'What's happened now, Rosie?' Laura said, her comforting arms going around her niece at once. 'Have they found Miss Pargeter?'

Rosie registered the significance of her words. Everybody assumed the worst. Her aunt didn't ask if Edith had turned up. She asked if they had found her. It was poignant and sad.

'No, they haven't. The police have asked me questions about her and it was horrible. I felt like a criminal.'

Laura looked horrified. 'Surely they didn't need to question you, and certainly not on your own.'

'I wasn't on my own. Charlie was with me. Charlie Walters, the reporter who came here last night. He was a great help, actually.'

Rosie's thoughts were immediately back with the Pargeter sisters. Both of them had favoured an old-fashioned, countrified Laura Ashley style of dress, and their dolls wore frocks in the same dainty prints. She could see why they called them their babies. The babies they never had.

Mechanically, she set the table for Sunday lunch, wondering vaguely what Charlie Walters would be having to eat at the pub. One of Mrs Gentry's meat and potato pies, no doubt, unless she rustled up a Sunday lunch for her customers. They rarely got too busy on a Sunday, but tourists did find their way here. And now, of course, Bately would be soon be on the map, if it wasn't already, which would benefit local traders and the like. A tragedy always lured tourists. It was human nature to be curious. It was why people automatically slowed down on a motorway at the scene of a crash, no matter how ghoulish. She shivered, and then jumped as she heard her uncle's voice behind her.

'Day-dreaming, Rosie? I thought you'd be solving the crime by now.'

'I've got my theories,' she said, wondering how he could look so relaxed this morning after such a night, when she was anything but.

'You should try not to feel so intensely about things, my dear,' Bernard went on, as if reading her thoughts. 'Working with your head stuck in books all the time isn't healthy, especially since most of your customers are pensioners.'

'I don't actually *read* the books at the library, Uncle. Not all of them, anyway, and I like dealing with people. So why don't you tell me your theory about last night as well. I'm sure you've got one,' she said, unable to resist asking him.

'On the surface it seems as though it was a terrible accident, but the thing that's most puzzling is where Miss Pargeter has got to. There was only one body in the factory, and it was definitely a man — what was left of him, poor devil. What he was doing there is another mystery, and of course, we don't know for certain Miss Pargeter went there last night. She could have left the village for some reason. Gone to visit a friend or something. We just don't know.'

'I know she was in the habit of working at the factory in the evenings, and she found it comforting to do so since her sister died. She told me that much, and she never mentioned any friends to me, or plans for going outside the village. She was as much a part of it as the church.'

She was no private eye, but she could still think for herself, and something certainly didn't add up here. And until Edith Pargeter was found, she knew she wouldn't be able to stop the questions in her restless mind.

5

Rosie Redman hadn't been the only one to wake up with a major headache after the night before, but it was twenty-four hours before Edgar Pargeter awoke with a mouth like cotton wool, feeling befuddled and nauseous. The repeated knocking in his head was driving him mad, and then he realised it was coming from the front door. He was lying in the dark, completely disorientated for a few minutes, until memory rushed back, and he realised he was in his sisters' cottage in Bately-sub-Mendip. There was something about a fire . . .

Christ Almighty, now he remembered! He slid off the sofa bed where he'd stayed all night after he'd refused to go upstairs and sleep in one of the bedrooms. He vaguely recalled the village doctor pumping his arm full of drugs and telling him he'd be sedated with all his nerves relaxed for the next twenty-four hours. Relaxed! He'd never felt so bloody thick-headed in his life as he did now. But through it all, something was telling him he had to get his thoughts in order.

His legs felt as though they no longer

belonged to him as he staggered upright and switched on the light, and then squinted them half-shut again at the feeling that a thousand pinpricks were invading his eyes. He yelled out as best his throat would let him that he was coming and to shut the effing hell up.

He wrenched open the door and saw the two dark-suited men standing outside. He wasn't so out of it that he couldn't recognise them for what they were. Bloody coppers. You could smell 'em a mile off. But then a smidgin of sensibility returned, and he held on to the door jamb, his eyes bleary and his voice hoarse. He wished to Christ the effing room wasn't still swimming in all directions, and that he didn't feel in danger of throwing up all over the buggers.

'You'd better come in, but I'm in no fit state to be able to tell you anything. I hope you're going to tell *me* something,'

He didn't know if he was making sense, but as he opened the door wider he registered the astonishment on the coppers' faces as they took in the state of the place. Cluttered wasn't the word for it, and besides the usual chaos there was stuff all over the floor by the bureau. *Wills and insurance claims* were the words hammering in Edgar's head now.

He thrust a hand to his throbbing temple, wishing to God the doctor was back here and giving him another shot of whatever magic substance he'd had last night so that he didn't have to think at all.

'My sister,' he managed to croak. 'Have you found her?'

The younger one of the coppers spoke quickly. 'Can I make you some black coffee, Mr Pargeter? It'll help to revive you.'

Edgar waved his hand towards the kitchen. 'Help yourself.'

He sank down on the sofa again, while the older man settled into an armchair, his incredulous eyes not missing anything; the crowded ornaments on every surface; the muddle of papers on the floor; the photos of the two sisters on the mantelpiece together with many more photos of their dolls. Especially those. God, he'd seen some places, but nothing like this. The only thing to be said for it was that it was apparently clean. The old girls didn't live in squalor, just in a muddle. They were like magpies, needing every item of familiar possessions surrounding them.

Edgar guessed what he'd be thinking as he'd looked at the chaos. What kind of crackpot old dames took photos of dolls, for Christ's sake?

'I'm Detective Inspector Forster,' he heard the man say formally, 'and Sergeant Locke is making your coffee. Can you tell me what you remember about last night, Mr Pargeter? I believe you were out with friends when you received a call that your sisters' factory was on fire?' he prompted, seeing that the guy still seemed totally bewildered.

As you would, if you'd been doped up to the eyeballs, after hearing that your last remaining sister was missing, and an unknown man was found dead in their factory. Forster made no concessions to sympathy at this stage. It was more important to find out if a serious crime was involved. The Redman girl had been indignant at his suggestion that the Pargeter woman had had a man friend, but there was no accounting for taste these days. In his experience nothing was impossible, or could be excluded from his enquiries.

'Do you want to have a quick wash before we begin?' Forster asked delicately. The place smelled like a brothel, despite the elderly inhabitants, or perhaps because of the sickly sweet smells of talcum powders and the like. The man who'd spent the night on the sofa smelled less than sweet now, with the lingering smell of drink wafting from him. For the time being, Forster ignored the fact that he must have driven down here at a hell of a rate, well tanked up.

'I need a pee if that's what you mean,' Edgar grunted, and made his way unsteadily up the stairs to the small bathroom.

It gave him time to collect his thoughts a little and to be on his guard to whatever damn fool questions he was going to be asked. You never knew with coppers, but nobody could accuse him of being in any way involved, since his drinking mates could all vouch for where he was last night. As if the fire hadn't been enough, hearing about the dead man had been one hell of a shock, and where the hell was Edith? He felt sick with anxiety.

He sluiced his face with cold water and ran a finger around his teeth, rubbing them clean. He was usually far fussier in his personal habits, but he just wanted to get this over and done with. A glance at his watch told him how late in the evening it was, and he'd need to get back to town in the morning. He certainly didn't have a hope in hell of driving back safely tonight.

By the time he went unsteadily back downstairs Sergeant Locke had his black coffee ready for him in one of Edith's dainty bone china cups and saucers. He could have swigged it down in one mouthful if it hadn't been so bloody hot, and he resisted the temptation.

'Are you ready, Mr Pargeter?

What was it those moron contestants always said on those effing TV game shows? *Ready as I'll ever be* . . . He grunted instead.

'You weren't in Bately-sub-Mendip last night, I believe.'

'You already know I was with some colleagues at a pub in Bristol, which they will verify. More importantly, have you got any news of my sister?'

The DI sounded patient. 'Not yet. I believe you received a call from a Doctor Redman to say that the doll factory was on fire, and you believed your sister to be in it. Is that correct?'

'No. I *thought* that she *might* be in it,' Edgar said, not falling into that trap. 'I know she sometimes liked to work there in the evenings.'

'It must have been a great relief to you to be told that it wasn't your sister who died in the fire,' the sergeant put in.

Edgar glared at him. He knew the methods. He'd seen enough cop shows on TV. One started the questioning, then the other one tossed out a seemingly harmless remark, and before the victim knew it, he was thrown sideways.

'Of course it was a bloody relief. How would you have felt?'

He'd dearly like to throw some insults at the pair of them for their inane questions, but he was too cautious for that. If he antagonised them, the next thing he knew he'd be in the frame for something he hadn't done. He wished he could get these effing TV cop show phrases out of his head. He brushed a hand across his forehead, knowing he was trembling in a way that was totally unlike his usual suave demeanour. Probably the after-effects of the sedative the doc had given him, he supposed, since his head still felt as if it belonged to somebody else.

'Look, man, I hardly need to tell you how worried I am about my sister,' he said more urgently. 'I don't know if she had any friends, but if she did, she couldn't have gone far since she never ventured out of the village as far as I know, so she would surely have got news of the fire by now and either come home or tried to get in touch with me.'

'Does she have a mobile phone?'

Edgar resisted the urge to scream obscenities at the fool.

'She wouldn't know how to use one if she did. When it comes to technology she was still in the Stone Age.'

'What does she like to do in her spare time?' the sergeant asked now. 'We've already heard from Miss Redman how much she liked her library books.'

'What did you speak to her for?'

'We're speaking to anybody who might have anything to offer as to Miss Pargeter's whereabouts or her frame of mind in the last couple of days, Sir.'

'You think something bad's happened to her, don't you?'

'It's impossible to say. I hesitate to ask you this, Sir, but does your sister have any men friends?'

Edgar laughed out loud, and immediately wished he hadn't as his head rocked. 'Sorry, but God, no. I mean, have you seen her? Take a look at the photos on the mantelpiece if you doubt me.'

'Isn't that being a bit uncharitable about your sister, Mr Pargeter?' the sergeant said, pausing in his note-taking, 'I presume you were fond of her.'

'I was fond of both my sisters,' Edgar said angrily. 'What are you implying?'

'Nothing at all. You were the one who sounded sneering.'

'Well, I didn't mean to, but I know that neither of my sisters was interested in men, so I can assure you she wouldn't have gone out on a date! Of course, if she had, she could be anywhere,' he added, as if the idea had only just occurred to him.

'But it's unlikely,' the DI said.

'Very.'

'So you don't think she could have known the man who died in the fire?'

Edgar was tiring of these questions that seemed to be going round in circles and getting nowhere. 'How can I possibly answer that? I didn't live here, and I don't know everybody that my sisters were acquainted with.'

'That's a reasonable assumption, considering they were so much older than yourself, and certainly the only person she seems to have confided to at any length is Miss Rosie Redman,' the DI said reasonably. 'Would you say she was a good friend to your sisters?'

'I suppose so. She's been to the cottage a few times, but my sisters never invited other people in, except for the odd job bloke.'

'On a more practical matter, Sir,' DI Forster went on more briskly, 'I trust you had the factory well insured. I believe you were the legal owner?'

'Of course it was insured, and I was the legal owner, since my sisters had no heads for business and preferred to leave that side of things to me. They insisted it was in my name so that they didn't have any legal worries.'

'And yet they ran a successful factory. I understand the dolls have had a modest success,' Sergeant Locke put in. 'They must have been shipped somewhere, so your sisters must have met people other than those in the village.'

'I see you've been doing your homework,' Edgar said, scowling.

The DI got to his feet. 'As it's getting very late I think we'll leave it there for now, Mr Pargeter, and thank you for your time. Just before we go, please give my sergeant your home and business address and telephone numbers, the name of your insurers, and of the personnel involved with distributing and selling the dolls. Then as soon as we have any more information we'll be in touch.'

★   ★   ★

'What do you think?' he asked Locke, as soon as the business was finished and they could get outside and breathe some welcome night air after the staleness of the cottage.

'A bit shifty, but probably not involved in any way. He must have cared for his sisters I suppose, and he certainly seemed anxious enough to find out where this one's got to. It might be worth contacting his insurers to find out how much he stands to gain from the factory fire — and how much he got from his first sister's death.'

'Exactly what I was thinking. As Arthur Daley might have said, he could have got himself a nice little earner.'

'Your wife still making you watch those old TV programmes, is she, Sir?' Locke said with a snigger.

Forster ignored the jibe and spoke thoughtfully. 'Except that Arthur Daley never included murder in his exploits, and for all we know, we could be including murder here. But we need to get the medical report on the dead bloke before we go any further along those lines. Let's leave it for now and get back to town.'

★   ★   ★

Edgar felt decidedly jumpy. All his nerves were on edge, and as soon as he was alone he reached for his hip flask and drained it of his remaining whiskey. Feeling in dire need of a drink to steady his nerves, he forgot that the effects of the sedative hadn't left him yet, and he felt groggier than ever, unable to remember what he'd been asked or what he'd said. One look at the clock on the mantelpiece told him it was after midnight and all he wanted to do was sleep.

The lure of a bed was calling to him, but he couldn't face going upstairs to one of his sisters' rooms, thank you very much, any more than he could last night. The ghost of Edna was still there, and Edith's bed had been too recently slept in. The smell of her would still be in her bedclothes, and he shivered. He was used to bunking down on the sofa-cum-bed-settee for a night or two whenever he visited, and that would have to do again.

The night had gone chilly and he needed a blanket. He fetched one from the airing cupboard, wrapped himself in it, and tried to get a couple of hours' sleep. He needed to get up early in the morning to get home and have a shower and get out of these clothes, knowing he stank. He wasn't in the habit of sleeping fully dressed, and he was going to look far less than his usual tidy self by morning, but he couldn't think about that now. He couldn't think properly at all.

He couldn't have said what it was that woke him, nor what time it was. He could see that it was getting light, and probably nearing dawn. Country sounds were different and unfamiliar to town dwellers, and somewhere in the ether an owl hooted, startling a dog and setting him barking, followed by the hectic squawking of chickens in a back yard.

Edgar wrapped himself more firmly in his blanket, but something was making his heart pound, and even through half-closed eyes he fancied he could see Edna and Edith drifting around the room as though their feet weren't touching the floor. The photos of his sisters and the dolls all seemed to be floating about the room as well, and he couldn't be sure if he was really awake or having a nightmare. It was a ghastly sensation, but his mouth was so dry he couldn't have croaked out a word if he tried.

He slid off the sofa with a bump, dragging his thoughts together, and switching on the light with shaking hands. There were no ghostly apparitions in the room, nor anything out of the ordinary, but he was totally unnerved now, and no matter what unearthly hour it was he had to get the hell out of there and back to the familiar surroundings of his own flat.

★ ★ ★

Outwardly, the village of Bately-sub-Mendip was returning to normal on Monday morning. The milkman whistled as he did his rounds, bottles clanking in his cart; the postman delivered letters and bills as usual; people got ready to go to work; the younger children walked to the village school; the older ones waited for the bus to take them to secondary schools and colleges.

The library didn't open until ten o'clock in the morning, but there was always admin business to attend to. Rosie was there as usual at nine, knowing that the main topic of conversation between her and Norman Youde, and any of their customers who came in for a book or a chat, wold be that of the factory fire.

'How are you?' Norman asked her cautiously.

Rosie shrugged. 'The same as everybody else in the village. Shocked. Worried. Upset. How else do you expect me to be?'

'I've got the kettle on,' he said. 'A good strong cup of coffee is what you need before the onslaught.'

She gave a small smile at that. Monday mornings were normally so quiet they might as well not open at all, but she guessed that today could be different. The library, the post office and the pub were focal points of information when anything happened, and since nothing much normally happened here, it was a fair guess that they'd be well used from now on.

'I see Edgar Pargeter's car has gone from outside the cottage,' Norman went on when he brought her a mug of coffee.

'Already? I thought he'd have the decency

to hang around a bit longer!'

'He'll have his own work to do, I suppose, whatever that is. I'm sure he'll be back. He'll want to know when Edith comes home.'

Rosie blinked hard. 'You think she's just going to walk back into the cottage as if nothing's happened, do you?'

'Of course not. But she must have gone to visit a friend or something. I just can't think of any other explanation. She wasn't at home and she wasn't at the factory, so I don't think you should see anything sinister in her disappearance.'

'I can't help it. I know something's not right. Oh, and you don't know the police interviewed me yesterday morning, do you?'

His face was a picture. 'Your Damien you mean?'

'No, I don't, and I wish people would stop calling him my Damien. These were a Detective Inspector and his Sergeant, and I was having a talk with Charlie Walters in the pub when they suddenly appeared. Made me feel like a criminal!'

'Who's Charlie Walters?'

Before she realised it was something he actually didn't know, they heard somebody rapping on the door. Norman yelled out that they didn't open until ten, and then saw through the glass panel that it was Damien Hall.

'Someone for you, I think, Rosie. We'd better let him in.'

She groaned. She'd been expecting him any time soon, especially after seeing her at the pub with Charlie.

For a policeman, Damien was often hot-headed, and he had a surprisingly jealous streak, and one look at his face told her that this wasn't going to be a friendly meeting, but then her heart jolted. For a moment she'd forgotten the most important thing that had been happening in this village.

'Have you had any news of Edith?' she said at once.

He shook his head. 'No news at all, but that's not what I want to talk to you about, Rosie.'

'We'll go through to the back room then,' she said quickly, not wanting Norman earwigging on what could be an uncomfortable five minutes.

Once there she faced him squarely. 'Let's have it, Damien.'

'All right. Who was that guy you were with yesterday morning at the pub? You looked pretty cosy when I arrived with the suits.'

She resisted the sarcastic remark that it sounded so bloody daft to call his superiors *suits* as though he was taking part in a TV show.

'His name's Charlie Walters and he works for the *West Gazette*,' she said evenly. 'He's interested in doing a feature on the Pargeter sisters and I was helping him with some background details about them. Is there anything else you want to know? His shoe size? His favourite movies?'

He stood there with his arms folded, and when he didn't answer, she spoke more impatiently.

'You don't own me, Damien. In fact, I think we both know we're going nowhere, so why don't we both accept it and move on?'

She didn't know where the words came from. She hadn't meant to say them. It wasn't necessary to be so sharp, and he hadn't deserved it. But it was true. She didn't want to be with him, no matter what the village might think about the two of them seeing one another a few times. Well, more than a few times. But she didn't love him.

And oh, Edith, you'd never advise me to marry somebody I didn't love, would you? You may not have had a love of your own, but you knew all about it from the pages of your romantic novels.

Damien spoke after a frozen moment. 'If that's how you really feel, then perhaps we should call it a day.'

'I think perhaps we should,' Rosie said. She

held out her hand. 'Friends?'

He took her hand reluctantly, staring at her as if he could hardly believe what was happening, and then he nodded and said he'd see her around.

He had dignity, Rosie reflected later. She'd give him that.

Norman was agog when Damien left the library, while Rosie merely said quickly that it was time to open up. She knew in her heart it had been the right thing to do to finish up with Damien, and that it had to happen sometime.

'Did I hear properly?' Norman said warily. 'Have you two broken up?'

'You know damn well what you heard, so don't pretend that you didn't.'

'Maybe so, but all I expected was to hear a bit of juicy beefing about you and this Charlie bloke. Does he have anything to do with it?'

'For heaven's sake, Norman, I think I should send you home with a pile of Edith's old books.' Thankfully, she heard the thin sound of the church clock striking the hour. 'Stop matchmaking and I'll go and open the door.'

Predictably, there was a rush of customers that morning. For a small village there was an inordinately large number of library readers, and they couldn't all have been ready to change their books that Monday. They mostly came in to congregate and discuss what was happening in their village, and today there was only one topic of conversation. What had started the fire? Who was the dead man? Where was Edith Pargeter?

If it was predictable, sad, and full of wild speculation, it also made the morning pass quickly, and it was nearing lunchtime when Rosie looked up to deal with the next customer and found herself facing Charlie Walters. This time she couldn't deny the familiar jolt in her heart. He looked different, fresher, and she realised it was because he was wearing different clothes from those he'd been wearing yesterday morning. Of course. He'd said he was staying at the pub for a few days. Was that only yesterday? It already seemed like a lifetime ago.

'What are you doing for lunch?' he said by way of greeting.

She replied crisply, aware that Norman was hovering. 'I usually go home for a sandwich.'

'Have lunch with me instead. There's something I want to talk to you about, and to save any local gossip, there's a place on the Mendip Road that's only a few miles from here. We can be there and back before you start work this afternoon.'

'As a matter of fact we close on Monday

afternoons,' she said before she could stop to think. 'We open for a couple of hours this evening instead.'

'Perfect. Then we can have the afternoon together.'

Rosie was beginning to get annoyed at his assumption. 'Why would I want to spend the afternoon with you?'

'Because I'm interested in your old ladies, and I know you are too. I promise I'm not going to make a pass at you. Deal?'

Actually, she wouldn't have minded if he did, she found herself thinking unexpectedly. There was an energy about him that was exhilarating. He knew what he wanted and came straight to the point. She liked that. It matched her own plain speaking.

'All right,' she said on an impulse. 'I'll phone my auntie and tell her I won't be home for lunch today.'

She didn't dare look behind her, but she could have sworn she heard Norman Youde give a soft sigh, as though he'd been holding his breath for her response. Romantic old fool, she thought, but she was smiling as she thought it.

6

Charlie drove fast and efficiently, and she was still wondering what he wanted to talk to her about. She'd told him all she could about Edna and Edith, and there didn't seem anything else to say. But she had overlooked his journalist's need for detail. It wasn't until they were sitting at a corner table in the roadside pub and had ordered a soft drink and a bar meal, that he finally came clean. When he did, she looked at him in fury.

'You can't be serious!'

'I'm perfectly serious,' he said, deadpan. 'My editor's keen on the feature, but so far it's incomplete.'

'You really want me to let you to see inside the cottage and take a few photos, so that your readers can gawp at them and mock them? You don't have a snowball's chance in hell of my agreeing to that. It's not my place to do so, anyway. You'd need Edith's permission for it, and she would never give it.'

'But Edith's not here, is she?'

'And if she was, the last thing she would want is for people to see inside her home,' Rosie said indignantly. 'It's a total invasion of privacy, and I'm surprised at you, Charlie.'

She was disappointed in him too. She'd thought he had more integrity, but why should she have assumed anything about him? She didn't know him, and if a slight attraction may have blinded her to other qualities in him, she was seeing them now.

'I can see I've upset you, Rosie, and it's the last thing I want to do, so hear me out, will you? At this moment I intend to simply write a feature about the Pargeter sisters with reference to the fire, of course. I give you my word that I wouldn't use any photos of the interior of the cottage or the ladies and their dolls unless the worst happens. That would be a separate feature altogether, and in the public interest. You must see that.'

'My God, you do think Edith's dead, don't you?' she said, ignoring the rest of his words.

'I don't know, but if that was sadly found to be the case, then the circumstances would change, and the sisters wouldn't be hurt by it.'

'But their brother would,' she stated.

'Well, that's where you come in. You know him, and you could ask him delicately if he would be agreeable to having a few photos taken. After all, the doll factory was a business venture, and presumably he's a businessman even if his sisters weren't commercially-minded. I'm not being crass about it, Rosie, and I know you'd be discreet about it. I simply want you to ask his opinion, that's all. He's still in the village, isn't he?'

'No, he's already left, and I don't think much of him for leaving so damn fast,' she said shortly.

'Well, that makes it easier. You have his phone number, I presume?'

If she had ever thought he was asking her out because he fancied her, she knew differently now. It was all part of his so-called charm, to worm his way into her friendship and then to pounce.

'You don't really expect me to phone him with such a request, do you? How gross is that in the circumstances?'

Their bar meal arrived, and she stabbed at her ham and cheese ploughman's with a vengeance.

'How gross is it of him to desert a sinking ship right now?'

Rosie glared at him, but damn him, he was only echoing her own uneasy thoughts. No matter what business Edgar Pargeter was in, surely he could have stayed in the village until Edith's whereabouts came to light.

'Anyway,' Charlie continued calmly, 'I reckon you can always gauge something out of a person's voice on the phone. He won't be able to hide his feelings, whatever they are.'

'I've always thought the same,' Rosie said reluctantly. 'But I wouldn't know what to say.'

'Let's just enjoy our meal and think about it afterwards,' Charlie said, and she knew he thought he'd won. But then another thought struck her.

'It's no good, anyway. I don't have Edgar's phone number. When my uncle needed it the other day we found it in Edith's little book that she keeps by the phone in the cottage.'

'It's fate then, isn't it? We can either go there to get the phone number, or I can just take a couple of photos, and job done.'

Fate had a habit of leading her to places she didn't really want to go, Rosie thought. She hadn't really wanted to go out for lunch with Charlie Walters, nor to feel a mild attraction towards him, no matter how much he irritated her. She hadn't wanted to get involved in any way with Edith's disappearance, but she had been interviewed by the police, and was now being asked to contribute to a newspaper article in what seemed a pretty clandestine way.

Was that fate? Or was she just letting herself be drawn along because of a smooth-talking reporter who was different in every way from Damien Hall, the man her family had had fond hopes of her marrying?

'You have my word that I won't use anything you think may be inappropriate,' Charlie went on. 'I know how fond you were — are — of Edith, and you'll be there to keep an eye on me, won't you?'

He could cajole with the best of them, Rosie thought. But before she could reply, he had continued.

'Listen, I have to go back to my office for a few things this afternoon. Do you want to come for the ride? We can be back at the village by early evening. You've got the afternoon free, haven't you? If nothing else, it will prove to you that I'm a bona fide reporter. We can always do the cottage thing later.'

She'd never actually doubted his profession, especially as his photo verified it in the newspaper. And it would get her away from the tension in the village for a few hours, so why not?

'All right,' she said casually, not wanting to sound too enthusiastic, and since there didn't seem any reason to hurry their meal now, they lingered over it for a while longer.

★ ★ ★

That afternoon, a nervous, dowdily-dressed woman in Bristol twisted her damp hands

102

together, trying to pluck up enough courage to go into the officious-looking premises. She had never done such a thing before, and it was giving her palpitations, trying to think of what to say. But she had got this far and she might as well do what she had come for. She opened the door and went inside, and an efficient receptionist looked up and smiled.

'Can I help you?' she said.

'Is this the Graham Fox Enquiry Agency?' the woman recited huskily.

'It is indeed. Do you have an appointment with Mr Fox?' the girl said, perfectly sure that she didn't.

'No. I didn't think. It doesn't matter,' the woman said, already backing towards the door and feeling decidedly faint.

'Hang on a minute,' the receptionist said. 'You don't look very well. Sit down and I'll see if Mr Fox is free.'

She helped the woman to a chair, pressed a buzzer on her desk and spoke quickly into an intercom. A grey-haired man appeared from another room and smiled encouragingly at the woman.

'I'm Graham Fox, and you wanted to see me, I believe. Come into my office, and Miss Jones will fetch you a glass of water.'

The woman followed as if in a dream, and sat down thankfully in the enquiry agent's small office. It didn't look terribly affluent, and in her anxious mind she guessed that business probably wasn't exactly brisk. She took a deep breath, hoping that this was a good sign. She said the words she had practised.

'My husband's gone missing,' she said, 'and I want you to find him for me. I can't pay much, but he don't have much truck with the police, so that's why I've come to you instead.'

'Let's have some details first,' Graham Fox was saying gently, seeing far more behind the stark words. 'Your name for a start.'

The woman took another deep breath and gulped at the glass of water she was handed. There. She'd said it now, and whatever else happened, she'd started the ball rolling.

'My name's Mrs Peggy Rawlings and my husband's been missing for three days. I saw this stuff on the TV about a fire in that Bately-sub-Mendip place, and a man's body being found in it, and I can't help thinking it might be my Wilf.'

Fox handed her the box of tissues he always kept on his desk for such occasions and she sniffled noisily into one of them.

'What makes you think it might be Wilf, Mrs Rawlings? Do you live in Bately-sub-Mendip?' he said.

'No, but one of his mates has done some work for somebody down there, which is how I remembered the name. He said there might be some odd jobs going, and Wilf was always ready to make a few bob on the QT if he got the chance.'

'What exactly do you want me to do, Mrs Rawlings?' Fox said, thinking it a pretty tenuous link.

She spread her hands. 'Well, I don't know. I thought, you being an enquiry agent, perhaps you could find out if they know who the man is yet. Like I said, I can pay a bit. If you could just give me a few hours of your time to put my mind at rest I'd be ever so grateful.'

She looked so pathetic that he forgot his usual resistance to a domestic enquiry where the bloke had probably simply gone out on the razzle. She was a nice enough little woman, but you never knew. In his business you learned that nothing was as it seemed. Everybody had secrets . . . but there was no use in letting his ideas run away with him before he knew what was what.

'Well, I can certainly check and see if they've identified the body yet. If not, I'll take a run down to Bately to see if there's any more news there. That's all I can offer at present, and after that, we'll see. Leave your contact details with Miss Jones and I'll be in touch.'

The receptionist came to join him once she had done what she was asked and shown the woman out of the office.

'Are you taking her on?' she asked her boss.

He shrugged. Business had been slack lately, and a trip out of town would clear his mind. 'She's willing to pay for a few hours of my time, so I'll go round to the morgue, and then to this village and see where we go from there.'

The first visit was an abortive one, to learn that the dead man had still not been identified, but he was told that dental records might have the answer, and that the police would be the first to know.

Fox had to be satisfied with that, and instead of taking umbrage at the response he had quite expected all along, he shook off the stuffiness of the city, and drove over the Mendip roads towards the picturesque village of Bately-sub-Mendip.

He couldn't deny that he'd been curious himself on hearing the brief details about these elderly women who had produced dolls in a small factory, and wondered about the identity of the dead man. Burnt to a crisp in a fire was tragic enough, but coupled with the mysterious disappearance of the woman who made the dolls, it was intriguing enough to put questions in anybody's mind, let alone an enquiry agent. But it wasn't his case, and it was left to the police to sort this one out, and good luck to them.

He swore as another car suddenly appeared from around a corner and narrowly missed him on the unmarked road.

'Bloody road hog,' he yelled, more for his own satisfaction than anything else. No more than two cars on the bloody road, and they had to meet at a junction. Out of habit and the nature of his job, he registered the colour and make of the car as it zoomed the other way towards Bristol, going too fast for him to check on the number plate. He never expected to see it again, anyway.

* * *

'You nearly hit that car!' Rosie Redman said accusingly.

'I didn't though; did I? It looked like some old guy cruising along with his mind somewhere else. You worry too much. Relax and enjoy the sunshine while it lasts. It's not bad weather, considering.'

'When you descend to talking about the weather, I know we've come to the end of the road,' Rosie said.

Charlie laughed. 'Rubbish. I'd say we're only at the beginning.'

She recognised the inflexion in his voice, and ignored the significance of the remark. It didn't stop her heart giving an extra beat, though. He was undoubtedly the most interesting man she had met in a long time, but that didn't mean she wanted to rush headlong into a relationship with him.

In any case, their brief association couldn't last much longer. As soon as his interest in Bately-sub-Mendip was over, he wouldn't be bothering to come there again. But his interest wouldn't be over until Edith Pargeter was found, one way or another.

Charlie heard her draw in her breath, and glanced at her.

'Have I said something to upset you now? God knows I go too fast when I see something I really want.'

She shook her head, ignoring that for the moment too.

'No. I was thinking of Edith again. In all of this, she's the most important thing on my mind, and I don't want to lose sight of that, Charlie. For a little while, having lunch, I almost forgot why we're here, and I don't want to do that for a minute.'

'Well, you should,' he said, to her surprise. 'You need to wind down occasionally.

Nobody can live at an intense level constantly. That's the way to a heart attack, and I should know. It happened to my father.'

She was startled at how serious he had become.

It was also the first time he had told her anything so personal about himself or his life.

'Do you want to tell me about it?' she said, hating the words as soon as she had said them. It was one of the stock sentences on any TV show, especially the soaps.

'He was a newspaperman, a foreign correspondent, and he worked abroad a lot of the time. He worked himself to death, and it happened when he was in Egypt, covering some coup or other. It broke my mother's heart, even though she never forgave him for leaving us when I was still a kid.'

Rosie's mouth had dropped open at hearing the clipped way he spoke, which revealed his distress far more than anything else.

'We've got something in common then.' It was all she could think of to say. 'My parents died abroad too, which is why my aunt and uncle brought me up. It hurts, doesn't it?'

'Yes, and I'd rather not talk about it, so let's forget it. I need to pick up the stuff from my office and then we'll get back to Bately.

Unless you'd like to see some of the delights of Bristol.'

He had forced his voice to lighten, and she gave a small laugh.

'I'm not a tourist, Charlie. I've been to Bristol before, thanks, despite living out in the sticks, and I don't want to be gone all day. Besides, didn't you want to see the inside of Edith's cottage?'

She bit her lip. She hadn't meant to say that, nor to agree to his request. But she'd said it now, damn it, and she knew he wouldn't let her off the hook.

By the time he'd done his business at the office and they'd taken a more leisurely drive back to Bately, she was still wondering how she could get out of it, short of flatly refusing to agree to any more of his requests. But without thinking of a more reasonable excuse, they were already parking the car in the pub car park and walking through the village towards Edith's cottage in Butcher's Lane, one of the narrow lanes off the village green.

And then Rosie stopped, her heart jumping.

'Oh God, Edgar's back,' she said in a panic, seeing the sleek black car that took up most of the road. 'I wonder if this means he's had some news. In any case, we can't go there now.'

'Why not? It would be the most natural thing in the world for you to enquire about the old girl, wouldn't it?'

'And you think he'll ask us in, make us a cup of tea, and let you take photos, do you?' Rosie said sarcastically, nerves making her sharp.

'No, but I might be able to get a glimpse inside.'

She had to know, anyway, unable to bear the knowledge that Edith had been found, and not knowing. Perhaps she was even inside the cottage with Edgar right now, Rosie thought hopefully, and all the worry would be over.

'Come on,' she said, almost breaking into a run.

* * *

The minute she saw Edgar Pargeter's frowning face she knew it wasn't going to be anything as simple as that.

'What do you want?' he said ungraciously, as though she was the last person in the world he wanted to see.

'I wondered if you've had any news of your sister, Mr Pargeter,' she said. 'I was hoping she might have returned home when I saw your car outside.'

'Well, she hasn't, and since she seems to have confided in you, if you've got any idea where she might have gone, you should have told the police, and you should tell me right now.'

'I wish I did, but she never said anything like that to me,' she said, his tone making her more nervous.

'And who the hell are you?' Edgar said, eyeing Charlie suspiciously.

To her horror, Charlie produced his card and handed it to Edgar. Big mistake, she was thinking hysterically. She'd never really got on with Edgar, and now he'd think she'd got Charlie here under the pretence of asking about Edith.

'I want to do a sympathetic feature about your sisters, Mr Pargeter, and I wondered if you had any photos of them that I could either borrow or copy.'

'No, you bloody can't. My sister's missing, not dead, and if I knew anything I wouldn't give you effing toe-rags houseroom, always sniffing around other peoples' grief,' Edgar shouted, and slammed the door shut.

Rosie flinched, feeling her face burn with humiliation at such a reaction. She couldn't help thinking that he didn't actually look eaten up with grief, and you didn't really feel *grief* unless somebody had died, did you? He looked more annoyed at being interrupted in something, and she also couldn't help noticing that he'd swept aside some of Edith's knick-knacks on the table, and that it was now spread with papers.

She was so jittery she couldn't think coherent thoughts any more, except to be sure that she had definitely scored another black mark as far as Edgar Pargeter was concerned.

'Don't let him get to you, Rosie,' Charlie said as they walked away. 'In my job, you're used to doors being slammed in your face.'

'Well, I'm not,' she snapped. 'That was horrible.'

'So let's go to the pub and have a stiff drink while you calm down. Or a strong black coffee if you prefer.'

'I'm fed up with drinking coffee, and a stiff drink sounds good to me,' she muttered.

She didn't object when he tucked her hand in the crook of his arm. God knew she felt she needed it to steady her nerves.

They walked inside the pub to find a grey-haired man standing at the bar talking to Mrs Gentry. As he turned around, his eyes widened.

'Good God, it's Charlie, isn't it? So you were the young devil who nearly ran me off the road. I thought I recognised the car outside.'

'Mr Fox, how great to see you,' Charlie said with a surprised smile as he pumped his hand. 'How's Foxy these days? I haven't heard from him in ages.'

The older man chuckled. 'Clive's fine. Working in Paris now, and flat sharing with a lovely young French girl. At least, that's what he calls it for his old man's benefit,' he added with a wink. 'I read your column in the *Gazette* now and again, so I guess you're down here on the scent of a story.'

As he glanced at Rosie approvingly, Charlie nodded and turned to her.

'Clive Fox and I were great mates at college and this is his father. Mr Fox, this is Rosie Redman. But what are you doing here? You haven't got involved in this Pargeter business, have you?'

Seeing how the landlady was trying not to look interested while staying very close, Graham Fox laughed.

'Let's sit down and have a drink first,' he said. 'Or is it too early?'

'Not for us. We're in need of one,' Charlie said before Rosie could speak. 'Something pretty strong, I think.'

They sat in an alcove well away from the bar while Graham Fox ordered the drinks.

'Why would he be involved?' Rosie said when they were alone.

'Oh, he'd be right up your street. He's an enquiry agent.'

She perked up at once, her fury over Edgar Pargeter's reaction fading away at the thought of actually meeting an enquiry agent. He didn't look anything like she might have imagined. But why would he? They didn't come rubber-stamped, or like clones of Columbo or Poirot. The best way was for them to travel incognito, and this guy certainly fitted that part, grey hair thinning on top and a bit paunchy. He could be anybody's dad.

'Do I have a smudge on my nose?' he asked her with a smile as he set the tray of drinks on the table.

She blushed, realising she had been staring. 'I'm sorry if I seemed rude. It's just that I've never met an enquiry agent before.'

'Rosie's a librarian,' Charlie said, to cover her embarrassment. 'She's a mystery addict and fancies herself as a bit of an amateur sleuth. She already has her own theory over this case, since she's a friend of Miss Pargeter.'

As Rosie glared at him, Fox spoke smoothly.

'Well, I'm sorry to disappoint you but I don't have any professional interest in the lady's disappearance, only the identity of the dead man. A lady came to my office this morning saying her husband had been missing for three days, and she thought it might be him.'

'Really? What was she like?' Rosie said eagerly. 'Was she elderly, and a bit old-fashioned in the way she dressed? I don't know what she'd be doing in Bristol, but it could have been Edith, pretending to be a married woman, and trying to find out who the dead man was.'

Even as she said it, her voice full of hope, she knew how far-fetched it sounded, and immediately felt stupid at being so impulsive.

Fox smiled at her kindly. 'She wasn't elderly, and her name was Mrs Rawlings, so I'm afraid that's one theory that won't wash, Miss Redman. But I can see the way your mind works, and it's always good to think laterally.'

His mobile rang, and he moved to the other side of the bar while he took the call. He came back a few minutes later.

'That was my receptionist. Excitement over. Mrs Rawlings has called with many apologies to say her husband's turned up. It seems he was away on a drunken football weekend.' He glanced at his watch. 'So now that that little mystery's been solved and I'm not needed here any more, I must get back to town and get on with some real work.'

'Aren't you interested in what's happened to Miss Pargeter?' Rosie said quickly. 'I couldn't bear it if anything bad's happened to her.'

'It's up to the police to investigate, Miss Redman. The only way I could get involved is if I was asked by a relative.'

'Or a friend?'

'Rosie, stop it,' Charlie warned. 'You've got to let the police do their job.'

'What's your theory then, Miss Redman?' the enquiry agent said.

She wasn't used to strong drink in the late afternoon, and she became more talkative than she intended.

'I don't trust the brother. He's the one who stands to gain from all this. He bought the factory to indulge his much older sisters. Edna died from a heart attack when she couldn't find her pills, when I know she never moved anywhere without them. Now the fire has happened and poor Edith is missing, and nobody has a clue who the dead man could be or what he was doing at the factory. But the one person to gain financially from all this, including the sale of their cottage, is their brother, Edgar, who's just slammed the door in our faces, incidentally.'

'You have a pretty vivid imagination, Miss

Redman, and I'm not patronising you,' Fox said as she paused for breath. 'Everything you say could be true, and everything could have an equally logical explanation. It's not my case, but if you want a word of advice from an old pro, don't go bandying about these theories in public.'

'Just what I've been trying to tell her,' Charlie said.

'I'm not aware that you've been telling me any such thing,' Rosie said. 'But I understand what you're saying, Mr Fox, and thank you for the advice.'

'Good. Then I'm off, and I'll let Clive know I've seen you, Charlie. Oh, and if you ever want a change of job, Miss Redman,' he added jocularly, 'I could do with a new pair of eyes and a keen young brain in my business.'

He handed her his business card and she took it automatically.

When he had left she looked at Charlie.

'Did he just say what I think he said?'

'Offering you a job? It sounded like it. Would you be interested?'

'I'm sure he was just indulging me. Why would I want to leave Bately when my family and friends are here and I've already got a job that I enjoy? It's fantasy land, Charlie.'

'The kind of fantasy I bet you've been half imagining, with yourself as Miss Marple, but much more glamorous, of course. Between us, you, me and Graham Fox are going to solve the mystery of the missing doll maker,' he teased her. 'I can see the headlines now! In fact, it already has the makings of an Agatha Christie title!'

She grinned. 'Put like that, I think I'll stick to my library work. Now I really must go home. My head's starting to feel woozy.'

'Then I'm driving you. Your car will be all right at the library for tonight, and I'll pick you up for work tomorrow morning, no arguments.'

She didn't feel like arguing. It had been a strange day, driving to Bristol with Charlie, the upsetting encounter with Edgar Pargeter and then meeting a real life enquiry agent. Her heart thumped. Just for a second, she wondered what it would be like, working undercover on actual cases instead of just reading about them and solving them before the end of the book.

And then she forgot about such things as her footsteps stumbled a little on the way to Charlie's car, knowing that her auntie wasn't going to be best pleased if she turned up looking the worse for wear.

7

Thankfully, there was nobody else at home, so Rosie went upstairs to lie down on her bed for a while until the dizziness passed. Inevitably, her thoughts went back to the meeting with Edgar Pargeter earlier that afternoon. He was a strange one all right. Supposedly devoted to his sisters, and yet he had always done his best to keep people away from them and their cottage. Perhaps he was more embarrassed by their quaintness than simply protective. He clearly fancied himself as a man about town.

Rosie never knew what he did, although Edith had once mentioned something about books, and also that he did the book-keeping for their little business, as she called it. Maybe he owned a bookshop, but somehow it didn't seem to be his style. The thought of it was bugging her now.

After a while, when her head no longer seemed to be spinning, her thoughts were clearer. It was obvious, really. She could look him up in the phone book, and ask Charlie to check out the address. What was the use of having a sidekick of sorts, if she didn't use him! Edgar might occupy some business premises, or simply a house in a respectable road. Whatever it was, Rosie knew she simply had to know now.

With a definite purpose in mind, she went downstairs to find the phone book. Pargeter wasn't a common name, so there weren't many entries, but the one that stood out was a north Bristol address. As soon as Rosie saw the phone number she knew it was the same one she had seen in Edith's little book. She felt a small sense of triumph, and tomorrow morning she would give the details to Charlie.

★   ★   ★

'What do you want me to do with this?' he asked when she handed him the piece of paper before he drove her to work.

'Find out where he lives and where he works.'

'Don't you think you're taking this too far, Rosie? If there's anything to find out, I'm sure the police will do their job.'

Rosie looked stubbornly ahead. Beyond the village there was still a haze over the factory site. Unfamiliar vehicles were still there, plus uniformed people milling about, and the firefighters were still probing the ashes. Surely something had to come to light soon. Strangers didn't enter factories and get burnt to death without something evil being involved. She couldn't rid herself of the gut feeling that Edgar Pargeter had something to do with it. Even if he had a cast iron alibi for the night of the fire, it didn't mean anything. Everyone knew that murderers could be proved guilty without actually being at the scene of the crime. She shivered, but went on determinedly.

'I'm not asking you to do much, Charlie. I just want to know, that's all. If you won't do it, I'll phone Graham Fox and ask him,' she added recklessly.

'You think you can afford his prices, do you? I still think you're taking this too much to heart, and Edith's bound to turn up sooner or later.'

He didn't sound convinced, and she changed tactics. When needs must, and all that tosh . . . She put her hand on his knee for a second.

'Please, Charlie. Just do this for me. It's not asking much, is it?'

He sighed. 'All right. I'm going back to Bristol as soon as I've dropped you off, anyway.'

'For good?' Rosie said.

'Do I detect a note of sadness in your

voice? No, not for good. I'm getting clearance from my boss to stay on and cover this event, whatever happens, so I'll be back later today. I'll check out this address while I'm there and report in later, Ma'am, providing you have dinner with me.'

'If that's a bribe, I accept,' Rosie said. If it got what she wanted . . .

They had reached the library now, and she got out of the car quickly. She didn't know what she might be putting in motion, if anything at all. She just knew in her bones that Edgar Pargeter wasn't all that he seemed. It was instinct, not certainty, but perhaps that was the essence of being a good private detective . . . All the fictional ones had it in abundance, and she wouldn't mind betting that Graham Fox had it too. It was a good name for a PI. A wily old fox . . .

* * *

After his mid-morning break, Norman Youde was bursting with news.

'Rosie, there was something on the radio about the man who was found dead at the factory. Apparently he had a deep indentation on his head as though he'd either been hit with a heavy object or fallen and struck his head. They still haven't identified him yet, but what do you make of that? Do you reckon Edith hit him when he surprised her and then ran off in a fright?'

'Don't be daft! Edith couldn't run anywhere!'

'Where is she then? That's if she was there at all. We don't even know that for sure, do we?'

'I hope she wasn't,' Rosie said feelingly. 'I can't imagine where she might have gone, but I just hope it was anywhere rather than the factory that night. She'd have been terrified.'

'Well, even if she was somewhere else, she must have heard about what's happened by now. We know she was as deaf as a post, but if she'd been with a friend or something, they'd surely have helped her to get in touch with her brother to let him know she's all right, wouldn't they? Something's happened to her, Rosie, and it's no use pretending it hasn't.'

She felt numbed by his words, knowing they were appallingly logical. 'I know you're right, even if I'm trying not to believe it. But if the man was hurt before he died, Edith couldn't have done it. She *couldn't*.'

'Anything's possible when people are threatened, including gaining all kinds of strength they never knew they had. You know that from some of those mystery novels you read. And what about the *Incredible Hulk*?'

he added for good measure.

She ignored such a daft remark.

'Other people, yes. Edith, no,' Rosie said stubbornly.

As he turned to deal with a customer, still chuntering on about the news he had just heard to anyone who would listen, Rosie wished desperately that Charlie was still here, so that she could talk to him about it sensibly and from a different perspective. She could put all her ideas to Damien, of course . . . but she rejected that immediately. With his nose still out of joint at being dumped, he'd just call her a madwoman.

She wished Norman would stop going on and on about it, but there was little chance of that. He was the kind of nosey parker who would carry on gossiping and ferreting about a topic until it made his listeners reach screaming point. And she was already there, thought Rosie, even though she knew that some of what he said could be true.

But to think that Edith, sweet little old Edith, could be capable of striking an intruder, leaving the factory to burn with him still inside it, was simply too bizarre to think about. In any case, by the end of the day, things took a different and more sinister turn, and Bately-sub-Mendip had something else to talk about.

By mid-afternoon school was out, and two small boys left the village, full of curiosity about all the activity around the site of the burnt-out factory. They hovered around the site and were told sharply to keep well away by their local copper and the other police constables, who grinned at the rude gestures the boys gave them as they headed for the fields beyond. As Damien made a mental note to let their father know what they were up to, he forgot them as the painstaking work continued to try to comb the ashes for anything of significance left there.

A short while later they were alerted by the almighty shrieks of the two young boys as they came hurtling back towards them. The smaller of the boys was holding tight to his crotch and snivelling loudly. The older one was still shrieking and hopping up and down with nerves as he rushed up to the familiar figure of Constable Hall and grabbed his arm in a vice-like grip.

'We've seen 'em, mister. We was looking for birds' eggs, and we seen them over there in the ditch, all 'orrible and staring up at us.'

Ignoring the fact that they were looking for birds' eggs for the moment, Damien grabbed his shaking shoulders as the other policemen came to hear what was going on.

'What have you seen, boy?'

'It's them dolls that the witch woman makes,' the boy hollered. 'There's two of 'em, and there's summat else in the ditch as well, only we didn't stop to see what it was 'cos our Dave's peed his trousers and our mum'll give him a walloping when we get back home. But we think it's *her*!'

Damien tried to calm him. 'Slow down a minute. You're one of the Wilkinson boys, aren't you? What's your first name?'

'It's Tony,' he said, trying to twist away.

'All right, well just hold on, Tony. Show us exactly where you saw these dolls, and then one of us will take you and your brother home.'

'It's over there, in the ditch,' the boy said, pointing, his voice rising in panic again. 'But I ain't going back there and our Dave won't neither.'

With a last great wrench he got free, and the next minute the two of them were tearing back towards the village. By now they were screeching and bellowing over what they had seen, leaving Damien cursing that it would be all around the village before anything definite was found. But that was the least of their problems right now, as he and his fellow officers sprinted across the field between the factory and the ditch.

The weed-filled ditches were swollen after a dismal summer of heavy rain, and the men strode along the length of it before they found what they were looking for. Two of the Pargeter dolls were half-submerged, but lying face up on top of the dank water, their white faces festooned with weeds, their blank eyes staring, their flouncy skirts spread out all around them.

'No wonder the kids were frightened out of their wits,' one of the men said sharply. 'Probably thought they were seeing ghosts. Let's get the damn things out of there.'

He poked at the dolls with a stick, disturbing the water as he lifted one and then the other one out of the filth.

'They were right, though. There's something else here as well, Jim,' Damien said sharply. 'It looks like — oh Christ, we've found her, lads.'

He recoiled in horror for a moment and then grabbed the man's stick and pushed gently at the object in the water, rolling Edith neatly over on to her back. It was obvious now that the dolls had been kept afloat by her body. One of the younger officers leaned forward to take a look and immediately puked as he saw the woman. After four days in the ditch, as far as anybody knew, she was a nightmarish sight, her features distorted, the bruises around her eyes and on her forehead blackened and swollen, the wispy hair matted.

In seconds Damien was on the phone to his superiors, and after a quick consultation he then phoned for an ambulance, doing the efficient job he was trained to do while trying to keep down his own bile. None of the other policemen here knew Edith Pargeter personally, but he did, and it turned his stomach to see the poor old dab looking like this.

'DI Forster is informing Mr Pargeter of what's happened, so let's try to get her out,' he said, his voice hoarse with shock. 'We can't leave her there until the ambulance arrives.'

Between them, several of the men lifted Edith out of the ditch and lay her on the ground. Sodden with water and filth, she was surprisingly heavy. One of the men removed his coat and put it over her, preferring to shiver in the late afternoon chill rather than expose her in such a state.

'Why didn't anybody look for her in this direction?' somebody said.

'Why would they? You don't expect an old woman to go traipsing across a field at night, do you? Especially with bruises on her head. There was no trace of blood surrounding the factory as far as anybody knew.'

'If there had been, with so many vehicles and feet tramping down the ground, it wouldn't have been easily seen. It was always assumed that she was the one in the factory at first. We weren't looking for anybody else.'

Damien ignored their arguing and speculating as they stood guard, not quite knowing what else to do until the ambulance arrived. But it was pointless speculating. Forensics and the pathologist would have to do their job, and he admitted that the sight of Edith had turned his normally strong gut.

He didn't know much about the forensic side of things, nor if there would be much evidence left on her after all this time under water. He was still trying not to think too deeply about that when to his fury he saw people running towards them from the village. The sight of them reminded him that as a local man he was in charge for the time being, and he shouted to the men to make himself heard above the din coming their way.

'We need to keep these buggers away. Let's get up a tape barrier as quickly as possible and don't answer any questions, even though they've obviously got wind of it from those bloody kids, and there's no chance of it not being common knowledge by now.'

* * *

Rosie was finishing work for the day when the library door burst open with a crash. Bert Smith almost fell inside, his face redder than if he'd drunk half a dozen pints as he gasped out the news.

'They've found her! Edith Pargeter, I mean. The two Wilkinson kids thought they was seeing demons when they saw two of her dolls staring up at 'em in a ditch over beyond the factory, and they reckon 'twas Edith down there as well. I just seen a couple of the women coming back from there, and they say 'tis true and that she was a horrible sight,' he elaborated wildly, 'all covered in weeds and slime. The police won't let anybody near her while they wait for the ambulance to come and take her away.'

He gasped for breath again, holding on to the stitch in his side as Rosie and Norman took in all that he was saying with growing horror.

'You'd better sit down before you fall down, man,' Norman said sharply, 'and you too, Rosie,' he added, seeing that she was as white as a sheet in contrast to Bert.

But she was already grabbing her coat and rushing out of the library. Nothing would have kept her away from the scene, despite how much she knew the police would keep people away from it. She was sobbing as she ran, her worst fears coming true. Poor, poor Edith . . .

There were people everywhere now, jostling and pushing, as news flew around the village like lightning. Somebody caught hold of her, rudely pulling her to a halt, and she turned in a fury at being stopped.

'Hang on a minute, darling,' Charlie said. 'I've just got back to the pub and people are saying all kinds of things. Is it true? Has Edith really been found?'

She looked at him wordlessly. How much did he know? How much had he heard? She would have given the earth to smile and say yes, Edith's been found, safe and well . . . but it wasn't like that. It had never been destined to be like that.

'She's dead,' she said shrilly. 'Drowned in a ditch with a couple of her babies. Can you believe that?'

She felt hysterical at the sound of her own words, and she clung to him as he held her very tight.

'Come on. Let's go and see if we can find out any more,' he said roughly. 'I know what this means to you, but hold on, Rosie. Don't go to pieces now.'

They walked quickly to where the crowds of people nearing the new police tape were falling quieter now, muttering among themselves. It was almost like a silent wake for a community mourning the death of someone who had lived among them all her long life.

Rosie saw her uncle arrive, and after speaking with Damien he went towards the policemen still guarding Edith and knelt down beside her body.

'Somebody will have to let Edgar know,' she said, her voice shaking.

'That's not your job, Rosie. The police have their own procedure to follow. By the way, in case you're interested, he runs a betting shop.'

She hardly took in what he was saying. What did it matter now? All that mattered was that the ambulance was going to get here quickly and put an end to this macabre tableau where nobody seemed able to move away. After what seemed like an age, at last they heard the siren, and the vehicle lumbered over the grass towards the police officers, effectively blocking out the scene from the onlookers.

'I've got to see Damien,' Rosie suddenly gasped, breaking away from Charlie and running towards him.

'What the hell for?' But he was talking to himself as she sped across the grass until she reached Damien, who was deep in conversation with her uncle now. The both looked at her warily, seeing how wild-eyed and distressed she appeared.

'It's true, isn't it? You've found Edith.'

Doctor Redman spoke sharply to her. 'Rosie, go on home. There's nothing you can do here, and nothing more that can be done for Miss Pargeter.'

She turned to Damien. 'Can I phone her brother?' she said in a shaky voice. 'I know it's your job, but I think it would be kinder coming from me.'

Though why she should bother being kind to him, she didn't know. It was more that she wanted to hear his reaction to the news at first-hand.

Her uncle was sharper than before. 'Rosie, you've had a shock, the same as we all have, so leave it to the police, my dear.'

'Please, Damien,' she spoke to him again. 'This is really important to me.'

He was at once the efficient policeman, following procedure.

'This is a police matter, Rosie. DI Forster already has all the details and will be contacting him as soon as possible to let him know we've found someone we presume to be his sister, and to ask him to formally identify her. It's not your place to interfere, and the last thing the man will want is umpteen people phoning him.'

'I'm not umpteen people. I'm the person who knew her best around here.'

Seeing how determined she was, her uncle spoke quickly. 'You must do as Damien says, Rosie, and leave it to the police. And I must get round to the Wilkinson house and check on those small boys. It must have been a terrible shock for them as well.'

She kept her voice as steady as possible. 'I understand.'

If she was shivering violently inside, outwardly she tried to appear as calm as possible in the circumstances. She didn't want either of them thinking she was in danger of falling apart. Instead, she tried to behave as Graham Fox might behave, doing the job that had to be done and leaving emotions aside.

She hurried back to where Charlie was standing with his arms crossed, looking at her as if she was a lunatic.

'What was that all about?'

'We're going to the cottage. I told Damien I wanted to phone Edgar to tell him that Edith's been found dead,' she recited.

'How the hell did you get the copper to agree to that?'

'I didn't. He couldn't really stop me, but I suppose it was a bad idea, since that DI bloke's probably already told Edgar, anyway,' she said, 'but at least you'll get what you wanted, and get a few photos of Edith and Edna.'

'Won't it be locked?' he said, as they began walking quickly back to the village, through the crowds of people unwilling to go back to their homes yet, as if it was a mark of respect for Edith to stay for a while.

'I'm sure Edgar locks it now. But I know she kept a key underneath a flower pot, even though she and Edna never locked their door.'

She felt her throat thicken, remembering how easy they had always been about that, saying who would want to rob a couple of crazy old biddies like themselves? But nobody would want to kill them either. Would they?

Edith's cottage was right at the end of Butcher's Lane, and thankfully nobody was around to stop them. As in every other crisis, there was comfort of a sort in people huddling together, and right now the emphasis was on the place where Edith's body had been found.

Rosie's heart was thumping, unsure if she was doing the right thing or not, but just wanting to do the best by Edith, whatever that might be. She was fully aware that hearing of her death, and in particular the way she had been found, hadn't really got through to her yet. She was doing it the PI way, she kept telling herself, keeping all her emotions at bay until later.

She found the key, still not sure why she was even doing this, but if Charlie was going to do a proper feature about the Pargeter sisters, then it made sense for him to have at least one photo of them. Providing it was a photo of them in a good light, she thought fiercely, still protective of their way of life.

'Good God!' he exclaimed, as they walked inside.

She gave a half-smile. She was used to the chaotic interior, and the need to sweep things off chairs before anybody could sit down on them, but he wasn't, of course. He'd be seeing it all with fresh eyes, the way those detectives would have done. They would have been sneering. She hoped Charlie wouldn't.

'So that's them, is it?' she heard him say, as he went straight to the mantelpiece after a startled look around. He picked up one of the photos, clearly taken some years ago. The sisters were smiling into the camera, wearing their favoured style of dress that had never changed, each of them holding an armful of dolls dressed exactly like themselves. It could have been endearing or spooky, depending on your outlook.

'Do you think that was what she was doing?' Rosie said involuntarily. 'Saving a couple of her dolls before she got out of the factory, I mean?'

She swallowed, knowing it sounded slightly mad. But knowing Edith, it was exactly what she would have done. And in the end it had been the means of finding her. In a weird way, she'd have liked that. Oh *God* . . .

'Look, Charlie, we'll have to go. People will be going back to their homes, and it won't look good if we seem to be prying.'

'All right. I'll take a photo of this one and that will do.'

'Can't you just take their head and shoulders?'

'I need the dolls as well, but I agree that the full-length picture makes them look too eccentric.'

He took a couple of photos on his mobile and showed them to her to make sure she was satisfied. There were so many photos of the dolls as well, that he said that one surely wouldn't be missed, and Rosie found herself agreeing as he slipped it into his pocket. By now all she wanted was to get out of there. The place had always been oppressive, and it was even more so now that she knew Edith was never coming home.

Once outside she took a few deep gulps of fresh air, locked the door and replaced the key under the flower pot, and slowly let the breath out of her lungs.

'I'm going back to the library to fetch my

car and then I'm going home,' she said, knowing she sounded like an automaton.

'Fair enough,' Charlie said, tucking her arm in his. She was glad of his support, thinking she might fall down without it. 'We mentioned dinner tonight. I suppose that's out of the question now?'

She looked at him as if he was stupid. The last thing she could face was food. In fact, she felt as if she never wanted to eat anything ever again. And that was daft, if anything was. Life went on, and all that stuff . . . Somebody had died, but it wasn't one of her family, and if she felt as though she wanted her own family around her right now, she guessed her uncle would say that was a natural reaction as well.

'Sorry,' Charlie went on. 'In any case, I've got work to do tonight, and I'll want to send these photos off to my editor with a bit of copy. I'll walk you to your car if you're sure you're OK to drive home.'

'I'm fine,' she said huskily, knowing she was anything but fine. But she appreciated his consideration. She squeezed his arm as they reached her car, and then he pulled her close and kissed her hard.

'You're a great girl, Rosie, and it's the copper's loss. Don't brood too much, and I'll see you tomorrow.'

She slammed the car door shut and drove

off through the village with her eyes starting to smart. *Hold on*, she told herself. Not long now and she could indulge herself in all the weeping she needed, once she had relayed all that had been happening to her auntie.

Her uncle Bernard would have told her the news that Edith had been found after Damien had sent for him, but he probably wouldn't be home yet if he'd had to see to the Wilkinson kids.

Poor little devils, she thought sympathetically, to stumble across something like that. It was the stuff of nightmares for kids of that age.

And for her too . . .

8

It was nearing the end of a poor working day for Edgar Pargeter and he was totting up the meagre day's takings, when the door of the bookmaker's opened and the two detectives he'd seen before came inside. His gut tightened. He didn't like coppers. They probed into things people didn't want them to know, and considering how he always liked to be in control, they made him edgy. Business was bad enough too, without them scaring off his customers, and now he'd lost the thread of what he was doing, so he'd have to start totting up all over again.

Still griping inwardly and wondering what damn fool questions they were going to ask him now, he saw the younger one slip the lock on his door, and from the grim look on their faces he knew it wasn't going to be good news.

'I've told you all I know, so get on with it,' he began belligerently, and then his voice altered. 'Unless you've found Edith. Have you?'

'Mr Pargeter, it would be advisable for you to sit down, so is there somewhere we can talk in private?'

Edgar stared at them, hating them for who they were, and even more for obviously knowing something he didn't.

'Who the hell's going to overhear? Let's just have it,' he snarled.

'Very well, Sir.' The DI's voice was grave. 'Then I'm very sorry to tell you that the body of your sister has been found.'

Even though anybody with any common sense must have known that this was likely to happen, without warning Edgar felt as though his bowels were turning to water. It was a sensation he had never felt before and never wanted to feel again. Any minute now and he thought he was going to crap himself.

He sat down heavily on the chair behind the counter, his face suddenly devoid of colour.

'Head between your knees, Sir,' he heard the sergeant order.

Before he had time to do as he was told, the sergeant had thrust his head downwards, and he forced himself not to throw up as well as the other thing. The last thing he needed was to disgrace himself in front of these buggers. He took the deepest breaths he could, considering how his head was pressed tightly over his belly, and then he pushed the man away as he sat up slowly.

'Can I fetch you some water, Sir?' Sergeant

Locke said politely.

'I don't want bloody water. I need a drink,' Edgar snarled again, reaching for his hip flask on the shelf beneath the counter. Uncaring of their opinion, he took a long draught that made his head spin, and he immediately slowed down, instinct telling him he should stay alert for whatever he was going to hear.

'Where was she? What happened? Was she hurt? Who found her?'

He listened to himself as the questions croaked out of his shaking lips. *God*, he was worse than a babbling old woman . . .

DI Forster kept his voice detached, knowing of old that it was the best way to deal with people in this situation. He had to admit that the poor devil looked totally shocked, which threw him for a moment. But only for a moment.

He was still of the opinion that Pargeter was somehow connected with the cause of the fire and the death of his sister — or maybe both sisters. Alibis could always be arranged, and families were more often involved in crimes than many people would believe. But until there was enough evidence to pin anything on the man, those theories would have to wait.

'I've heard from my colleague in Bately-sub-Mendip that Miss Edith Pargeter's body was found in a nearby ditch by two young boys out looking for birds' eggs,' he said, sparing him none of the facts. 'She had presumably been there since the night of the fire, and had apparently drowned, but she had considerable facial bruising as well, so foul play can't be ruled out until we get the pathologist's report.'

Edgar's throat was filling with bile again, and he swallowed the vile tasting muck down. He closed his eyes for a moment. The idea of Edith lying dead in a ditch horrified him as much as the thought of her being burnt to death in the fire had horrified him earlier. For a second, his thoughts wavered to a place he didn't want to go, to the time when he'd been a small boy, the late baby of elderly parents, and his two much older, plain-faced sisters had petted and pampered him, treating him like one of their dolls, calling him their baby . . . For one ghastly moment he thought his emotions were going to overcome him, and he swallowed hard.

'So what — what's happening to her now?' he managed to say.

'In due course you will be required to formally identify her, Mr Pargeter.'

'Of course,' Edgar said, dragging himself together.

Sergeant Locke spoke again. 'Is there

anyone else we can contact for you, Sir? Do you have a wife or partner, or are there any other relatives, or a close friend, perhaps? I believe you were out with friends on the night of the fire.'

'No. There are no other relatives, and I'll see to anything else myself.'

'Right,' DI Forster said. 'Then we'll be in touch again soon. Please don't leave town until we need you for the identification. I'm sure you'll want to go to the village to arrange for the burial, although it may be a while before the body can be released. Meantime, let me say that I'm very sorry for your loss.'

It was the kind of trite remark that didn't mean anything. Why should he be sorry? It wasn't his sister, or his factory that had gone up in smoke.

For a long while after they had gone, Edgar kept the door of the betting shop locked. Not that there were likely to be customers now, but in any case he didn't want to see anybody. He just wanted to think, and it was a pity that the whiskey on top of an empty stomach was making his thoughts so muddled. Or maybe it was better so, because right now, all he could imagine was Edith's poor old pudding face, swollen and bruised after being in the ditch for a few days.

She'd have been so cold too, and she

always hated the cold. It was the reason she'd had the little electric fire put in the factory, so she could keep warm while she worked. To his horror, he found himself dangerously near to sobbing, and he took another swig of whiskey to ward it off.

The hell of it was, he couldn't stop imagining what she must have looked like when they found her. Four days in a filthy ditch couldn't have improved her looks, and he tried to squash such an unworthy thought. What had the police said? Two kids looking for birds' eggs had found her. Poor little sods. They must have thought Hallowe'en had come early. But how the hell had she got there? Had she been in the factory at all that night?

His thoughts went off at a tangent, as he remembered that nobody had mentioned anything about the man who had died in the factory. Presumably they hadn't been able to identify him yet. Perhaps they never would.

So many questions were swirling around in his head now that he needed to get out of the claustrophobic atmosphere of the betting shop and into his own flat where he could breathe. He'd been sweating so much since the coppers arrived that the rank smell of his own sweat was making him want to puke all over again, and he was badly in need of a shower.

Clean in body, clean in mind was one of his sisters' favourite sayings, especially when he was a small boy and they'd had the job of scrubbing him in the bath tub. And he wished to God he hadn't thought of it right then, nor the smug, self-righteous smiles on their faces when they'd said it!

★　★　★

'What do you think?' DI Forster said to his sergeant when they left the bookie's and breathed in some welcome fresh air for themselves.

'Not sure. He looked pretty cut up to hear that his sister's dead, and I wouldn't have put him down for much of an actor.'

'Maybe,' Forster said thoughtfully. 'I reckon he's not as flash as he appears to be with his big cigar and tidy clothes, and if he was banking on the insurance money from the factory, he'll have to wait awhile until the cause is determined.'

'Same goes for the life insurance on his sister. Some companies won't pay out if it was a case of murder, but unless somebody actually shoved her in the ditch, there's probably a loophole of death by drowning.'

Forster looked at him sharply. 'So what do you think? Is he involved?'

'I'm still keeping an open mind until we know about the cause of the sister's death when we get the pathologist's report.'

'Right. So let's go and see if there's any news yet. You can forget your supper for a while, and you probably won't feel like it when we've had a look at Edith, anyway,' he finished with a grin.

Heartless bastard, Locke found himself thinking. But in their job it was the way you had to be sometimes, to offset the horror of the sights you saw.

★　★　★

There was only one topic of conversation in Bately-sub-Mendip that evening, and it wasn't going to stop for a long time. Clusters of people still hung around on the Green and in the pub. There was shock and there were tears. Edith Pargeter may have been an eccentric, but she was one of *their* eccentrics, who had never done anyone any harm, any more than her sister Edna had done. They were part of the fabric of the village, and now, in the space of months, they were both gone.

Rosie had firmly intended staying home that evening, but in the end, she knew it was impossible. In times of crisis, you needed to be with people, and after her auntie had phoned Doctor Redman, she had immediately said she would go to the Wilkinson house to see if she could offer any help with her boys. Rosie drove her there, and seeing her uncle's car still outside the house, she went to the pub to find Charlie. It was crowded, but he stood up as soon as he saw her and made room at the table where he was sitting with Bert Smith and a few others.

'I thought we said dinner was out for tonight,' he said, trying to cheer her up and avoiding any mention of her red eyes.

'It is,' she said abruptly. 'I couldn't eat a thing. It would choke me if I tried. It's such awful news, Charlie.'

Her eyes welled up again, and he squeezed her arm. 'I know it is, but I think in our hearts we knew it had to be something like this, didn't we?'

'Not like *this*! Not to be found in such a state! She was such a dear old soul, and nobody deserved such an end, least of all Edith.'

Bert Smith agreed. 'Somebody should be hung, drawn and quartered for doing such a thing to the poor lady.'

'You don't think it was an accident then, Bert?' Charlie asked.

Bert snorted. ''Course it was no accident. Don't ask me how she got there, 'cos I don't know, but I'm telling you 'twas no accident. Somebody wanted to do away with the poor lady, and they did it in a horrible way.'

The little group at the table fell silent, and Rosie didn't dare look at Charlie. She wondered how much of all this he was going to send off to his editor, or how much he had done so already. It was hot news now. Two deaths in a small village like Bately, plus an unexplained fire, would definitely put them on the map in a way nobody here had ever wanted to be.

'I'm going to see Damien,' Rosie said quietly to Charlie once general conversation had resumed. 'I want to tell him what I think.'

'Are you sure that's a good idea?'

'I don't know. I just know I can't sit here speculating.'

'Then I'm coming with you,' he said.

'Not this time, please, Charlie. I'll come back to the pub after I've seen him. I'm sure I'll be in need of a drink by then.'

She knew it was best if she went alone, knowing how Damien would resent her being seen too often in Charlie's company. As if he had any claims on her! But she knew how his mind worked. She and Damien had officially broken up, but in his eyes he would see Charlie Walters as an interloper who had suddenly appeared on the scene, and not only taken up residence at the local pub, but taken over his girl as well.

But she couldn't think of that now. She wanted to put her theories to somebody in authority as well as Charlie, to see if there was any substance in them, or if she was simply weaving stories in her head, and making mysteries where there were none. Perhaps the fire had been accidental. Perhaps the man had seen a light in the factory and had been merely asking for directions. Perhaps Edith had needed fresh air and gone for a walk, tripped, and fallen into the ditch.

And pigs might fly.

It was already dark by now. The evening was cold, and she shivered as she hurried round to the small police house cum police station. She still wasn't sure what she was going to say, or if Damien would take her seriously. He knew her of old, and how much she was in the habit of making mysteries where there were none. He might not even be there. He might be interviewing people on the streets, but the light streaming out told her that he was at home. She pressed the bell and took a deep breath as he came to answer it. In his small office, she could see he had been working at his computer.

'I want to talk to you about Edgar Pargeter, Damien,' she said.

She felt oddly nervous, knowing damn well that his own feathers were ruffled, since he could have been in charge of the investigation if those interfering Bristol coppers hadn't taken over. But he knew it had to be like that. He didn't have the facilities or the manpower here — had never needed such things — to deal with serious crimes. His incidents were more in the case of lost car keys, or cats stuck up trees, or the occasional fracas outside the pub by some of the local lads. He'd never had to deal with a murder, if murder it was.

And he didn't care to be tackled in his own police station by Rosie Redman suggesting that that was exactly what it was.

'It's obvious that Edar Pargeter had to be involved,' she virtually exploded as he glared at her as though she was a lunatic. 'He had everything to gain, didn't he? The insurance from the factory fire, his sisters' life insurance, and the sale of the cottage!'

'I always thought you were slightly mad, Rosie,' Damien snapped. 'So are you suggesting that everybody who dies in the village is a potential murder victim, simply because their relatives are going to gain from their life insurance?'

'Of course not,' she snapped back. 'But he will.'

'Why did you mention both sisters?' he said

next. 'Edna died from a heart attack, which was hardly a surprise, since the whole village knew how frail she was. God knows how she ever went back and forth to the factory all the time, and you know very well that your uncle told her she was being foolish to do so, and that she risked this happening at any time.'

'And I know that she never went anywhere without her pills. They were always in a pocket of her dress or coat, and when she went to bed they were always on her bedside table so she could get to them quickly. So why weren't they there that night?'

Damien was impatient with her. 'Look, I've got more important things to do than rake over old incidents. It's Edith's death that I'm more concerned with now, and I have to send in my report to Bristol as soon as possible. I suggest that you keep your theories to yourself, Rosie,' he warned her.

'Why? Do you think I'd be in any danger if Edgar thought I was on to him?' she asked wildly.

She didn't think it for a minute, but with a sudden shiver, she supposed it was possible, Anything was possible.

'Just remember what I say, that's all. This is police work, and we'll get to the bottom of it, don't you worry.'

He stood up pointedly, leaving her in no

doubt that she'd said enough and he wanted her out. *God*, when did he ever become so pompous, she raged, or perhaps he had always been like that, and when she was going out with him, she had just been too blind to see it.

She went straight back to the pub, needing the comparative security of Charlie and the group of people still there, rather than register the beginning of darker thoughts about her own position in all this. Though why Edgar should think she was a threat to him in any way, was ludicrous. Even if he was guilty of something too awful to contemplate, it had nothing to do with her, other than that she liked the Pargeter sisters and always felt ready to champion them if need be.

Admittedly, there had always been those in the village who were ready to snigger at their old-fashioned ways, particularly the schoolkids, while older people were more than ready to tolerate them. And for God's sake, Rosie admonished herself, here she was, thinking like an oldie when she was barely twenty-four herself!

'So how did it go?' Charlie asked, seeing her angry face and tight lips. 'Not well, I'd say.'

'I don't know what I ever saw in him,' she snapped without thinking. 'For a copper, he's completely blinkered. He sees things one way, and as long as it's his way, that's the end of it.'

'My God, you do need a drink, don't you? Mrs Gentry's rustled up sandwiches for anybody who wants them, so what do you say? Cheese and pickle, or ham and mustard?'

She hadn't been able to face the thought of food, even though it seemed daft to starve yourself. It didn't change the fact that Edith was dead. It wouldn't bring her back, and at the suspicious rumbling in her stomach at the mere mention of ham and mustard sandwiches, she gave in.

But she didn't want to stay long. People were starting to drift away now, and the news of Edith's death was no longer the stark and terrible shock it had been a few hours ago. The circumstances would always be terrible, but if time never really healed, at least it gave some perspective to the needs of everyday living. Half an hour later she said goodbye to Charlie and drove home.

Her aunt and uncle were still out, and she wasn't sorry. She needed time on her own now. Switching on the television for the late night local news, her heart jumped as she saw how Edith's death was already being reported. The same woman reporter who had been here before was superimposed over a picture postcard image of the village, and she ended by saying that police were continuing to investigate.

'Vultures, all of them,' Rosie muttered, knowing it wasn't strictly true. It was news, and the woman was only doing her job, the same as Charlie was doing his. Damien too.

How scathing he had been, as good as telling her get on with her job as librarian and leave police work to the police. Perhaps she should do just that, she thought, even though library work seemed so dull now, when she had always enjoyed it. And if she hadn't been there to help Edna and Edith with their weekly choices of romances, and listened to their chatty bits of news, she would never have become so fond of them, and so anxious and defensive over what had happened to them.

She swallowed back the lump in her throat, switched off the TV and went to bed, hoping she would be able to sleep. And hoping too, that somewhere out there, whoever it was who had done this dreadful thing to Edith, would be brought to justice.

★　★　★

The following afternoon, Edgar Pargeter was visited by the police again, and invited to come and formally identify his sister. *Invited* was the last word he'd have used for it, as they drove him away from the betting shop that afternoon. A fine thing this was doing for business, he thought savagely, to have the police sniffing around all the time. Most of his customers wouldn't like that one bit.

His nerves were shot to pieces by now, afraid of what he would see, afraid that if Edith's eyes were open, they would be staring at him reproachfully for not being there when she needed him. But they wouldn't be open, would they? Didn't dead bodies have their eyes closed, and all orifices plugged, in whatever Goddamn way they did it? He didn't know, and didn't want to know. It sounded so bloody undignified, and a bloody revolting job for somebody to do, but he remembered that he'd read about it some-where after Edna died, and desperately wished that he hadn't.

He'd been dreading this occasion. He hadn't been able to sleep because of it. For an outwardly bragging, bolshy individual, he was particularly squeamish about hospitals and needles and the sight of blood. He dreaded the antiseptic smells, and the mere sight of doctors and nurses in their uniforms, especially when they were wearing surgical masks. He failed to understand how people could watch those damn hospital dramas on TV. As for watching the procedure of a real operation, they were nothing short of vampires.

'When you're ready, Mr Pargeter,' he heard DI Forster say when they had covered the short distance across town, and were standing outside the room where Edith's body lay ready for his inspection. Until that moment he'd deliberately kept his thoughts away from what was actually going on today, but he knew he couldn't avoid the moment any longer.

He nodded. 'I'm ready,' he said in a strangled voice.

They went inside together, to where he could see a female shape beneath a covering sheet on a gurney, and a man wearing a pale green gown and surgical gloves pulled back the sheet covering Edith's face.

Edgar made himself look down, and almost fainted. Didn't they have some kind of make-up artist at the undertaker's who doctored the deceased's face for viewing before burial, he thought hysterically? But this wasn't ready for burial. This grey-faced, bulbous thing with the dark bruises over the closed eyes and cheeks was just as it had been recovered from the ditch, minus the weeds and muck. This thing had once been his sister. He forced down the vile taste in his throat and nodded.

'This is Edith Pargeter,' he said hoarsely. 'Now can I get out of here?'

* * *

By the time the latest edition of the *West Gazette* came through his letterbox that evening, he had drunk an entire bottle of whiskey to try to rid his mind of the ghastly image he had seen today. He tried to tell himself it wasn't Edith lying there, glacier-cold and still, at least not the Edith he knew, fussing and flapping over him in her well-meaning, maddening way. It was a waxwork, a model, a hideous *doll* . . . and that was a word that made things worse.

He grabbed the newspaper and took it back to his flat on unsteady legs, intending to fill his mind with other things. He needed to see nonsensical features and council pomposity and football crap. He flopped down on an armchair and unfolded the paper. And the first thing he saw was a large photo of Edna and Edith smiling up at him, holding armfuls of their effing dolls.

He let out a howl of horror and threw the newspaper away from him, his heart pound-ing. They were after him. For some

159

Goddamned reason, they were out to get him. They never wanted him to consider selling the factory and he had placated them on that, even though he knew he could get a good price for it. Now they were both gone, and just when he could do as he pleased with it, the factory was gone too. And here they were, gloating at him.

But how the hell had their photos got into the paper? That effing reporter who was hanging around with Rosie Redman and obviously trying to get his leg over, would be first in the frame, of course. He snatched up the paper again and read as much as his drink-sodden eyes would allow him to do. The Walters chap had written up a sympathetic report of the way Edith had been found, and the sadness of it all, which Edgar impatiently skimmed.

There was a second photo of a group of the dolls as well, and the more he looked at their inanimate faces, the more enraged he became. It was that bloody girl. Rosie Redman. It had to be her who had let the bloke into the cottage to take the photos. She had always taken too much effing interest in his sisters' business for his liking. Probably trying to get a mention in their Wills, he thought next, his thoughts becoming ever more vicious. Well, even if there was anything

160

to her advantage in Edith's, he'd see that nothing came of that!

He stared at the photos for as long as his eyes would hold up, and then he screwed up the paper and hurled it across the room in a fury. The little bitch should have known that his sisters would never want publicity of this kind. Unless she was being paid for the photos. That was probably it. Out for herself, and scoring points with the newspaper hack at the same time. They might even have done it in Edith's bed. The very thought made his stomach curdle.

But after seeing what the little bitch had done, he had more than a score to settle with her once he got back to Bately-sub-Mendip.

He blundered into his bedroom and sprawled across his bed, fully dressed, too stupefied to think of getting undressed, or even to realise that his rage at the newspaper photos had taken his mind off the horror of the afternoon for the moment. That would return in his nightmares.

9

Bately-sub-Mendip was swarming with people for the next couple of days. Without seeing the irony of her words, the one good thing to come out of all this, Mrs Gentry remarked to Charlie Walters, was that it was good for business. The village shops were doing well, and so was the pub. TV crews and newspaper reporters and curious visitors all had to eat, and needed a drink when they had done their share of fact-finding or sheer damn nosiness.

Charlie had always known that his wouldn't be the only paper to report the goings-on in Bately. But he had been the first, and he would always have the credit for that, even though it was turning out to be a gruesome credit now, and initially he had simply come to report on a small factory fire.

He had also met Rosie Redman, and as far as he was concerned, that was far and away the best thing to come out of it all.

*   *   *

On that first day after the discovery of Edith Pargeter's body, Norman Youde was preparing to close the library for their lunch hour, and Rosie was re-stacking some books in their right order on the shelves when she heard her name called.

'Miss Rosie Redman?' a male voice said, and she turned with a smile, which faded at once as she saw the TV camera right in front of her.

'I've got nothing to say,' she said quickly.

The male interviewer moved closer, followed by a small retinue crowding into the small library space behind him.

'Just a few questions for our viewers, Miss Redman. I believe you were a close friend of the deceased Edith Pargeter?'

'I was a friend to her, the same as the rest of the village,' she snapped. 'Miss Pargeter was a well-liked person in Bately, and if you'll excuse me, I have work to do.'

'Was she not something of a recluse?' the man persisted.

Rosie just managed to resist the urge to be overly sarcastic. 'Hardly. She did her shopping in the village and she worked at her factory, which I'm sure you know, and I saw her once a week when she came to renew her library books.'

'What kind of books did she read? I imagine it was the kind of lurid love stories an elderly spinster liked to indulge in. Would that be about right?'

Rosie didn't like the picture he was painting of a recluse, who avidly read love stories in lieu of a romance of her own. It almost made her want to laugh to think of Edith reading the kind of erotic novels he was implying. She was nothing like that at all — and nor did she really feel less like laughing, Rosie thought angrily, seeing the smirk on the interviewer's face.

'It's not my place to discuss Miss Pargeter with you, and her brother is the person to tell you anything more you want to know.'

'Thank you, Miss Redman,' the man said smoothly, and almost as one, the retinue turned and moved out of the library, leaving Rosie to slam the door after them and lock it with shaking hands.

'Why did I say all that!' she raged at Norman.

'You didn't say anything out of place and I think you did very well,' he told her. 'Come and sit down a minute.'

She shook her head. 'No thanks. I'm meeting Charlie for lunch at the pub, so I'll see you later, Norman.'

She was upset at being caught unawares. She hadn't wanted to be interviewed at all, but if she'd known it was coming, she might have had a few prepared sentences instead of babbling the first thing that came into her head. But that would be the way they operated, of course.

The first thing she saw as she neared the pub was the same camera crew moving towards it, probably with the intention of getting some more candid observations about Edith. *Vox pops* they called them, and they could cobble them together in any way they liked to make their report as sensational as possible. Poor Edith, who never wanted to be famous, and would hate all this.

But that decided it. There was no way Rosie was going inside the pub now. She ran back to the library, jumped in her car and headed home for a quick snack with her aunt and uncle. She called Charlie on her mobile and told him she'd see him later, unable to say anything more.

'You look flustered, Rosie,' her aunt Laura said at once. 'Surely nothing else has happened?'

'Don't be surprised if you see me on TV this evening,' she replied shakily. 'They came to the library, assuming I was a close friend of Edith's and wanted me to tell them more about her. I didn't say much, but I've no doubt they'll edit it so that they get what they want.'

'It's a pity you said anything at all,' her uncle said.

'It's a bit difficult not to when you suddenly get a camera thrust in your face!' she said, more upset that he seemed to be censuring her.

'Yes, but these people are clever at putting words in your mouth that you didn't intend to say.'

'Well, I told them that Edith's brother was the person they should be talking to, and they couldn't argue with that, could they?'

'Come and sit down, Rosie, while I make you a sandwich,' her aunt said soothingly. 'I'm sure they'll have so many people to interview they'll just use a few words from each person.'

They all heard the sound of a car on the drive, and the next minute there was a hammering on the door.

'Good God, who's that?' Bernard Redman exclaimed angrily. He went to answer it and was almost pushed aside as Charlie came into the house.

'Sorry about that, Doc, but I was anxious to know if Rosie's all right after that garbled message on my phone.'

'Of course I'm all right,' she said. 'I didn't mean to alarm you, but I didn't want to face that TV crew again.'

'Norman told me what happened. I did warn you to be careful what you said, didn't I?'

'Oh God, don't you have a go at me too!'

He was suddenly sitting beside her on the sofa and gripping her hand.

'I'm not having a go, sweetheart. I was worried, that's all.'

Rosie realised that her aunt and uncle were looking startled at this show of affection from a man she barely knew, and she felt her face go hot.

Then Laura took control. 'Well, as you can see, Mr Walters, Rosie's fine, and since you probably haven't eaten, either, shall I make you both a sandwich?'

'That would be great, Mrs Redman, and I was going to suggest, Rosie, that we get right away from here this evening, and go and see a film in Bristol. What do you say?'

'I think that's the best idea I've heard yet!' she said fervently.

To Rosie, Charlie was like a breath of fresh air. He was in the business of interviewing people himself, and he could always calm her down, and put everything into perspective. She liked him more and more, and it was obvious that her aunt liked him too.

The TV crews had gone by the time she returned to the library for the afternoon, and she admitted later that she had probably been getting in a tizz over nothing. It was as her uncle said — there would be others who would be interviewed, and her contribution would be small, if used at all. The fact that it was going to be used in its entirety that evening at the end of a local news transmission, and that Edgar Pargeter would be watching it, was something that may have unnerved her still further.

But she didn't know it, and after they had laughed and cried through the daft comedy film that Charlie took her too — to get her mind off things, he said — they went outside into the cool evening air and he suggested going back to his flat for a nightcap before they went back to Bately.

'Is this a good idea?' she murmured.

'Why not? Are you afraid that I'll ravish you?' he said, sounding like the villain in a melodrama.

Maybe I'm afraid that you won't . . .

'I think I can trust you,' she said, smothering the thought.

'Pity. But never mind. We've got time on our side.'

'Have we?' she said in surprise.

He laughed 'Of course. You don't think I'm letting you go now, do you? Even if you don't throw up your job and go to work for Graham Fox and become a super sleuth, we're going to keep seeing one another, aren't we?'

'Yes, we are,' Rosie said after less than a moment.

She hadn't been inside his flat before, and it was a mixture of everything she might have expected, healthily disorganised, and yet with the sense that Charlie knew exactly where to put his finger on anything he wanted. He was that kind of guy. He made a good cup of coffee too, she thought, as she curled up companionably on the sofa beside him.

'We'd better see what they did with your interview,' he said, as the time for the local news approached.

'Must we?' she muttered as he switched on the TV.

'It's always better to know your enemy, Rosie. It might be a trite old saying to say that forewarned is forearmed, but it's true, for all that.'

She reluctantly agreed, and when the item came on, there was the smugly earnest interviewer, doing the *vox pops*, turning to one and another of the people in the village, and clearly looking for *characters*.

Bert Smith was as garrulous as ever, his accent even more countrified on television; the lady at the post office mentioned how the sisters chatted for a while when they came to draw their pensions; Mrs Gentry said the Pargeter sisters weren't drinkers so they never came inside the pub; several shop keepers mentioned what they bought for their tea; and the vicar gave his views of two God-fearing women who had sadly both gone to their Maker now, and would be their loss, but God's gain. His piety made Rosie squirm. Then finally, she had to sit through an embarrassing few minutes watching herself giving her answers to the questions she'd been asked.

'That was all right, wasn't it?' Charlie said. 'Or are you going to do the female thing and ask *does my bum look big in this*?' he teased her to take the sting out of it all.

'Shut up a minute, Charlie,' she said, sitting up straight. 'What's happening now?'

The announcer was busy shuffling the papers he had been handed, and then looked straight into the camera.

'Since we've been on air, there has been a development in the Bately-sub-Mendip case. It concerns the identity of the person who was burned to death in the Pargeter doll factory there. Dental records are being examined, and police are hopeful that these will confirm the area where the man lived. It is thought likely that he was a Bristol man, and police are now following up this lead before the man's name is released and any relatives are informed, and also to see if there

170

can be any clue as to what he might have been doing at the factory on the outskirts of the village on the night in question. We'll bring you any more news as soon as we have it.'

The local weather forecast map appeared on the screen next, and Charlie switched off the TV quickly. Rosie's face was white as she looked at him.

'I know it has to be followed up, and if I was doing the investigating, I'd probably be elated that something's happening at last. But part of me doesn't want to know, Charlie. I don't want to know that some thug went there with the sole intention of beating Edith up, or even worse. Does that sound crazy to you?'

He held on to her hands, just as he had done at her aunt's house.

'No, it's not crazy. You don't want to know, because you're too close to the people concerned. If you were really on the case as an independent PI, it would be different, because however hideous it all became, you would still be detached from it all. That's the difference, darling. But reading between the lines of that statement, it's pretty clear that as yet the police know nothing. There were too many likelys and hopefuls, and nothing definite in the announcement at all. It's the usual police method of letting people know that they're doing something when they probably still haven't got a clue.'

'I suppose so,' Rosie said reluctantly. 'Look, I'm sorry, Charlie, but can we go back now? I know I'm ruining what's been a lovely evening, but I've lost the taste for coffee.'

And for whatever else might or might not have happened this evening.

'I think you're right. You need a good night's sleep, and you can think about it tomorrow, as Scarlett O'Hara said in *Gone with the Wind*.'

'My God, for a newspaperman you're a bit of a romantic after all, aren't you?' Rosie said, with the ghost of a smile.

'You have no idea,' Charlie said, and kissed her for the second time.

⋆ ⋆ ⋆

Edgar Pargeter sat as though transfixed as he watched the local news on the TV screen. After sneering at the words of the various kooks in Bately-sub-Mendip, especially the snot-nosed vicar, who was nearly as old as Edith had been, and scowling at the interview with Rosie Redman, he had also sat up straighter as the final item was broadcast.

He wasn't as canny as Charlie at

deciphering police jargon. They were on to something, and he was as keen as the next person to know exactly what it was. He tried not to imagine the poor bugger in the fire leaving nothing but a set of teeth, if that was what it was, nor the gruesome findings by the firefighters before they handed them over to the police.

The trouble was, he was becoming so sodden with drink he found it hard to think straight at all. He knew he was drinking far too much, and had done so ever since he'd had to identify Edith's body, which had been a shock of the first order. In death, Edna hadn't looked anything like that despite the ghastly faces she must have pulled as she gasped for air. But then, Edna hadn't been lying in water and filth for four days, with her face all beaten up.

Hardly knowing what he was doing, he automatically reached for the whiskey bottle again as the image came into his mind. It was his one way of warding off the images and allowing him to sleep, at least until the effing nightmares began again. And now he had another vision crawling into his brain, that of sets of chattering false teeth calling for help as the flames began to consume their owner. He didn't even know if false teeth were involved, but he couldn't get the bloody things out of his head now. Dozens of them *Hundreds* of them, clacking away in a macabre dance in front of his eyes.

Bloody hellfire! His throat caught on a tortured sob. Why hadn't the stupid sod got out of there before he burned to death? Did he even know what was happening? And had he done that terrible thing to Edith? So many questions to which there were no answers. The shock of seeing her, and now hearing this latest news was turning his guts to water again.

By now his mind was so befuddled that he blundered off to his bedroom, still clutching the whiskey bottle, wishing to God that this was all over. He wished he could turn back the clock to yesterday, to six months ago, to God knows when. He wished he'd never bought the damn factory. Wished he'd never got greedy and thought he could sell it at a profit. Never got so angry with his sisters for their refusal ... and wished for one stupendous moment that he could go back to the child he'd once been, with those two adoring, pudding-faced older sisters pampering him and calling him their sweet baby doll.

★ ★ ★

'I wonder when the funeral will be,' Rosie said sadly to Norman Youde. 'I shall go to it, of course, and I'd think that half the village will turn out.'

She shivered as she spoke. It seemed hardly any time ago that they were turning out for Edna's funeral, never thinking that her slightly more robust sister would be so soon afterwards.

'You don't want to dwell on things like that,' Norman said.

'I'm not dwelling on it. I just wonder when it will be, that's all, and if Edgar Pargeter will have the decency to let people know. They may not have cared much for him, but Edith was part of this village.'

'She was a character, that's for sure. Your boy-friend certainly seemed to think so, from what he wrote about her. Nice photos in the *Gazette* as well, though I doubt that Edgar was too pleased to see them. I wonder how your bloke got hold of them.'

She ignored the suspicion in his voice. 'I thought Charlie did a nice piece about both sisters,' she said defensively.

'Oh ah, I'll give you that. He's still around then.'

'Well, not for much longer. He's going back to his office today and he'll be back as and when his paper thinks there's anything more for him to cover.'

Rosie kept her voice non-committal,

though she had been surprised by her own feelings when Charlie had told her. She had known him for a very short time, but because of the circumstances in which they had met, their relationship had become more intense than she had ever expected. She wasn't even sure if it was real, and being apart for a time was probably a good thing, despite the pang she felt at knowing how much she was going to miss him.

'You heard the news last night, Norman,' she said, switching her thoughts quickly. 'Do you think they'll find out who the dead man was?'

'Probably. They can do all sorts these days, and teeth can be a dead giveaway. Did you get my pun there? Anyway, I doubt if they'll be able to do much with poor old Edith. Any evidence there was on her will be long gone after being stuck in that ditch for four days.'

Rosie wished he hadn't said that, reminding her of that awful moment when they had all heard of the discovery. She wished she hadn't brought up any mention of the funeral, either. But there was still hardly any other topic of conversation in Bately now, and the last thing any of them could do for Edith would be to give her a decent send-off in the local churchyard. Although they wouldn't have any hand in it, of course, except to turn up. The details would be up to Edgar.

She wondered how he was feeling now. For the life of her she couldn't dredge up any feelings of sympathy for the man, but he certainly had a lot to think about. For the first time, she wondered if he had any real money troubles. He had lost his factory and his last remaining sister, and there would be insurance claims to be made, plus whatever Edith had left him in her Will. There was the cottage, which presumably he would sell. Despite what he had lost, he was still going to come out of all this with money in the bank.

'Rosie, stop day-dreaming and see to the customers,' she heard Norman say, and she realised she had been staring into space as the word *motive* started drumming into her mind.

She reminded herself of where she was, smiled and chatted with the customers bringing back books for exchange, and discussed the inevitable comments about Edith mechanically. At the same time she went through the rest of that day with all kinds of possibilities spinning around in her mind. There had to be a motive for any crime, apart from the mindless ones you read about where the perpetrators were high on drugs or addicted to killing for killing's sake, as in the case of those revolting sex or serial killers. Greed was a powerful motive, and so was need.

But surely Edgar Pargeter wasn't in such need of money that he would hire somebody to burn down the factory, and kill off both his sisters. He always looked affluent enough. He drove a big car and smoked those evil-smelling cigars, and he ran his own bookmaking business. The idea was too ludicrous for comfort, and yet, regardless of whether or not he needed the money that would come out of all this, wasn't it the idea that had been in the forefront of her mind all this time? That somehow all this was down to Edgar and nobody else?

Rosie wished Charlie was still around, so that they could thrash this out between them that evening, but he wasn't here right now. But there was somebody else who might listen. The library was always closed on Saturday afternoons, and it was late in the day when she knew where she had to go.

'Good God, what are you doing here?' Damien Hall said, not exactly welcoming when he opened the door to her.

Rosie took a deep breath. 'Can I talk to you, Damien? Right now I'm too confused and upset about Edith to think straight, and you could always put a logical take on a problem.'

She cringed as she said it, knowing she was doing the girly thing and flattering him. But hell, she *was* a girl, and if it took a bit of flattery to get what she wanted, so what?

'You'd better come in and sit down. Do you want some coffee?'

This wasn't intended to be a social occasion, and his voice was grudging, but she accepted anyway. She had known him for ever, and not so long ago she knew he'd expected them to eventually walk up the aisle together. She had squashed all that, and now that she was here, she felt jittery, wanting anything to delay the moment before he told her she was out of her mind.

'You'll probably think I'm mad,' she said when he handed her the coffee.

'I think that already, so get on with it.'

Rosie glared at him. 'Let me put a hypothetical question to you. If a person was seemingly very fond of another person, but unknown to them they were so desperate for money that when they saw how to get their hands on it by way of a crime, how would you go about trying to prove it?'

Damien banged the table in front of him.

'You're as transparent as glass, Rosie,' he snapped. 'This is all about Edgar Pargeter, isn't it? I don't know what you've got against the man. Don't you think he'll have enough on his plate right now, coming to terms with what's happened, without you accusing him of being behind it all?'

'Well, don't you think he could be?'

'Of course he could. So could I. Or you. Or Bert Smith or the vicar if you want to go to extremes.'

'Well, now you're being stupid. What would Bert Smith have to gain by Edith's death, or the factory being burnt down? What would *you* have to gain, though I can't see you doing so much as pinching a bit of office stationery, Mister Upright Public Citizen,' she snapped at him.

'It's nice to know what you really think of me.'

'I was being sarcastic, in case you hadn't noticed. But why won't you take me seriously, Damien? How often is it found that family members are behind a crime? Don't you think that Edgar Pargeter could have been involved in this one? Think what he has to gain. Does anybody know what state his business is in for a start, or if he has any financial troubles? Has anybody tried to find out?'

After a minute Damien gave an impatient sigh.

'You really are in the wrong business, Rosie, but I'm perfectly sure that DI Forster has got everything in hand, and has examined all the points you raise. We're not stupid, Rosie.'

'Have you asked him?' she persisted.

'What, and find myself accused of being an interfering village copper when the big boys are on the track?' he burst out.

'That's the problem, isn't it? You've been overlooked in all this, and you don't like it. Whatever theories you may or may not have had, you won't go to them now, and you should, since you knew the Pargeter sisters, and they didn't. You're taking the easy way out, Damien, and you're letting Edith down.'

She hardly knew where the words came from. But she knew they were true from the furious reddening of his face.

'I think you'd better get out, before I say something I'll regret, Rosie.'

'Don't worry, I'm going. And if you won't say something, I will.'

She turned and went out, slamming the door behind her before she could hear anything more. Her eyes were smarting with fury, and she wondered what she had ever seen in him. But she knew that. It had been prestige, no more. Going out with the handsome village copper had given her a boost, and she was ashamed of that now, just as she was ashamed of him for being such a wimp.

Damien Hall was the acknowledged authority figure in Bately, where crime wasn't exactly rife and where everybody looked up to him. But he wasn't God, just an ordinary man — and right now not much of one.

Rosie drove off with her car wheels spinning, and the wild thought that if Damien had any gumption about him, he'd come after her and give her a warning for speeding. But fat chance of that. He was probably sitting there fuming now, and thanking his stars he was no longer involved with the irritating Rosie Redman who thought she had a better brain for solving crimes than the police.

She got as far as the end of the village and was nearly home, when she thought better of it and turned the car towards Bristol. She'd threatened Damien with what she would do, so why didn't she just do it? She'd had one brush with DI Forster before, but that time he'd taken her unawares and scared her silly. This time it would be on her terms.

10

Less than an hour later Rosie was in Bristol. She drove into the police station car park and then marched into the building. Still fired up, she told the duty sergeant behind the counter that she needed to speak to Detective Inspector Forster.

'What's it about, Miss?' he asked politely.

'It's about what happened in Bately-sub-Mendip.'

She didn't want to talk to him, or any one of the DI's minions. She stared him out as a flicker of recognition dawned in his eyes.

'You're the young lady who was interviewed on TV last night, aren't you? Miss Redman, isn't it?'

'Yes, and I want to speak to DI Forster,' she said again.

'I'm afraid he's not here tonight, Miss Redman.'

It was Rosie's turn to stare now. Not here? Where was he, for God's sake, when there was a serious crime going on?

'Where is he, then?' she demanded.

The duty sergeant gave a slight smile. 'Even policemen have private lives, Miss. DI Forster is off duty for the weekend, and I daresay he'll be spending it with his wife and family.'

Rosie hated his patronising tone. But the fact that Forster wasn't here knocked the stuffing out of her for a moment. But only for a moment. She wasn't going to be put off that easily.

'I need to speak to someone else then. The sergeant who was with him was called Locke or something. I suppose he's not off duty as well, or does all crime stop for the weekend?'

As the man's eyes hardened, she knew it was a mistake as soon as she had said it. She groaned inwardly, and she spoke quickly before he could answer, uncaring if she was humbling herself. This was too important to her.

'I'm sorry, I shouldn't have said that. It's just that I'm anxious and I know the officers concerned would be interested in what I've got to say.'

'Take a seat and I'll see if Sergeant Locke is free,' the man said after a freezing moment.

The bizarre thought flew through Rosie's head that if looks could kill, she'd be joining Edith now. She sat down on a chair beside a gum-chewing girl wearing flashy make-up and a skirt as short as a belt.

'Don't worry, love, you'll get seen soon

enough,' the girl drawled. 'Get pulled in, did you?'

'Leave it, Queenie,' the desk sergeant called out to her. 'This is nothing to do with you.'

The girl grinned and leaned towards Rosie as if they were conspirators. The smell of her perfume was overpowering.

'I'm a reg'lar, see? They all know me, and it beats walking the streets all day.' She gave a huge wink as she spoke, showing misshapen teeth.

The sight of them was an uncomfortable reminder to Rosie of the dental records the police were following up regarding the body in the fire. She edged away from the girl as the desk sergeant made a snide comment about her preferring to walk the streets at night, which brought on peals of laughter from Queenie. Then Sergeant Locke appeared, and Rosie breathed a sigh of relief as he motioned her to follow him to an interview room.

A policewoman hovered by the door. Was this for moral support for herself or Locke, Rosie found herself thinking in mild hysteria? Now that she was here, what was she going to say to him that wouldn't be thought of as the ramblings of someone with an over-active imagination?

'So, Miss Redman, what is it you have to say?' he said, sitting back on his chair with his

185

arms folded behind his head.

A sudden wariness came over her, remembering Charlie's warnings about not getting in too deep, and accusing Edgar when there was no proof that he was responsible for any of this. A gut feeling probably wouldn't go down too well with this so-superior-looking man. Her thoughts flew around in her head like quicksilver, and she gulped out the words.

'It's about Miss Pargeter and the man who died in her factory.'

'I thought it might be,' Sergeant Locke said smoothly.

'You know she was my friend, well, a sort of friend,' Rosie floundered, 'and the way she died was so awful that I've been racking my brains to think how she got into the ditch at all.'

Locke gave an almost imperceptible glance at his watch. 'Do you have any thing concrete to say that will help our investigations, Miss Redman?'

'Yes. Supposing the man was just a vagrant with no devious motive for being there, other than to get somewhere warm.'

'It wasn't a cold night, as I remember.'

Doggedly, Rosie continued inventing. 'Supposing he saw an opportunity to steal something — anything! He went inside, startling Edith, who was so deaf she wouldn't have heard him coming, and when she shouted out for help, he panicked and hit her. She wasn't afraid of anything, despite her age, and she would almost certainly have hit back. They could have knocked over the electric fire between them and the man could have fallen and knocked himself out before the fire took hold. Meanwhile, even if Edith was concussed and hurt, she would probably have grabbed some of her precious dolls before rushing out of the factory. We know the two little boys who found her saw the dolls first. But she would be disorientated, going the wrong way instead of heading back to the village, and finally reaching the ditch where she fell in and drowned.'

There was silence in the room by the time she had finished speaking, and then, to her fury, there was the sound of slow hand-clapping.

'It's a good story, Miss Redman. Tell me, have you ever thought of writing such tosh yourself?'

'Can you see anything wrong with it?' she demanded. 'Don't you think it's a reasonable explanation for what happened?'

'Anything's possible. So you think it was all no more than a terrible accident brought about by circumstances, do you?'

'I think it *could* be,' Rosie muttered, feeling more and more deflated. She glanced for help or sympathy from the policewoman standing motionless by the door, but her face was completely impassive.

'And you came all this way just to tell us your theory. Do you know how many crackpot theories we have to listen to in the course of an enquiry, Miss Redman?'

She felt her face flush. It may seem like a crackpot theory to him, but it was still completely feasible, and far better than blurting out that she thought Edgar Pargeter was responsible for it all.

'I'm sorry to have wasted your time,' she said stiffly.

To her surprise his face softened a little.

'Miss Redman, we're always ready to listen to ideas from the public, but in this case, perhaps your personal interest in the deceased lady has distorted your viewpoint. Rest assured that we want to solve this case as quickly as possible, and we will certainly keep your thoughts in mind.'

She was dismissed, and once outside the police station again, where it was already dark now, she sat and fumed inside her car. Well, what had she expected? She had come here, determined to tell DI Forster exactly why she thought Edgar Pargeter had done away with at least one of his sisters, however obliquely he had managed it, and was set on profiting from her death and the sale of the cottage, plus the fire at the factory.

She was convinced of it in her own mind, and his eventual comeuppance would be that the perpetrator of a crime couldn't benefit from it. So why in God's name had she concocted the tale she had just told Sergeant Locke?

But what if it hadn't just been an unlikely tale? What if it had happened just like that, whether or not the man was a vagrant, or someone sent there on a more sinister errand? All the rest of it could be true. Though how it could ever be proved was another matter, since there was nobody alive to tell it.

She was more jittery than before now, and not ready to drive home yet. She knew Bristol moderately well, and by now she knew that Edgar Pargeter's betting shop was in one of the side roads off Whiteladies Road. She had a sudden urge to see just where he worked and lived, and she drove around slowly until she saw the name of the road. And there it was, the betting shop with the flat above where Edgar lived. She parked the car on the opposite side of the road, staring up at it, longing for some telepathic answers to it all.

There was a light in the front window of

the flat, the curtains not yet drawn, so he was evidently at home. Rosie wondered just what thoughts were going through his head now. Was he truly mourning Edith's death as a good brother should, or was he mentally counting up the coffers of what was coming to him? Did he know the identity of the man who had died in the fire, or had it truly been a vagrant as she had suggested in her wild theory to Sergeant Locke?

Her head ached, and she leaned her head on the steering wheel for a moment and inadvertently pressed the horn, startling herself when it went off. She had been here long enough, anyway, and she was achieving nothing.

A final glance up at the uncurtained window of the flat made her heart give a massive jolt. Whether or not it had been the sound of her car horn or not, she could see the dark outline of Edgar Pargeter's shape staring down at her car. She drove off in a rush, well away from the city centre, her heartbeats drumming furiously, and hardly knowing where she was going until she found herself in a road where she had been once before, and a familiar-looking flat.

Oh, please be in, she thought frantically. She stopped the car and rushed up to the door of the flat, almost falling into Charlie's arms when he answered it.

'Thank goodness you're home. I think I'd have crashed my car if I'd driven back to Bately in the mood I'm in,' she gasped.

'Rosie, what's happened? You're shaking like a leaf. Come inside and sit down before you fall down.'

After the scene with Damien, the embarrassment of speaking with Sergeant Locke, and then the shock of seeing the illuminated outline of Edgar Pargeter at his window, his concern was just too much, and she burst into tears.

'I don't know if he saw me,' she babbled. 'If he didn't see me, I bet he recognised the car. He's seen it enough times in Bately, and now he'll think I'm stalking him.'

'What the hell are you talking about, Rosie?' Charlie said, becoming really alarmed at the wild look on her face now. He led her into his sitting room, brushing the scattered magazines from the sofa before sitting down beside her and holding her hands to try to stop them shaking.

'Edgar Pargeter. He was silhouetted in his window. I couldn't see his face, but the look of his body language was enough for me.'

Charlie's mood quickly changed from concern to anger. The hands holding Rosie's were gripping hers now, tighter than ever, hurting her.

'Are you saying you've been outside Edgar Pargeter's flat and that he saw you there? Don't tell me you've done anything so bloody stupid, Rosie.'

She flinched visibly. 'I just wanted to see where he lived. I didn't intend to do so at all, but after going to see DI Forster who wasn't there, and having to talk to Sergeant Locke instead, I was too uptight to go straight back home.'

'God Almighty, it gets worse. I leave the village for twenty-four hours and you get into all kinds of trouble. You're not safe to be out on your own. You'd better start at the beginning and tell me everything that's happened. Take some deep breaths and take it slowly.'

She did as she was told, feeling like an automaton, but unutterably relieved that he had been close at hand when she needed him. If she'd had to drive back over the notoriously lonely Mendip roads in the state she was in, she was sure she'd have had an accident. And out there, with the autumn evening mists already closing in, and so little traffic, she might not have been found until morning, if at all. One more casualty to add to Bately's misfortunes.

Much later, feeling like a complete idiot for getting so het up over everything, and gladly accepting a few glasses of wine to steady her nerves, Charlie's calm words finally settled her down. Yes, she had been a fool and she admitted it, and the most foolish thing of all was her curiosity over where Edgar Pargeter lived. Without warning, she gave a nervous giggle.

'You don't really think he'll think I was stalking him, do you, Charlie?'

He took the empty glass out of her hand. 'I don't know about that, but I do know one thing. You're not driving back to Bately tonight in your condition.'

'What condition is that?'

She was unconsciously provocative, and he sighed. 'Sweetheart, I wish I could say that you're to stay here with me and to hell with the consequences, but I'm too much of a gentleman to take advantage of you right now.'

'So I can't stay here then?' Rosie said, her woozy head already starting to feel double its size.

'Well, I could drive you home, but I don't think your family will be too pleased to see you like this. You can stay, and I'll sleep on the sofa, but first of all, you'd better phone your aunt and tell her you're spending the night with a friend. OK?'

'OK,' she said in a muzzy voice.

★ ★ ★

When she awoke it was daylight and she was completely bemused to find herself in a strange bed, unable to think how she had got there, or why she was only wearing her bra and pants. Turning her head a little, she could see her jeans and other clothes on a chair, her shoes on the floor beneath. So she had either undressed herself, or someone else had done it for her.

'Tea and toast if you're up to it,' she heard a voice say, and her face flooded with colour as she saw Charlie come into the bedroom wearing a dressing-gown, his legs bare beneath it.

Oh God, oh God, oh God . . .

'Don't worry, nothing happened, tempting though it was,' he said with a half-smile. 'How are you feeling?'

'Ask me that a bit later when my mouth doesn't feel as if it's stuffed with cotton wool,' she said faintly. But it was all coming back to her now, and if she could have wiped yesterday out of her memory, she would gladly have done so.

'I have to get out of here,' she said next, struggling to sit up, and then sliding down beneath the bedcovers again.

'I've seen it before, Rosie. Who do you

194

think got you ready for bed? And you don't have to go anywhere until you're ready. It's Sunday, in case you've forgotten,' he said calmly.

Sunday. And in the village church the vicar would be saying prayers for Edith Pargeter, and asking God to save her immortal soul. Not much doubt about that, since Edith was a good-living woman who had never done harm to anybody.

'I can't stay here all day,' Rosie said more hurriedly, as more uneasy memories crowded in.

'I'd have no objection if you stayed for ever but we won't go into that now. Eat that toast to settle your stomach. I'll make something more substantial later on if you think you can stand it, but I've also brought you some towels and you can have a shower before you think about that.'

'Why are you being so good to me when I'm such a blessed nuisance?' Rosie said huskily.

'I'd have thought that was obvious,' he replied, before he left her.

By the time she had had a shower and got back into yesterday's clothes again, she began to feel more human, if still embarrassed at the way she had burst in here and imposed herself on Charlie.

'I'll get off home as soon as I've had another cup of tea,' she said quickly, declining a larger breakfast that she knew would choke her.

'You don't have to. Stay all day if you like.'

'I won't, Charlie. I'm so thankful you were here when I needed you, but I have to sort myself out, and I can't do that here.'

Besides, who knew what might happen if she stayed any longer? And she wasn't ready for that yet, not while the shadow of what had happened to Edith was still hanging over her. She knew she shouldn't take it all so personally, but she couldn't help it. Maybe she would never have made much of a PI, if this were to happen every time. But logic told her it wouldn't, because she would never be so deeply involved with the clients as she was with Edith Pargeter.

It was late morning when she finally left Charlie's flat, thanking him again, and assuring him she was quite all right and promising to keep in touch. This time, his kiss left her in no doubt about his feelings for her, and she knew damn well that it was only a matter of time . . .

★　★　★

'We were worried about you last night, Rosie,' her aunt exclaimed as soon as she returned home to the succulent smells of Sunday dinner roasting. 'You sounded so odd on the phone.'

'Did I?' she replied, trying to laugh. 'It was probably because I'd had a little too much wine, and it didn't seem a good idea to drive back. A few drinks turned into a party, and it was no problem to stay at a friend's house.'

It was partly true, and she hoped her aunt wouldn't probe any farther. Staying the night with a man she had only known for a week wouldn't be on her aunt's agenda, even though nothing had happened.

'Oh, by the way there was a phone call for you earlier this morning,' Laura went on casually. 'He apologised for calling us at home, but he didn't have your mobile number.'

'*He?*' Rosie said, with a swift sense of premonition. It wouldn't be Charlie, who she had just left, nor Damien or Norman, who both knew her mobile number. Besides, why would either of them be calling her on a Sunday morning?

'It was Edgar Pargeter,' her aunt went on. 'I must say it took me by surprise to hear his voice, but he's come down for the day and to see the vicar about arranging Edith's funeral as soon as her body can be released. He thought you might like to know, and also, he wondered if you'd care to help him sort out the cottage this afternoon. I wasn't at all sure how you'd feel about that, and I told him you were away at present, but I'd let you know.'

'You didn't give him my mobile number, did you?' Rosie said quickly, her mouth suddenly dry.

'No. Should I have?'

'Absolutely not. The less I have to do with that man, the better.'

Laura looked startled at the aggressive response.

'Has something happened, Rosie?'

'I just don't like him, that's all,' she muttered, with no intention of telling her all that had happened yesterday. So much had been packed into those few hours since she tried to get Damien to listen to her, and until this moment she had been desperately trying to forget the sight of Edgar Pargeter's dark silhouetted shape at his window, looking down at her.

All the way home she had been telling herself she had imagined that he recognised her or her car, that it was just coincidence, and that he had merely been about to close his curtains for the night. But in her heart she knew it wasn't like that. She knew it even more now that he was here, had tried to contact her and wanted to see her.

Her immediate instinct was to phone Charlie and tell him, but it was crazy to go to him for every little thing. She wasn't his responsibility, and even if she was daft enough to go to the cottage to help Edgar, both her aunt and uncle would know about it, and no harm could possibly come to her. Could it?

'You don't think I should do as he asked, do you?' she said to her aunt, willing her to say no.

'Well, it would be a kindly gesture, and I daresay he wants some of the personal things removed for charity shops or something,' her aunt said vaguely.

'Maybe,' Rosie said uneasily.

'It's not really a man's job, is it?' Laura went on. 'He's clearly aware of all that you did for his sisters, Rosie, and how much they thought of you, but if you don't think you could face it alone, I could always come with you.'

'*Would* you?' Rosie said, almost faint with relief. 'I'd really appreciate it, Aunt Laura.'

And let him try anything then, she thought, almost triumphantly. But why would he? Wasn't it enough that he had two deaths on his conscience — and maybe three, she thought, remembering Edna?

'I'll phone him and let him know we'll be

there sometime this afternoon then,' she said, before she could change her mind, being careful to use the house phone rather than her mobile.

The moment she heard his voice, she felt sick, but she steeled herself to speak as normally as possible.

'I'll be glad to help you at the cottage this afternoon Mr Pargeter, and my aunt will come with me. Two pairs of hands are always better than one,' she added, uncaring if she sounded twee, and knowing it was the kind of thing that Edna and Edith would have said. Maybe she was turning into them . . .

'That will be very helpful, Miss Redman,' Edgar said after a small pause when she could hear him breathing. As a smoker, his breathing was thick and heavy, like one of those anonymous phone calls beloved of stalkers . . .

'I shall look forward to seeing you again,' he added, and she didn't fail to notice the imperceptible pause before the last word as she put down the phone.

He knew. He had seen her last night, just as she thought, and this was his way of telling her. She should be scared, and so she was. She was angry as well. But almost to her surprise, something else was taking over now. Instead of the nerves she had felt previously, a strange calm was filling her. A sense of needing to see justice done for Edith was overcoming all other feelings. As much as possible Rosie knew she had to keep herself detached from the horror of it all, and think of it as a tragedy in which an elderly woman had been wronged and for whom right had to be done.

Perhaps nobody else but Rosie Redman truly suspected Edgar Pargeter of being the prime suspect in what had happened to his sisters and the fire at the factory, but she was also in the prime position of being involved closely enough to find out anything that she could. This afternoon, for instance, might throw up some clues as to their real relationship, and she would have the security of her aunt being there to be a buffer between her and Edgar.

Because one thing was for sure. However noble her sentiments, and her determination to see that Edith's death wouldn't go unpunished, she vowed that from now on she was never going to be alone with him. If what she believed was true, there was no point in putting herself in unnecessary danger. And the first thing to do about that was to defuse any suspicion he might have that she had been in Bristol looking for him last night.

She wouldn't even let on that she knew he

had a betting shop. She had merely been in the area looking for a friend's flat where she was going to a party and had stayed all night. Her aunt would vouch for that . . .

11

The first thing Rosie noticed was the strong smell of cigar smoke in the cottage. On the few occasions she had been there before when Edgar was around, it had always seemed odd to her that neither Edna nor Edith had objected to it. They had once remarked that it was fragrant and homely, and as it was so typically dear Edgar, how could they ever object!

Laura had never been inside the Pargeters' cottage before, and Rosie could see at once how astonished she was at the sight of it all. So far Edgar had touched very little, except for his sojourns to the bureau, which now looked closed and locked. The table was still covered in ornaments, the stacks of magazines and newspapers still in a corner of the room. But there was something missing. For a moment Rosie couldn't think what it was, and then she realised that although the photos of the sisters still adorned the mantelpiece, all the pictures of the dolls had gone. *Curiouser and curiouser*, as Alice would have said . . .

'It's kind of you both to come,' Edgar

Pargeter said solemnly. 'As you can imagine, this a particularly upsetting task for me, and it's good to have a woman's help. Or two women, in this case,' he added with a smile that was totally false to Rosie, but to which Laura warmed at once.

'Tell us what you would like us to do, Mr Pargeter,' she said gently.

'It would be a great help if you would go through my sisters' wardrobes and drawers and put the things in the boxes you'll find in their bedrooms, ready for sending to Oxfam, or possibly to a third world charity, since I can't imagine many ladies here would care for their style of dress. I can deal with most things here, but this is one job that is out of my domain.'

'And understandably so,' Laura said at once, while Rosie marvelled at the way he could put such sincerity in his voice.

She didn't believe it for a minute. It was more likely that, for whatever reason, he couldn't bear to be handling clothes that still had the scent of his sisters. It wouldn't be conscience, since Rosie didn't believe he had one, but he could still be spooked by the sight of all the old-fashioned clothes they had worn.

'Miss Redman has been here before, and will show you the bedrooms,' he said, looking directly at Rosie now, his eyes cold and unblinking. To anyone else, they might convey grief, but not to her. 'Meanwhile, if I may leave you here, I want to see the vicar about a possible date for the funeral. I don't know when it might be yet, but I know that as her friend, my sister would be comforted to know that you attended, Miss Redman.'

'Of course I will,' she said stiffly. 'There was never any doubt about that.'

Any minute now and he'd be backing away like the slimy slug that he was, she thought furiously.

'And I do hope some of the village will turn out as well, since I'm now the only family Edith has left,' he went on.

Laura's eyes were suspiciously moist by now. 'You need have no fear of that, Mr Pargeter. Everyone knew your sister, and I'm sure she will be duly honoured. Have they found the identity of the poor man who died in the factory yet, by the way?'

'Not as far as I know,' Edgar said. 'Now if you'll excuse me, I'll get down to the vicarage and I'll see you both later.'

'Poor man,' Laura said to Rosie when they were alone. 'This has all hit him terribly hard. Did you see how his hands were shaking?'

'I daresay that's down to the drink,' Rosie replied dryly.

Her aunt looked at her in surprise. 'It's not like you to be so cynical, my dear. I know you don't care for Mr Pargeter, but remember he's a man in mourning, and even if he did take a drink or two to dull the grief a little, it's perfectly understandable. I think you could show a little more compassion.'

'I'll try,' Rosie muttered, knowing that she couldn't.

They went upstairs, and with every step Rosie felt more and more uneasy. It was unbelievable that she should be here doing this task, when a little over a week ago, Edith had come into the library, chatting away as usual and taking away her armful of romance novels. She supposed she should return them herself, she thought, with a mild burst of hysteria.

'Shall we take a bedroom each?' she heard her aunt say.

'I couldn't bear that. Let's do it together.'

There were cardboard boxes in both bedrooms, and Rosie tried to avoid looking at the expected knick-knacks on the dressing-tables. It was all so personal and intimate — and so heartbreaking. But better for her and her aunt to do it than leave it to Edgar.

They tackled Edna's bedroom first, but Rosie knew it would be a replica of Edith's. They were so alike in every way except for their separate health problems, Edna with her weak heart and Edith with her deafness. Other than that, they were like the proverbial peas in a pod, especially in the long dresses they favoured. She took them from the wardrobe with almost reverent fingers, folded them neatly and placed them in a box, trying to be as detached as possible.

Then there were the dressing-table drawers, filled with underwear and yet more knick-knacks, and even a few discarded half-finished dolls' dresses. Finally, the items on top of the dressing-table had to be wrapped and placed on the clothes, the hair brushes and combs, the pots of hairpins and odds and ends.

'I feel worse than an intruder because we know exactly what we're doing here, and who the owner of all these things was,' Rosie said.

'Then let's sort out Edith's things as quickly as possible,' her aunt said briskly. 'Or would you rather leave it to strangers to do? I'm sure that's what would happen if we didn't get on with it. I can't see their brother doing it. What's his business, anyway? Do you have any idea?' she said curiously, hoping to take her niece's mind off the job in hand.

'He's a bookmaker,' Rosie said, as they went into Edith's bedroom. Her mind balked for a moment. Edith had always been her favourite, and here she was, about to expose her private space.

'Well, I know one shouldn't stereotype people, but perhaps it explains that almost *risque* air about him,' Laura said.

'If you were Norman, you'd use one of his dreadful puns and call it a *racy* air, ha ha,' Rosie said with a faint smile.

But the brief pause in proceedings had brought her back to her senses. They were here to do a job for Edith now, and they had better get on with it. Once they had finished they could get out of there before Edgar came back, she thought hopefully. But that chance was dashed as they heard him coming upstairs a while later.

'Nearly finished?' he said, glancing at the filled boxes. 'I can't thank you ladies enough. I need to get the place cleared out as I'm putting it on the market right away. It holds too many painful memories for me to hold on to it.'

I'll bet it does, thought Rosie.

'That's perfectly understandable,' Laura said. 'So did you speak to the vicar, Mr Pargeter?'

'Yes, and you'll be sure to know when the funeral has been arranged,' he said, clearly wanting to get them out of here now.

That suited Rosie. She found herself

breathing deeply once they were out in the open air. She told herself she must be imagining things every time Edgar looked at her. *Giving her the evil eye* was what came to mind, and she didn't like it one bit. She hadn't liked being here. It made her uncomfortable and uneasy. The whole cottage still held so much of Edna and Edith. It was a sad place now, where it had once been so homely and pleasant. Did places hold memories and the essence of their owners, she wondered? Could the people who had passed over, to use the vicar's words, ever be trying to tell a sympathetic person something? And was she going completely bonkers now?

The sisters had been scrupulously clean, but there was an inevitable amount of dust from the inside of wardrobes and drawers and old clothes. But it was more than that. Mingling with the smell of Edgar's cigar, she needed to get the taint of the place out of her skin, and she intended to have a shower the minute she and her aunt returned home.

★ ★ ★

On Monday morning DI Forster was frowning over the photos of the two elderly sisters and their dolls in the pages of the *West*

Gazette, and still pondering over the unlikely threesome of the Pargeter family.

'It didn't take Charlie Walters long to go sniffing over all this, did it?' he grunted, as his sergeant brought in two mugs of coffee to his office.

'I bet that's not the only thing he's been sniffing around. Probably getting his leg over with the Redman girl at the same time,' Locke sniggered.

Forster ignored him. Silly young bugger, always thinking about sex.

'But why would anyone want to kill these two old biddies? They look harmless enough,' he persisted.

'Who says either of them was killed? The first one had a heart attack and the second one fell in a ditch. She must have been a nutter to be out in the dark with those creepy dolls, unless she thought she was taking them for a moonlight stroll,' he finished with a snort of derision.

'You don't have an ounce of compassion in you, do you, Locke?' Forster snapped. 'No, there's something about all this that stinks. She was definitely scared into leaving the factory before falling into that ditch. That's if she was in factory at all, of course. We don't even know that for sure, and there's nothing to tell us now that the place has gone up in smoke.'

Later in the day he got the confirmation he needed about Edith's death. The blows about her head may have been cause by a fall, but there was also internal bleeding in her stomach from what could only be construed as having suffered some brutal blows. The verdict given on Edith was one of accidental death by drowning, brought on by concussion and severe beating or kicking by a person or persons unknown.

'In my eyes, it amounts to murder,' Forster said, 'but proving it is something else. In any case, if the poor bugger in the factory did it, he's already had his punishment.'

'So all we need now is to find out who he was and what he was doing there,' Locke said, with heavy sarcasm.

'Right, but at least the old girl's body can be released for burial now, so let the brother know, Sergeant, and he can start making arrangements. And for now, we'll keep some of the details under our hat,' he added. 'If the general public think the old girl was just wandering about in the dark and struck her head as she fell in, so much the better.'

The buzzer went on Forster's desk at that moment and he was told that somebody had some news concerning the dead man at the factory. He held up his hand as the sergeant was about to go out of the door.

'Hold everything, Locke. We may be getting a breakthrough at last. Let's go and see what this joker has to say.'

They went quickly to the interview room where a burly man in working clothes was sitting nervously, accompanied by a young policeman.

'I don't have time to sit here all day,' the man said. 'I only wanted to give you a bit of information that may be of use to you. I've got to get back to my gov'ner and he don't like to be kept waiting.'

'Don't worry, Sir,' DI Forster said soothingly. 'We won't keep you any longer than necessary, Mr — ?'

'John Philips. I'm a lorry driver, see and I've been doing the Continental run for the past week, and it was only when I was clearing out the old newspapers for my missus that I came across the stuff about this fire at Bately-sub-Mendip and the bloke who died, and I remembered.'

'Right,' said Forster briskly. 'Then before we go any further, you won't mind if we get your statement on tape, will you, Mr Philips?'

The man shrugged. 'It's no skin off my nose, but there's not much to tell. I just gave the guy a lift, that's all.'

'All in good time, Mr Philips,' said Locke,

adjusting the tape machine. Once it was up and running, Forster spoke to the man briskly.

'Your full name and address please, Mr Philips.'

'Is that necessary?'

'If you wouldn't mind, Sir,' Forster said, wondering why the hell these people had to be so bloody reluctant when they'd come in of their own accord. The fact that they were being recorded got some of them agitated, but they couldn't deny saying it later.

Once he'd got the man's details, he prompted him to go on.

'Well, it was like this. I drive all over the place, and I was delivering a lorry load of stuff to Yeovil, and taking the Mendip route, when this guy nearly jumped out in front of me. Good job I'd slowed down at a crossing, or he'd have got himself killed for sure. He gave me the fright of my life, I can tell you, and I was still yelling blue murder at him when he just stood there and waved me down. I had no choice but to stop if I didn't want to kill the bastard.'

'Then what happened?' Forster said, ignoring the swear word as the guy got more heated, and preferring not to stop him in full flow.

'He said he needed to get to Bately-sub-Mendip to do a job, and I said I wasn't going anywhere near there as it's right off my route. Then he said he'd pay for the lift. Next minute he was flashing this wad of notes at me. God knows how much he was carrying, but he said it was payment for the job. Well, I wasn't turning up my nose at that, so I told him to get in and I'd drop him as near as I could. My artic ain't suited for them narrow village roads, so I told him he'd still have to walk quite a way, and he said that was all right. It was getting dark by then, so I assumed he knew where he had to go.'

'Why do you think this was the man who died in the factory fire, Mr Philips? Did he give any indication that that was where he was going in Bately-sub-Mendip, or that he was involved in any way with the doll factory?'

Philips snorted. 'That was the funny thing. He never said another bloody word all the way. Usually if I pick anybody up we have a bit of a chat, but not this guy. He just sort of clammed up, went into himself, if that makes sense. I'd say he had a lot on his mind, despite the amount of cash he was carrying. I only came here today 'cos my missus nagged me into it.'

'Well, we appreciate your co-operation, Sir,' Forster said, sensing that he was becoming belligerent now. 'So just one last thing. Could you describe the man to us, please?'

Philips narrowed his eyes in thought. 'Pretty nondescript, I suppose. About forty maybe, wearing jeans and one of them army combat jackets you can buy in second-hand stores. He was a bit weedy, and looked in need of a good meal, which made it all the more surprising that he had so much money on him.'

'Was he clean-shaven? Wearing glasses?'

'No glasses and just the usual stubble. Look, can I go now? I've got places to be.'

'Of course, and thank you very much for coming in, Mr Philips. All this information is very useful.'

It was the first bit of concrete information they had had leading to a possible identity of the dead man, and it began to tie up a few loose ends. If the hitchhiker was the man who died in the fire, which seemed increasingly likely, then it also seemed as though someone had been paying him well to go to Bately-sub-Mendip and do a job. But whether that job was to set fire to the doll factory or dispose of the elderly Miss Pargeter was something they had yet to discover.

All the same, Forster was jubilant that at last somebody had had contact with the likely victim of the fire, and who could now be considered a highly suspicious one at that.

'Once we get a transcript of that tape, fax it over to the forensic boys, Locke, and see if you can gee them up about those dental records. We might be on to something at last.'

★   ★   ★

Edgar Pargeter had mixed feelings when he got the message that he could now arrange Edith's funeral. Nothing much else was going right at the moment. The insurance company wasn't ready to pay out on the fire yet, and nor could he get his hands on Edith's insurance money until the cause of death was firmly established on a death certificate. Nobody could dispute her Will, which he knew would leave everything to him, but how soon he could get his hands on that was something else that was bugging him.

At least the bloody village wouldn't be getting their knickers in a twist when they saw the For Sale sign going up at the cottage before Edith's body was cold. Although it must have been colder than an eskimo's balls, he thought graphically, to be immersed in that filthy ditch water for days. He didn't want to think about it too much, nor to have the image of it constantly in his mind, but it wouldn't go away no matter how much he drank to try to blank it out. But once the day's business was over, he meant to phone the vicar for a definite date and time for the burial, and he'd also give Rosie Redman the news as promised, and then maybe things would get moving.

He scowled, thinking about her. It had given him a hell of a shock to look out of his window prior to pulling across the curtains the other night, to see her car parked in the road opposite, her face illuminated by the street light outside. He reckoned he'd given the little bitch a shock too, and a bloody good job. But it was what she was doing there in the first place that was niggling him.

He had no idea she knew where he lived and worked, and she could only have known it by deliberately trying to find out. She was becoming a thorn in his flesh that he could do without, and the only reason he had enlisted her help at the cottage on Sunday afternoon was partly because he truly couldn't face the thought of sorting out his sisters' personal belongings; and partly because he wanted to judge whether or not she had some crazy idea that he was somehow involved in Edith's death. And he still didn't know what to make of her.

All the same, it wouldn't hurt to give the interfering bitch a little fright now and then. Once he had phoned the vicar and made the tentative arrangements for the funeral, to be confirmed once he had been to see the undertakers to take control of Edith's body and do the necessary, he phoned Rosie's home number that evening.

That she answered the phone herself was an added bonus.

'Hello. *Hello. Hello*! Who is this, please?' he heard her say when the caller said nothing at first.

Edgar had no intention of replying immediately. Instead he breathed heavily and deeply into the phone, and he heard the change in her voice as she spoke again. It was both efficient and suddenly wary.

'*Hello*. This is Doctor Redman's house. Is something wrong? If you wish to speak to the doctor, please give me your name.'

Pargeter cleared his throat in an unpleasantly gutteral way, and then he spoke slowly and hoarsely.

'This is Edgar Pargeter, Miss Redman. I've spoken to the vicar, and my sister's funeral is provisionally booked for next Saturday afternoon at 2pm. I thought you would like to know.'

Rosie's heart thumped as she swallowed hard and paused for a moment.

'Thank you. So they have found nothing untoward about her death then?'

'Did you think they would?' Edgar said.

Rosie was suddenly angry. She wasn't stupid, and she knew when somebody was baiting her, playing with her in a cat and mouse game.

'Of course I did. It's hardly a natural occurance for an elderly woman to fall into a ditch at night. I thought you'd want to know more details than that.'

'If I do, it's a family matter, and families look after their own.'

'Goodnight then, and thank you for telling me,' she said in a strangled voice now.

She was still staring at the phone when her aunt came into the hall to ask her what was wrong.

'It was that man,' she almost choked. 'That horrible Edgar Pargeter. He's just told me about Edith's funeral next Saturday.'

'Well, that's a relief, isn't it? At least they must be satisfied with the cause of death if they're allowing her to be decently buried.'

'He didn't say anything about that, and I'm not so sure about it, anyway. No, it was just the way he spoke to me. Or rather, the way he *didn't* speak at first. He just breathed heavily into the phone like one of those awful stalkers you read about, and then he was all croaky and weird.'

'Rosie, I'm sure you're imagining things. I

219

know you've got a bee in your bonnet about Mr Pargeter, but didn't it occur to you that he was probably upset at just having arranged his sister's funeral? It's one thing on top of another for the poor man, isn't it?'

Poor man indeed! To Rosie it seemed as if her aunt had been taken in by Edgar Pargeter's so-called indulgence towards his sisters, and the way he had seemed so genuine at the cottage on Sunday afternoon. Well, Rosie wasn't taken in by him at all. Call it intuition or what you will, she *knew* there was something evil about him. But it wasn't something you could bandy about in public, without other people thinking you were crazy. Damien had already warned her of that. There was only one person who was always ready to believe her.

She passed off her aunt's comments with a murmur of acceptance, and said she was going up to her bedroom for a while. Once there she pressed Charlie's speed-dial number on her mobile phone.

When he answered she could hear the sounds of music and laughter and the clink of glasses in the background. So he was out socialising. Well, she didn't expect him to be always at her beck and call, did she? All the same, she was embarrassed at having called him on a whim.

'Rosie, hang on a minute while I go somewhere quieter,' she heard him say with a laugh in his voice, and a quick apology to someone.

He was obviously having a good time, she thought with sudden and unreasonable misery. So much for thinking there had been an instant attraction between them. Maybe it had all been on her part after all. She resisted the small sense of pique that tempted her to switch off her phone.

'Sorry about that, darling,' she heard him say next. 'One of the reporters is retiring and we're giving him a bit of a send off in the office.'

'Oh, I see.'

Come on, girl. No need to think the world was turning the right way up again just because it was a bit of an office do rather than a date . . .

'What's up?' Charlie said. 'Not that it's not great to hear from you. You've been on my mind a lot, and I was thinking of coming down tomorrow night, if you fancy going out for dinner. What do you say?'

'That would be good. I've got things to tell you, Charlie, and it's much better said face to face.'

'I'm all for that,' he said cheekily. 'Listen, I'll have to get back to the party now. They're about to present the old boy with a leaving gift, but I'll see you about sevenish tomorrow night then, OK?'

'OK,' Rosie said, and she was still smiling as she closed down her phone.

12

'So you're seeing the newspaper guy again,' Norman Youde said the next day. 'Damien's going to have his nose put out about that.'

'It's none of Damien's business,' Rosie said. 'Nor yours, come to that.'

'All right, hold your horses! If you didn't want to make it my business, why did you bother telling me?'

Rosie bit her lip. 'Sorry. I'm a bit on edge today. Pargeter has been in touch with me, and Aunt Laura and I sorted through Edna and Edith's clothes at the cottage yesterday and it was a bit upsetting. He's going to send all their stuff to charity shops.'

'Well, that's sensible, isn't it? You didn't want any of it, did you?' he finished with a snigger. 'I can't you wearing flowery frocks.'

'Don't be daft. I brought Edith's library books back as well,' she told him.

It was the last thing she had thought of before she left the cottage. It was one more thing to finalise a life that had once been happy and contented. First the clothes, then the books. On Saturday it would be the funeral, and soon the cottage would be sold.

223

The factory was gone, and to all intents and purposes it would soon seem as though Edna and Edith had never existed. Rosie gave a shudder, thinking what a tenuous hold on life any of them really had.

'You want to pull yourself together, girl,' she heard Norman say as she stared vacantly into space. 'Ask your uncle for some magic pills or something.'

'I don't need magic pills. Just to see justice done, that's all.'

Before he could delve any further into just what she meant by that, several of their regular customers came in for a chat and an exchange of books, and the moments passed. Rosie was looking forward to this evening when she could see Charlie again and get some of his no-nonsense conversation. He wasn't so involved with the village as she was. He was on the outside looking in, but still with a keen interest in all that happened. It wasn't just for his newspaper either, Rosie knew. He was interested in her too, and it was the one thing to calm her jitters amid all this upheaval.

They went to the same pub restaurant where they had been before, and it was a relief to get away from the village and relate all that had gone on since she last saw him.

'I couldn't get past the feeling that Pargeter

had invited me to the cottage mainly to suss me out,' she told him.

'Or simply to do as he asked and sort out his sisters' clothes. It's not something that a man would want to do, and maybe you're reading too much into it, Rosie,' he pointed out.

She shook her head. 'I know I'm not. Every time he looks at me I'm uneasy. It's too much to suggest that he hates me, and my feelings may be no more than intuition, but I just know I don't ever want to be alone with him.'

'Well, there's no reason why you ever have to be, is there?' Charlie gave a sigh. 'And since we're never going to get through this evening without thrashing out everything there is to know, I might as well tell you that I called in at the police station today to see if there was anything more I could use in the paper.'

'And was there?' Rosie said sharply.

'Policemen can be closer than clams, even when you know damn well there's something they're not saying. All I could get out of them was the stock reply that there may be developments soon on the identity of the dead man.'

Rosie was disappointed. If she had hoped for some dramatic revelation concerning Edith's death, she didn't get it.

'They also mentioned they were releasing Edith's body for burial,' Charlie added, seeing the look on her face. 'I suppose that's good news of a sort. Have you heard anything about that?'

'It's on Saturday, 2 o'clock.'

'OK, then I'll be down to cover it for our readers.'

'Is that the only reason you're taking all this interest?' Rosie said angrily.

'You know damn well it's not, but I didn't think this was the time to declare my undying love,' he said dryly.

She gave a small smile. She had wanted so much to be with him, but her head was too full of Edith and Edgar and everything that had happened to relax properly. She wasn't being fair on him.

'Do you really think I'm getting all this out of proportion, Charlie? Tell me honestly. I know it should be left to the police to investigate, not for somebody like me to start dabbling, isn't it?'

'I think if you were doing this on a professional basis instead of being personally involved with the lady concerned, you'd be able to separate your emotions from the facts. As it is, I know you can't help yourself, which is why I'll be glad when it's all over and the right conclusions are reached, and then we can get on with our real lives.'

'You mean you'll go your way and I'll go mine,' she stated.

'Actually, that's not the way I see it at all.'

She wasn't going to press him any further on that score, and determinedly spoke of other things for the rest of the evening. When he drove her home later they had to pass the flattened site where the doll factory used to be. The earth was blackened now, and the police presence had gone, but to Rosie it still resembled a desperately sad patch of land on which there had once been a small, thriving business. In time, the grass would grow again, and future generations would be unaware that a crime had ever been committed there.

Rosie shivered, but then her resolve hardened. It was as Charlie said. She should try to keep her emotions out of all this as much as possible. She was no professional detective, merely a keen amateur, but to follow any of it through, she should try to behave in the way a professional would do.

And she still had her theories. No matter what the outcome or the final verdict, factories didn't burn themselves down. Strangers didn't walk into them and burn to death. And sweet old ladies didn't end up with bruises on them, drowning in a ditch. If all that didn't all add up to a crime being involved somewhere, she didn't know what did.

'I'm going to call in the local pub before I go back to Bristol, Rosie,' Charlie was saying now. 'I'll book myself in for the weekend and I'll be down on Friday evening, all right?'

It was more than all right. He might be at the funeral partly because of his job, but she knew it was also to give her moral support. Edgar Pargeter would be the grieving brother, and the village's sympathy would go out to him, but there would be at least one person in the congregation, if not two, who would suspect him of having a far darker heart than he showed.

'And if you hear anything more in the meantime, phone me, will you?' she said as they reached her house.

'I'll phone you anyway.'

He walked her up to the front door and pulled her into his arms, and she responded to his kiss with a passion that matched his. The last thought in her head as she watched him drive away was one that had been there before. Oh yes, it was only a matter of time . . .

* * *

DI Forster was gazing into space in a way that told his staff that he was either suffering from an upset gut or working something out in his mind. Either way, they all knew it was better not to disturb him at such time until he snapped his fingers and bellowed for somebody to come into his office. Sergeant Locke was there in an instant, and looked at him cautiously.

'Sit down, Locke, and answer me a few things,' Forster said tersely. 'What do we know about this joker who was found dead in the Pargeter factory? I'll tell you,' he went on, answering his own question. 'We know eff-all, except that he was given a lift by a lorry driver from the middle of nowhere, which tells us nothing about where he lived or where he came from on that day. All we know was that he was burnt to death and the only things giving any clue are his teeth. His *rotten* teeth, Locke.'

'That's right, Sir,' Locke replied, not too sure where this was going, and knowing better than to interrupt when the muse was flowing.

'*Rotten* teeth, Locke, which is why we've had no joy from any local dentists, because the bugger was obviously not in the habit of having them regularly checked! We were told that there was some evidence of having had an abcess and an extraction not too long ago, so if he didn't visit a dentist, where would he go for emergency treatment?'

'The dental hospital?'

'Bingo!' Forster said. 'So get a copy of the dental records over there and see what you can find out. I'll nail this joker if it's the last thing I do. One thing's emerging for sure. He doesn't fit the idea of a professional hitman, which I never really suspected anyway, so what did he have to gain from a doll factory or beating up a little old lady?'

He sat back with a mixture of satisfaction and annoyance, sure that his doggedness would get him somewhere eventually, but frustrated at every turn. Intuition wasn't the prerogative of the bloody female sex either, and he didn't deny that he had the Redman girl in his mind at that moment. She had a cute brain, and a vivid imagination to go with it, but when it came to policing, it was best left to the professionals. And with luck, he would finally get a lead from the dental hospital and find out where this guy had lived. Somebody must be missing him, and that was another thing that was frustrating as well as mystifying, since nobody had reported a missing person to them.

But nobody lived in a total vacuum. Didn't he have a home and a job, which entailed having a boss and workmates? Didn't he have a wife or family, a mother, brothers and sisters, or a partner, which was the poncey way to call them nowadays, of whatever sex? Forster shrugged. He wasn't here to make moral judgements, just to find out the truth and see justice done.

Unknowingly, he echoed Rosie Redman's words. But it was bloody odd to think nobody had missed the poor bugger at all. It made you think. It really did. Would anybody want to be so anonymous that nobody in the world cared a damn about him?

Later that day, his sergeant arrived back with some news. A couple of months back a guy had turned up at the dental hospital with rampant toothache due to an abcess.

'The bloke who saw him was pretty dismissive,' Locke said. 'He said the guy looked like a tramp and stank to high heaven. He was unshaven and dishevelled and obviously hadn't seen a dentist for years, and all he wanted was to be given some pills and be sent on his way, They weren't having any of that, and they yanked the tooth out, gave him some antibiotics and told him to come back in a week, but that was the last they saw of him.'

'Name? Address?' Forster said, registering the details automatically, but waving it all aside for more vital facts.

'Nothing much, I'm afraid. He said his

name was Denny and he moved around a lot. He could give no permanent address, except that he sometimes stayed on a farm outside Bristol. They couldn't get anything else out of him.'

'Well, what bloody use is that?' Forster almost exploded. 'Do you know how many farms there are outside Bristol, man? He could have lived anywhere, and we're no farther forward.'

'We are a bit, Sir.' Locke became calmer as the older man started to get red around the gills. 'If the lorry driver picked him up on the way to Bately-sub-Mendip across the Mendips, then the farm was most likely in that area. The farms are pretty scattered in those parts, and we do know his name was Denny. At least, that was the name he gave.'

As his voice took on a slightly patronising tone, he suffered the glare of his boss. But what else did they have? And then Forster nodded.

'So let's get moving on what's we've got so far. I'll need a survey of all the farms in the likely area. Then we'll make a systematic enquiry of them about any occasional help they've got now, or have had recently, by the name of Denny. It may be his first name or his surname for all we know. Start looking, and then start phoning.'

By now Forster knew that it was definitely his gut that was playing up. No wonder so many coppers ended up with stomach ulcers and worse. Sometimes he wondered why he didn't just work at a supermarket, with none of the hassle and responsibility of dealing with peoples' lives — and deaths. He reached for the bottle of antacid tablets he always kept handy and angrily chomped on a couple.

Nearing the end of the afternoon he was thinking of packing it in for the day, when Locke burst into his office again in triumph.

'I think we've found the farm, Sir.' He stabbed his finger at the map in front of him, unable to conceal his excitement. 'It's across the top of Mendip, not far from Priddy. A Farmer Brownley says a chap's been living on and off in an old caravan on one of his fields. He never bothers about him, since the guy sometimes does odd jobs for the farmer, mends a few fences when required and wards off the odd fox. It's a mutual arrangement, and apart from that the guy keeps to himself. That's all the farmer can tell us, except that the chap calls himself Denny. He hasn't seen him lately, but apparently that's nothing unusual as he comes and goes as he pleases.'

'Right! Good work, Locke. It sounds as if this is our man and we've got a lead at last. We'll leave it for today, and first thing tomorrow we'll get over there and take a look at this caravan.'

★ ★ ★

It was a pleasant drive out of the city the following morning, with the thin rays of the sun low in the sky now that the year was moving towards autumn. Mendip was still green, and the scattered villages and hamlets looked picturesque enough, but it could be a bleak place in winter. Being city born and bred, Forster wondered why anybody would want to live in such remote places at all. Farms held no thrills for him. Nasty, mucky places, always smelling of cow dung, but today he and Locke were on a mission, and he forgot all about that as they found the farm they sought.

The farmer's wife pointed them in the direction of one of the barns, and Forster swore as his smart shoes immediately became caked in something unmentionable. The farmer looked up from doing something equally unmentionable to one of his cows and looked at the visitors warily.

'Farmer Brownley?' Forster asked, showing him his ID card. 'I'm Detective Inspector Forster, and this is Sergeant Locke, whom you spoke to yesterday about a man living in a caravan on your farm by the name of Denny.'

'Oh ah,' the farmer said con-committally. 'Denny's what he called himself, as I told your man.'

'Did you have any reason to doubt it?'

'Made no never mind to me,' Brownley shrugged. 'I never asked any questions. He was no trouble, and if it looked as if somebody was living in the old caravan, it kept predators at bay from my beasts.'

'Do you mind if we take a look at the caravan?' Locke asked.

'Why would you want to do that? It's an old thing, on its last legs if you get my meaning, and it'd fall to pieces if anybody tried to move it.'

'We're investigating a man's disappearance, Mr Brownley,' Forster said, not inclined to give him any more information as yet. 'We have reason to think this Mr Denny might be the man we're looking for, so with your permission?'

'Do you have the key?' Locke added.

Brownley guffawed now. 'There ain't no key. The van's never locked, and nobody would want to pinch anything from it. It's a couple of fields from here, so if you've got some boots in your car I'd advise you to put them on.'

'Thank you, Sir. We'll carry on then,' Forster said.

Ten minutes later he wished they'd been able to take the farmer's advice. The fields were heavy with dew and filth from where the ground had been churned up by animals. Their shoes and trouser bottoms were soon caked with the stuff, and both men were wishing themselves anywhere else but here, and the air was soon rich with their cursing.

'There it is, Sir,' Locke said at last as the decrepit old caravan appeared.

'Thank Christ,' Forster said. Both men pulled on rubber gloves before they handled anything, including the grubby door latch. 'Now let's see what delights are inside.'

The caravan was small and dirty with a definite lean to the right. Locke opened the door gingerly and immediately recoiled as he stepped inside.

'Bloody hell, what's died in here?' he croaked, holding his hand over his face to keep out the stench.

Forster followed him inside and resisted the urge to do the same. The interior bore all the signs of a vagrant. There was no comfort, just a sofa bed covered with an old blanket and a stained pillow, a table, a small grimy cooker and a filthy sink piled high with used plates and cups and cutlery.

'Get a couple of those utensils into a bag for DNA testing, Locke,' Forster said, already opening the narrow cupboard that held a few scruffy clothes and then pulling open stuffed drawers that held little more than old comics, a few girlie magazines and general rubbish. It all pointed to somebody with little education and little need for material things. A bum, in other words.

'Well, well, and what do we have here?' he said softly, after tipping one of the drawers out onto the table and prodding through the various bits of paper.

'What is it, Sir?' Locke said, zipping up the plastic bag containing several items of cutlery, and already desperate to get out of there to have a shower. He was starting to itch and was convinced the caravan was full of fleas.

Forster held up a tattered piece of paper. Locke stared at it for a minute, and then nodded.

'It's a betting slip.'

'Correct. And who do we know who has a betting shop?'

'Edgar Pargeter,' they both said in unison.

Forster snorted. 'Unfortunately, this slip is so old, with half of it torn away, and unfortunately the date and place of origin is indecipherable. It may be a long shot, but if it comes from the betting shop owned by Edgar

Pargeter, then this opens up a whole new can of worms.'

And not too far from what the irritating Redman girl had been implying all along . . .

'So can we get out of here now?' Locke said, almost in desperation.

'Might as well. We've got enough to think about for now,' Forster said to his sergeant's relief. 'We'll get this cutlery off for DNA testing, and then we'll give Mr Edgar Pargeter a visit to see if he can identify this betting slip as one of his, and when it might have been issued. Hopefully, we'll surprise him.'

'But before all that, can we please take a shower and get a change of clothes?' Locke almost pleaded.

Forster grinned. 'I should say so. You stink as though something's crawled up your ass and putrefied there.'

'I know, and if I could get the hell away from myself right now, I would! I can't say you're smelling too sweet yourself, Sir, and Mrs Forster won't thank you for turning up in this state!' he added tartly.

With relief, they staggered out of the caravan and took some deep breaths of air. Even the usual farmyard smells were preferable to what they had just encountered. They returned to the car and drove quickly back to Bristol, anxious to fumigate themselves and the car as soon as possible.

★ ★ ★

Edgar Pargeter was opening up for the usual punters for the afternoon's races, and didn't welcome the sight of police officers whose presence was always bad for business. Even in plain clothes, you could smell 'em a mile off, and today you could smell 'em even more than usual. Even though they were smartly dressed as usual, they brought in a whiff of something that made him wrinkle his nose.

'Have you two taken up farming or something?' he said by way of greeting, and partly to smother the little knot of anxiety he always felt in the presence of coppers.

'You could say that, Mr Pargeter,' DI Forster said smoothly. 'We've been visiting a farm near Priddy recently.'

Pargeter stared at them warily. 'Taking up country pursuits now, are you? Is this supposed to mean something to me?'

'I don't know. You tell us.'

Pargeter scowled. 'I'm not in the habit of visiting farmyards, so what's this all about? Make it snappy before you start putting off my customers.'

Forster produced the betting slip in its

plastic bag and showed it to Edgar, studying his face closely, but there was no indication of recognition.

'You know what this is, of course.'

'Naturally. What's this, twenty questions?'

Forster took it out of the bag and handed it to him. 'Please take a closer look, Mr Pargeter, and tell us if you can, if this came from your establishment, and when it might have been issued.'

'Good God, man, I issue hundreds of betting slips. Look at the state of it! It could be from here. It could be from anywhere. I can't help you.'

He handed the slip back and turned away to deal with a client. But not before the police officers had noticed the beads of sweat on his forehead and the way his fingers shook. It all told Forster more than words that he knew something all right. If the betting slip had been purchased here, then he knew Denny. And since Denny was the man with the rotten teeth who had been burnt to death in Pargeter's doll factory then there was a definite link between them. The hell of it was, they couldn't interview Denny to find out what. But even dead bodies could tell them more than people suspected, and so could their belongings. Reluctantly, he decided that a second visit to the old caravan would have to be on the agenda, however much he and Locke were repulsed by it, and neither of them would be exactly keen to go back there too soon.

Truth was, he had never been totally convinced that the Pargeter brother had had a serious hand in the events at the village, certainly not in the way the Redman girl seemed to believe. But things were beginning to look interesting in that respect now, and their visit to the betting shop with news about the betting slip found in the old caravan had definitely made Edgar Pargeter sweat a little.

★   ★   ★

The following evening, a small item in the *West Gazette* sent in by one of their trainee roving reporters looking for any kind of news to get his name noticed in the paper, mentioned a burnt out caravan on a farm owned by Farmer Martin Brownley. The farmer had stated that it was falling to pieces anyway, and was of no value at all, and that no-one had been living it in recently. How it had caught fire was a mystery. The trainee reporter had clearly found it of little interest after all and hadn't pursued the matter further.

DI Forster's wife read the item out to him

as he was eating his supper, causing him to choke over his cottage pie.

'I bloody well knew it!' he bellowed, ignoring her tut-tutting, and livid that he hadn't followed his instincts and re-visited the farm as quickly as he should have done.

Whatever evidence might have been found in the caravan was gone for ever now, and the question of just who had started the fire was in no doubt in his mind. It had to be bloody Pargeter . . . even though he couldn't imagine him driving his posh car down there or striding across those filthy fields to torch the caravan himself. But Forster was old enough and canny enough to know that where there was a will there was always a way, and always a minion well paid enough to carry out any job. It had to be down to Pargeter . . . but he knew he couldn't prove it, and Pargeter would know it too.

13

Saturday arrived and with it virtually the end of summer, as a cold misty rain covered the entire Mendip countryside, creating a strange, ethereal effect on hamlets and villages. At times like this, the imagination could run riot. Bately-sub-Mendip was no exception to the general hush of silence the penetrating rain and mist evoked, and on any other weekend people would simply huddle indoors with the papers and the telly and ignore it. But this Saturday was a special day in the village, because the funeral service for Edith Pargeter was due to begin at the church at 2 o'clock that afternoon.

Charlie Walters turned up at the doctor's house during the late morning, having been invited to lunch so that he could attend the funeral with Rosie's family. He usually dressed casually, but today he was dressed soberly in the kind of dark suit normally reserved for weddings and funerals, Rosie thought, with a lump in her throat. She wished she dared to wear a bright summer dress that she was sure Edith would have approved, but the village was far too conventional for such frivolity.

'It couldn't be a worse day for it, could it?' Charlie said, giving a small shiver once he was inside the warmth of the house.

'There's never a good day for a funeral, is there?'

He squeezed her hand. 'Of course not, but let's hope the rain clears up, so that at least Edith will get a good send-off.'

'There's no doubt about that,' she said, wondering why they were talking like strangers now. When conversation descended to discussing the weather, it was never a good sign. But as the misty rain turned to a steady downpour by midday, with no sign of it letting up for the rest of the day, nobody seemed to be talking much at all in the Redman household.

Rosie had been dreading this day. She had been so fond of both the old ladies, and it was hideous to think that they had to watch Edgar Pargeter grieving over his sister in a way that to her was going to be completely false. When Edna was buried, Edith had clung to him in a way that was both sad and pathetic, and he had shown such courtesy and kindness towards her that nobody could have thought anything bad about him. The whole village had sympathised with their loss and the care he had given to Edith at that time. Now Edith was about to be buried alongside her sister, and people would have even more sympathy for the man and the terrible circumstances that had brought him to this.

'Am I the only one?' she murmured to Charlie after a lunch that nobody felt much like eating, and they had finally set out in his car for the short distance to the church. Her aunt and uncle led the way in the doctor's car. Normally they would have walked, as befitted weddings, christenings and burials in a small country village, but it was no day for walking and getting soaked before they had even reached the church.

'What? The only one to think that this is all a farce on Edgar's behalf?' he said, knowing instinctively where her thoughts were going. 'He must have felt something for his sister, Rosie.'

'But not enough to stop what happened.'

She couldn't stop the bitterness in her voice, and she took a deep breath as she saw the many cars parked in the lane outside the church, with soberly-clad people carrying umbrellas as they hurried towards it. It was just as she had thought. No brightly coloured summer dresses today, and no fashion parade.

'All right,' she went on. 'I'll try to put my prejudice aside for the time being, and just remember that I'm here to honour an old friend.'

'Good girl,' Charlie said, putting his hand over hers for a moment. 'I'd say I'd race you to the church to get out of the rain, but I guess that wouldn't be a good move, would it?'

She managed a small smile at his attempt to cheer her up and said that no, it wouldn't! Instead, they got out of the car and hurried as best they could, along with the many others milling inside the small church, which was soon filled to capacity. They were all neighbours, in the way that only a small village could be, and she nodded briefly to Damien Hall and Norman Youde and everyone else that she had known all her life.

Everybody stood up as the coffin arrived, with Edgar walking behind it, head bowed and looking neither to left nor right. He looked the part of the grieving brother all right, and Rosie had to forcibly stop herself from allowing her thoughts to be mocking. She found it hard to concentrate on anything other than the back of his bull-shaped head in the front pew, and when the service was over, she couldn't remember a word that was said, except for the vicar saying that there were to be no eulogies, as their dear sister Edith had requested.

Was that Edith's wish, or Edgar's? They all trailed out of the church and over the sodden ground to the grave side. It still seemed so unreal to Rosie. Such a short time ago, she had been chatting with Edith as usual over her romances and her favourite authors. Despite her deafness, Edith could always tune in to Rosie's voice, as she called it. And now they were here in this dismal setting. She was aware of the vicar intoning the final words as the coffin was lowered, and then the dull sound of the handful of wet earth that Edgar threw over it.

She couldn't bear to look at him any more, nor at the scene unfolding in front of her with all the familiar faces she had known since childhood expressing murmurs of sorrow and affection for Edith, and sympathy for Edgar . . .

She deliberately looked past it all, to where the small copse of trees at the edge of the churchyard was dripping with rain now and adding to the general misery of the occasion. And then her heart jolted.

Two swarthy men she had never seen before were lurking between the trees. *Lurking* was the only word she could think of that moment, since they looked so shifty and out of place. They weren't the coppers who had been here before. These two were huddled into anoraks, large and unkempt as far as she could tell because of the slanting rain, but one thing was certain. They were strangers and had no place here at the funeral of a well-loved old lady. The second thing she was sure about was that they gave her the shivers.

She gave Charlie a nudge, trying to attract his attention to the two men without being too obvious. Even as she did so, she saw Edgar Pargeter look up from his dutiful actions, and as he caught sight of the two men as well, Rosie saw his manner change. He visibly stiffened. His face blanched and he looked suddenly hunted, and Rosie grabbed Charlie's arm more firmly.

'Look over there,' she breathed urgently.

'I see them,' he replied, 'and I don't think they're invited guests.'

As a few people began to move away from the grave side, Edgar started to clear his throat and spoke hurriedly in a tense, choked voice, as befitted a man who had just buried his only surviving sister.

'As you all know, my sister's cottage is very small, but I would appreciate it if as many of you as would like to, would come to the village pub and take a few drinks with me, to honour my sister's memory,' he said. 'I'm sure that many of you have memories of

Edith that you would like to share on this sad day, and I know she would appreciate the fact of her friends staying together for a while longer yet.'

There were murmurs of assent and surprise at the unexpected offer.

'That clumsy little speech was a sudden gesture, wasn't it?' Rosie said suspiciously. 'And an unlikely one too, knowing how Edgar never wanted to socialise with the villagers before. Do you suppose it could have anything to do with the fact that he didn't want to risk those two uninvited guests getting him on his own?'

'Maybe. Maybe not. He could just be feeling charitable,' Charlie said.

'And you don't believe that any more than I do! They looked like thugs to me, and he looked damned scared of them.'

She felt an uneasy shiver of excitement. But why wouldn't they be thugs? She wouldn't discount anything as far as Edgar Pargeter was concerned. But why would Edgar feel threatened by them, unless he wasn't in financial trouble and desperately in need of the money that was presumably coming to him? It would explain why he had put the cottage up for sale with indecent haste.

Her aunt came to join them for a moment. 'Are you coming to the pub, Rosie? I think most people will want to do so, and I see that Mr Pargeter's already asked Damien to join them.'

'Does he think he needs police protection then?' she said without thinking.

Her aunt frowned. 'What an odd thing to say, Rosie. Sometimes I think you're developing a mean streak, and on such a day as this too. I think you should be more careful in the things you say.'

Rosie bit her lip as her aunt turned away.

'Now I've upset her, and I shall have to apologise later,' she told Charlie.

'Does this mean you're not going to join the party at the pub then?'

'Are you kidding?' she said more aggressively. 'I'm keen to see if those two gorillas turn up, and I'm going to stay there until the last person goes home. They're not going to be the only ones to ruffle Edgar's feathers today.'

His small sigh told her he approved of her spirit, if not her sense, but as far as Rosie was concerned, this seemed a highly sensible thing to do. With many other people at the pub taking advantage of Edgar's generosity, it wouldn't be too difficult to gauge his reaction while he remained in Bately for the rest of the day. He was obviously more than put out by the two unexpected guests at the funeral and not in any hurry to get away from a crowd of people.

'Aren't you in the least curious, Charlie? I thought it was what you reporters were all about,' she said as they got in the car to drive to the pub. The rain was slanting down even heavier than before now, blotting out much of the landscape, and walking was out of the question without getting drenched.

'Of course I'm curious, but not to the point of obsession.'

She stared at him. 'Is that what you think this is?'

'Well, how many other people do you suppose even noticed those two men, and put your devious interpretation on why they were there?'

'I don't think it was at all devious. So why do *you* think they were there? It's hardly the day for standing around in the pouring rain at a stranger's funeral unless you had some kind of motive for doing so, is it?'

He didn't reply, turning the car into the pub car park after the short distance from the church. 'I don't know who they were or why they were there, but I concede that you have a point. So can we drop it for now and go and spend some of Edgar's money with a few drinks?'

She couldn't resist one last comment. 'All

right. I suppose he's splashing out now that he'll be able to get his hands on whatever Edith's left him, and I'm sure the sale of the cottage will go through very soon. Desirable country cottages in picturesque villages are well sought after. If he's been having money troubles, they'll soon be over.'

He never looked as if he had money troubles. He was always well turned out, smoking his large Havana cigars and driving his flash car. He always gave the appearance of the well-heeled businessman, but she couldn't forget the almost stricken look on his face when he had seen the two thugs at the churchyard. They were after him for something, and if it wasn't money, then what was it?

The pub was soon filling up as people removed their wet outer clothes and took advantage of a warm and social environment on such a dismal day. It was the best place to be. Edgar was already at the bar, advising the landlord that people were to have whatever they wanted. Since many of the mourners were elderly and not given to drinking, Rosie guessed there would be more cups of tea and coffee and the occasional glass of sherry than any hard liquor, so Edgar wouldn't have to foot too hefty a bill. And for the first time, she wished she could get these uncharitable thoughts out of her head, while knowing that she couldn't until the truth came to light.

She and Charlie were joined at a corner table by Norman Youde and Bert Smith before her aunt and uncle appeared with Damien Hall. Bert was as garrulous as ever.

'It were a nice do for the old girl,' he commented, already slurping deeply at the first pint of the day. 'She'd have liked the service, and being planted next to her sister in a nice corner of the churchyard. They've got a good view of the village from where they are. Might have had a good view of the factory too, if it hadn't been burned to Kingdom Come. They'll miss that.'

Rosie managed to resist looking at Charlie as his artless words continued. In Bert's simple philosophy you were born, you lived your life, and then you died. No matter what the circumstances, you couldn't change the order of things, and a belief in the hereafter was something that you didn't tinker with.

Instead, she looked across the room to where Edgar was conversing with one and another of the villagers. Snatches of conversation drifted across to her as he was holding court, and relating stories to them of when Edith and Edna were the older sisters and had pampered and petted the baby brother, when he came along such a long time after them.

'She'll have left everything to him, o' course,' Bert Smith went on, oblivious to anything but his own rambling thoughts. 'The sisters never spent nothing on themselves, so there's probably a tidy sum.'

'That's hardly the right thing to be saying today, Bert,' Rosie said. 'I'm sure Mr Pargeter's not thinking of anything like that. He's still grieving and getting over the shock of what happened to Edith.'

And who was the prize hypocrite now! She couldn't believe she had just said those words, and as Charlie cleared his throat she knew he was thinking exactly that. But the less Bert or anyone else knew of her suspicions regarding Pargeter, the better, or it would be all around the village in no time that Rosie Redman was shamefully stirring things up for the poor man

While they began talking quietly about their own shared memories of Edith, she suddenly looked up to see that Edgar had reached their table. He looked large and dark and menacing, and even his smile was false and didn't reach his eyes, and that wasn't her imagination either.

'I want to thank everybody for coming here today,' he said, repeating what Rosie guessed

254

had been said many times now. 'It means a lot to me to know that my sister was so well thought about in the village. I know she would have been glad to know that her many friends and neighbours saw her finally laid to rest.'

If that was a barbed comment on Rosie's behalf that now that Edith was laid to rest, then that should be an end to it, she simply stared him out, while Bert became louder than ever in his fulsome remarks about the dear departed lady. But everyone here had their own memories of Edith, no matter how quaint she had been to some people — and in death, it seemed that even the oddest person could suddenly become a saint. And yes, she *was* becoming mean-spirited if she could even think that way, Rosie thought shame-facedly, but she was thankful when Edgar moved on to speak with other people.

'Do you want to get out of here?' she heard Charlie say in a low voice. 'You look a bit pinched if I may say so.'

'I'm all right,' she said, making a determined effort to smile. 'There's nowhere much to go in this weather, and at least it's warm in here.'

As she spoke the pub door opened and a flurry of cold air and rain came inside. Someone in a heavy raincoat looked around the room and then headed for Damien Hall and spoke quickly. Damien immediately called for Edgar Pargeter, but for the moment he was nowhere to be seen.

'Probably gone for a piddle,' Bert Smith said lazily. 'Which is where I'm going. All this ale goes straight through me like a tap.'

Damien paused at the table near the door where Rosie was sitting.

'When you see Pargeter, can you ask him to come to his sister's cottage right away?' he said tersely.

'Why? What's happened?' she began, but by then he had gone, accompanied by the raincoat man.

'Pass on the message to Mr Pargeter, will you, Bert?' Charlie said, already on his feet, followed by Rosie. 'And don't broadcast it,' he added, knowing it was probably a futile remark.

Ignoring the rain now, Rosie and Charlie shrugged into their coats and raced through the narrow streets and alleys until they reached Edith's cottage in Butcher's Lane. Rosie's heart began to beat painfully fast as she saw the door swinging open on its hinges, and Damien and the neighbour were already inside as they burst in.

'My God, what's happened here?' Rosie croaked, as her horrified eyes took in the scene.

The whole place had been maniacally ransacked. Chairs and tables were turned over and thrown to the floor. Cupboards and drawers were flung open, and their contents strewn everywhere. Everything on the mantelpiece had been swept to the floor, glass-framed photographs stamped underfoot. The walls and carpets were covered in red paint, along with everything else.

The next minute Edgar Pargeter had arrived, his face gaunt with fury as he saw the carnage in front of him, and he was swearing loudly and colourfully as he was followed by Bert Smith and a dozen other locals.

'Unless anyone has any idea of who might have done this, will you people all please get out of here?' Damien shouted above the hubbub.

It was obvious that nobody knew anything, since they had all been at the pub. By now Edgar was blundering his way upstairs, and he came down again to report that everything in the bedrooms had been similarly trashed.

'It'll cost a bloody fortune to have all this put right before anybody will even look at it, let alone want to buy it,' he raged. 'Who's going to want to view this? And all this furniture will have to be carted off to the rubbish dump. There's not a damn thing that can be salvaged.'

'I'd have thought that was the last thing on your mind on today of all days, Mr Pargeter,' Rosie blurted out before she could stop herself, then she clamped her lips together, wishing she had had the sense to stay silent as Edgar rounded on her at once, his eyes murderous.

'Why the hell are you always around, Miss bloody know-it-all? You and your hanger-on.'

Charlie's eyes hardened, but ignoring the insult, he spoke smoothly.

'Would you like this break-in mentioned in the *Gazette*, Sir? If you'd like to say a few words for our readers, I'll be glad to send in a report.'

'No, I wouldn't like it effing-well mentioned in your rag,' Edgar shouted, almost beside himself now.

Damien stepped in, putting a restraining hand on Edgar's arm.

'I suggest you calm yourself, Sir. No good will be done by everyone shouting and arguing with one another. Perhaps you'd care to check whether or not anything is missing, and then give me a statement. We can go back to my office or to the pub if you prefer, since there's nowhere to sit down comfortably here,' he added delicately.

Edgar looked as if he was about to explode again, and then he seemed to take stock of himself, and spoke in his usual cold, calculated tone.

'What I *prefer* is for all these people to get the hell out of here,' he snapped. 'Then I'll take a proper look around and give you a statement at the pub if I must. At least it's warm there, and I'm damn sure I'll be in need of something stronger by then.'

'Very well, Sir,' Damien said. 'And I take it you won't be driving back to Bristol tonight? I'm sure Mr and Mrs Gentry can accommodate you at the pub for the night.'

Edgar glared at him, getting his meaning only too well. He had already had to bolster himself up with whiskey before he turned up at the church that day, and he needed a stiffer one right now.

'Since I've no wish to kill myself on these effing wet Mendip tracks you people call roads, you can be damn sure of it. Now, can we get on with it?'

He was still cursing freely as Rosie and Charlie, along with the few people remaining in the cottage, began making their way back along Butcher's Lane. Rosie had her own pretty good theory about who had done the trashing, and she was desperate to talk to Charlie alone, but Bert Smith seemed determined to tag along with them.

'Shows him up in his true colours, don't

it?' Bert said snidely, as he followed closely behind them. 'All the sod really wants to do is sell the place where the poor old ducks lived and get some money out of it.'

'He's never looked short of cash, Bert,' Rosie said.

Bert snorted, raindrops hanging from his nose and ears like dewdrops.

'Oh ah, that sort never does. He puts on a good show, but for all his finery, I reckon he's scratching for money, same as the rest of us. Stands to reason, dunnit? Otherwise, why would he have wanted to sell the cottage so quick?'

'Well, he won't sell it as quickly now,' Charlie said, thankful that they were nearing the pub again as rainwater trickled down their necks. It hadn't let up all day, and he pitied the poor devils at the churchyard, having to fill in Edith's grave with earth that had turned into a quagmire.

Once back inside the warmth of the pub, a large number of folk were still lingering and muttering and wondering what the commotion had been about. They left Bert with his bit of glory as he passed on the news, and sat as far from everybody else as possible, and Rosie couldn't contain her feelings a minute longer. She spoke with an urgent excitement now.

'You know who it was, don't you, Charlie? Who it *had* to be. And I reckon Edgar was pretty sure of it as well.'

'The two geezers at the churchyard, you mean. I'd say it was a fair guess. Nobody around here would have had any reason to do such a thing, would they?'

'Hardly. We've never had any vandalism in Bately before, and besides, nobody would want to hurt Edith's memory in such a horrible way. But they weren't hurting her, were they? They were hurting Edgar and ruining his plans to sell the cottage asap. He knew who they were when he saw them at the churchyard all right. All this was a warning, Charlie! But *why*?'

'I don't know, Miss Marple,' he said, trying to humour her. 'You tell me.'

'That's what I've still got to figure out,' she said with a frown. 'I should probably mention them to Damien sometime, providing he doesn't think I'm interfering again. But I know what I'd do if I was in charge of this case. I'd start taking a serious interest in Edgar Pargeter's finances.'

14

When Rosie went back to work on Monday, she was still uneasy and upset after the events of the weekend. It was inevitable that the talk of the village had switched from Edith's funeral to the vandalism that had been done to her cottage. It was dreadful that the dignity of an old lady's burial had been taken over by gossip about this crime, because crime was what it was. Damien had said so in no uncertain terms when she had gone to see him on Sunday evening after Charlie went back to Bristol.

'Why didn't you mention these two men at the churchyard before?' Damien demanded, clearly none too pleased to see her. 'And why would you think they were anything other than curious onlookers?'

Sometimes she thought he could be really dense.

'Because curious onlookers don't normally stand about in the pouring rain at a stranger's funeral, especially men who looked more like thugs than chief mourners, which they certainly did,' she snapped. 'And I tell you, Damien, Edgar Pargeter was definitely edgy when he saw them, and that's when he suggested we all went back to the pub. I know it was a spur of the moment decision, because Mrs Gentry said that nothing had been arranged beforehand, and my guess is that he hadn't intended staying in the village afterwards at all.'

'You do a lot of guessing these days, don't you, Rosie? And what does your new newspaper friend have to say about all this?'

'He agrees with me,' she said, refusing to be goaded.

'Well, thank you for the information. Was there anything else?'

God, how did she ever think she fancied him? He was a bigoted idiot.

'Not a thing, except that anybody with any sense might wonder if two strangers turning up at a funeral could have been responsible for what happened at the cottage. And in case any of my opinions should ever be needed for evidence at some future date, you will note what a concerned citizen has said, won't you? That *is* what police jargon calls interfering busybodies, isn't it?

She stared him out, still smarting at his crassness, and then left without waiting for an answer. Couldn't he see she was only trying to help? Knowing that his feelings had been hurt when she dumped him shouldn't blind him to the fact that there was something sinister going on here. But apparently it did.

Even her aunt and uncle didn't seem to believe there could have been anything untoward about the two men she and Charlie — and Edgar — had seen at the churchyard, and were more indignant that some one should have desecrated the Pargeter sisters' memory in such a terrible way. They didn't seem to connect the two events at all, and if Rosie hadn't been so fond of Edith she knew she should give up worrying about any of it, but she couldn't, and she wouldn't.

★ ★ ★

Now that he'd been deprived of the chance to go back to the caravan near Priddy and take a more thorough look around it, DI Forster was having to switch his thoughts again. He was convinced now that the guy who had perished in the factory fire was Denny. There had to be a connection there. And if he had had money to pay the lorry driver to take him to Bately-sub-Mendip, then somebody had to be paying him. With the tenuous evidence of the tattered betting slip he was damn sure now that there was a link to Edgar Pargeter. No matter how he had tried to brush it off, the man's agitated manner on being questioned was enough confirmation in Forster's mind. But it wasn't evidence.

The questions went round endlessly in his head. Bookies were often the affluent end of a society that could be full of highly dubious characters as well as genuine punters happy to squander their money on a bet or two just for the thrill of it. He wondered if Pargeter himself came into that category. It wasn't unheard of for a bookie to get into massive debt himself by taking chances and reckless gambling, and the lure of big money was right there at his fingertips, along with the risk of losing plenty.

'It was the Pargeter woman's funeral last Saturday, wasn't it? I wonder how it went,' he remarked to Sergeant Locke, with less enthusiasm than he should have shown. The constant wet weather since last weekend had blotted out any semblance of summer and had seen people scratchy and irritable at the beginning of the week. It was now Wednesday and they were no farther forward on the Pargeter case.

'I wonder what she left him as well,' Locke said with his usual snigger. 'I suppose they must have had some income from their weird dolls. From the kind of low-life we now think Pargeter to be, he wouldn't have sunk too much cash into a losing venture.'

'Maybe not at first. But consider whether or not he really did have a hand in what happened. Maybe sales weren't doing so well any more, and maybe he thought he'd get more from the insurance money from the fire than from keeping it going. I'm not saying he intended his sister to die, and her death may have been no more than a tragic misfortune after she got caught up in it. Unfortunately, we'll never know. Get on to that village bobby, Locke, and see if he knows how things went on Saturday. It was a lousy day for it, poor sods.'

It was a long shot, and he didn't really know how it could help the investigation, but he needed to be doing something, instead of getting frustrated at every turn. And a short while later Locke same back into his office, his face agog with news.

'You'll never guess what Constable Hall had to say, Sir!'

'No, I won't, unless you tell me,' Forster said dryly. 'What happened? Did somebody have a fainting fit and fall into the grave by mistake?'

'Better than that. No, scrub that! Bad taste. It was afterwards, when Pargeter invited them all to the pub to drink his sister's health and share their memories of her.'

'Oh? I wouldn't have said that was his style at all,' Forster said. 'A bit beneath him to socialise with a load of locals, wasn't it?'

'That what I'd have said. But Constable Hall said that's what happened, and it was all going all right at the pub until somebody turned up looking for him and Pargeter because of some rumpus at the woman's cottage. When he and Pargeter got there, along with half the village as far as I can make out, the cottage had been trashed.'

'Had it now? And who would do a thing like that on such a day? And why?' Forster said, his interest caught now.

Locke consulted his hurriedly written notes. 'Don't know, but the day after, Rosie Redman went to see Hall and mentioned two blokes lurking about at the funeral. She said Pargeter seemed very put out to see them, and that's when he suggested the get-together at the pub. Miss Redman thinks it was so that he didn't have to risk being alone with these guys, whoever they were.'

'Christ Almighty, is that young woman going to turn up everywhere?' Forster roared, echoing Edgar's feelings.

'Well, you must admit, Sir, she could have a point. Two strangers appear at the funeral so Pargeter goes against type and keeps himself surrounded by people. Next thing, the sister's cottage is trashed. He'd had plenty to drink by then, so Hall advised him to stay at the pub overnight, which he did, but he said several people then heard him driving out of the village like a bat out of hell on Sunday morning. Hall says he was in a terrible rage at the cottage, on account of not being able to sell it in the state it's in until he gets it fixed up.'

Forster nodded. 'Makes sense if he was hoping for a quick sale. The more I hear about that man the more I dislike him. And the more I think he may not be as flush as he likes to appear. So I think he's due for another surprise visit this afternoon.'

Locke groaned. It wasn't the weather to go visiting, but police work never stopped for rain or snow or anything in between, and at least it beat tramping over sodden fields to investigate a stinking caravan. He also knew that Forster was getting increasingly narked about the lack of any real progress in the Pargeter case.

So later that day they turned up at the bookie's establishment, only to find it shut up and silent.

'Understandable, I suppose,' Locke said with a shrug. 'I can't imagine he's doing much business on days like this, and it's already getting dark. Do you want to try his flat or shall we leave it until tomorrow?'

Forster was frowning. 'There are no lights showing in the flat upstairs or down here, and I don't imagine he's gone back to Bately-sub-Mendip cleaning up the sister's cottage himself, especially if he left the village like a bat out of hell on Sunday morning as reported, so where is the bugger?'

Locke was peering through the letter-box. 'There seems to be a hell of a lot of letters and flyers and other stuff strewn over the floor. Wherever he is now, he hasn't bothered to pick up anything for a few days.'

He hesitated, but he had to say what was on his mind, no matter how much it might inflame his boss. 'Sir, you don't think the Redman girl was on to something with those two jokers she saw at the sister's funeral, do you? If they were out to threaten him for some reason, the cottage may have been just a warning, and they could have followed him here.'

Before Forster could answer they heard a smoke-filled voice behind them

'You looking for the bookie bloke? You and a few others, I reckon. He ain't been seen since last Friday, and there's some of us reg'lars who ain't too pleased about it.'

Forster made a quick appraisal of the man,

about fifty years old, thinning hair, disagree-able mouth, wearing an anorak and woolly hat, army combat trousers of the kind bought from army and navy surplus stores, and scuffed boots.

'You're one of his punters?' he asked.

'Nothing wrong with having a few bets now and then, mate,' the man said with a scowl. 'But I'd like to know where the toe-rag's got to now. I got some winnings to come.'

'You say there's been no sign of him since last Friday?' Locke put in. 'What about his car? Where does he keep it?'

The man's eyes narrowed. 'You cops? What's he done, scarpered with last week's takings or summat?'

'Where does he keep his car, Sir?' Forster repeated, producing his ID card impatiently.

'God knows. There's a block of garages round the back of the shop, so it could be there, I s'pose.'

'Thank you, Sir.' But Forster was already talking to himself as the man sidled away. It didn't bother him, since it was a reaction he was used to.

'Right, Locke. Round the back to find this garage and locate Pargeter's car. If it's not there we may have a problem. And if it is — '

He didn't need to finish, If the car was here and Pargeter wasn't, then something must have happened to him.

Ten minutes later, with the help of a neighbour who pointed out which garage housed the flash bookie's car, they had prised it open and found the car intact. Nothing seemed out of place, and there was no sign of foul play.

'Do we try the flat now, Sir?' Locke asked.

'Too right we do. I've got a bad feeling about this, and that girl's instinct may not have been so far off after all.'

They bounded up the stairs of the flat and banged on the door. As expected there was no reply, and it didn't take a moment to force it. They went from room to room quickly, but there was no sign of any occupant, nor of any previous break-in or of a crime having been committed.

Pargeter had virtually disappeared since he had left Bately-sub-Mendip on Sunday morning, and not for one minute did Forster think there was any simple explanation for it.

'Sir, take a look at this,' Locke said suddenly, pointing to a flashing light on Pargeter's answering machine. 'We might get some clues from whoever was trying to call him recently.'

'Play it back,' Forster ordered.

There were two messages. According to the monotonous automated tone recording the date and time of the calls, one was on Saturday evening, and the next was in the early hours of Sunday morning. The menacing voice on each was the same.

'Time's up, Pargeter. You've had long enough to find the cash, and now it's time for you to pay up or take the consequences.'

Recorded time: Saturday, 20.34 p.m.

'Last chance, Pargeter, or you know what's coming to you.'

Recorded time: Sunday, 02.17 a.m.

'Get down to his office and bring up all that mail that's piled up, Locke. Go through it while I look for anything relating to debts here. From the sound of it, Pargeter could be massively in debt, which could explain a hell of a lot of things. We know he left the village in a hell of a tear on Sunday morning, and from what that punter told us he hasn't been seen here since, not in working hours, anyway. His car's in his garage, so at least he came back here. Whether or not he ever got inside his flat is something we don't yet know. But what we *do* know is that we could now be looking at a crime of a different kind,' he added grimly.

After some considerable research, it became clear that Pargeter had enormous debts. He had been gambling heavily himself, and got involved with loan sharks. There were unpaid and overdue bills everywhere, and his previous bank and credit card statements found in a drawer in the flat showed him to be hugely overdrawn.

'How can he have been such a fool, with a thriving business concern, and the doll factory as a sideline?' Lock said contemptuously.

'Unfortunately, he's in the right place for it. He sees these punters coming into the shop, placing bets, making money and bragging about it, so why not do it himself? Only it seems to have got out of hand in a very big way,' Forster retorted. 'We've seen what he's like. He's a man who likes to put on a big show, but deep down he's one of the world's losers, and he knows it. No wonder he revelled in the adoration of those poor little buggers who worked till all hours making their dolls.'

'Look here, Sir. Returns on the factory for the last six months,' Locke said, rifling through another pile of invoices in a file marked Pargeter's Doll Factory. 'It was losing money hand over fist.'

'So it would suit him very well if it burnt to the ground and he could cash in on the insurance money. That may have been his only plan, and he paid the wretched Denny to torch the place for him. Unfortunately for him, Denny surprised the sister still lovingly working on her dolls, and we know the rest.'

'Sounds more than feasible, Sir.'

Forster drew a deep breath. It might sound feasible, but he hated the sound of his own conclusions. That woman didn't deserve to die, and the thought that her scheming brother was responsible, whether he intended it or not, turned his already wrenching gut.

'Gather up all this stuff and let's get out of here,' he ordered. 'We'll get back to the nick and start going through it all methodically. And then get somebody to start phoning around the hospitals to see if anybody matching Pargeter's description has been brought in over the last few days, and let's just hope it wasn't feet first. This joker has still got plenty to answer to. He's got to be somewhere, and the sooner we track him down the less uneasy I'll feel.'

'You don't want to call it a day for now then, Sir?' Locke said hopefully.

The look he got in return told him Forster was prepared to stay up all night if need be, and that his sergeant had better get used to the idea as well.

★ ★ ★

Rosie felt her heart jump when her aunt answered the family phone and told her that Detective Inspector Forster was asking to speak to her. He made her nervous in the way that innocent people always did when an officer of the law wanted to question them. And in his eyes, she was probably guilty of putting her nose into affairs that were police business, not hers. But Edith Pargeter had been her friend, and therefore she *was* her business, she thought indignantly as she took the receiver from her aunt and spoke cautiously.

'I'm sorry to disturb you, Miss Redman,' Forster said smoothly. 'It's about the two men you reported seeing at Miss Edith Pargeter's funeral.'

'Oh yes,' she replied.

'Can you be a little more forthcoming about them? It would be useful to have a description in case we need to interview them.'

'Has something happened?' Rosie said, really anxious now. 'I'm sure it must have been those two who made such a mess of the cottage, and it was obvious that Mr Pargeter thought so too. Anybody could see he was put out when he saw them — at least, anybody who was in the least bit observant.'

She stopped babbling as he interrupted impatiently.

'Miss Redman, I am not interested in those particular observations right now, and I gather you have told Constable Hall all this already. What I want is a description of the two men if possible, please.'

'I couldn't see them that clearly, and don't forget it was pouring with rain at the time. They were some distance away from the rest of us, but they looked large and swarthy, and they wore dark clothes, which meant that they wouldn't have looked totally out of place at a funeral, except that they certainly didn't belong there. I know they didn't live in the village, and I'm also certain that Edgar knew who they were,' she finished defensively.

'So that's all you can give me?' Forster asked.

'Well, apart from the fact that for a man who had just buried his sister, Edgar was unreasonably nasty about not being able to sell the cottage quickly now that he'd have to get it all cleaned up. I thought he was being really hateful about it, if you want to know.'

'Thank you, Miss Redman. You've been very helpful.'

The line went dead. His manner was always cold and clinical, which was how she supposed policemen had to be. She wondered if he had a wife and maybe a family, but good luck to them if so. She couldn't imagine anyone warming to him.

'Are you all right, Rosie?' her aunt said, as

she put down the phone.

'I'm fine. He just wanted to know a bit more about the day of the funeral, that's all. Maybe he's starting to take my thoughts a bit more seriously. That'll be a turn-up, won't it? I think I'll have a chat with Charlie on my mobile and let him know the latest.'

She went up to her bedroom to be on her own, needing to hear his voice, to know that there was someone who definitely believed in her. And as she hoped, Charlie was interested to hear that Forster had phoned her, confirming that he too thought Rosie was on to something, even if he didn't say so outright.

'It's probably beneath his dignity to say as much, even though we all know that the police couldn't operate properly without the help of the public now and then,' Charlie said. 'You're turning into a proper little sleuth, aren't you?'

'Is that meant to be sarcastic or just patronising?' she demanded.

'God, no. I wouldn't dare to be either.'

She heard the smile in his voice and relaxed. Anyway, he was right. She was turning into a proper little sleuth, and she had to admit it gave her a heady feeling, despite the circumstances of trying to get justice done for someone she had known and liked. It didn't disguise the thrill of trying to unravel the puzzle of finding out the truth, and however avidly you read about fictional crimes it could never replace being actually involved in solving them.

'Charlie, do you think that private investigator in Bristol really meant what he said about giving me a job if I wanted one?' she said without thinking.

He laughed now, not sure if she was serious or not.

'I reckon he did. He certainly took a shine to you and your theories. Why? Are you thinking of applying?'

She took a deep breath before replying. 'Well, I might, but probably not. It's a daft idea really, isn't it?'

'It wouldn't be a daft idea at all if it meant you moving to Bristol so that we could see each other all the time.'

'Oh really? Then it's just as I thought,' Rosie said, laughing now. 'I might have known you'd have some ulterior motive behind it. Goodnight, Charlie!'

She switched off before he could say anything more, still smiling at the thought of her ever turning into a real private eye. Just as if!

* * *

After DI Forster and Sergeant Locke had gone through Edgar Pargeter's pile of papers, invoices and bills meticulously, it became clear that he had a serious financial problem. In view of the threats on his answering machine — if he had even heard them — it would be understandable if he had simply gone to ground. But there was still the little matter of his car being in his garage. He had definitely returned home at some time on Sunday, so where was he now?

'What worries me,' DI Forster said, 'is the time gap between Pargeter leaving the village and getting back to Bristol. He left on Sunday morning and he put his car in the garage. But did he ever reach his flat, and if not, why not? It would certainly seem that he didn't, otherwise he would have checked his answering machine, and probably gone down to his office to collect any mail. Although some of that has probably been accumulating since the weekend.'

'Maybe he drove around all day, and when he finally got back home somebody was already waiting for him to arrive back at the garage, and once the car was inside, they pounced,' Locke offered.

'It's one possibility, I suppose, and probably the most likely one, since we've got nothing else.'

'Did the Redman girl give you any description of the two goons at the funeral?'

'Nothing worth mentioning. They could have been anybody. Have the other blokes had any joy with the hospitals?'

'Not as far as I know. What with twenty-four hour drinking and the pubs staying open all night, the city's hardly a quiet place.'

Forster grunted. Weekends were the worst, of course, when the hospitals were usually inundated with drunks and petty injuries, and frequently something worse. Binge drinking had definitely accelerated the city's crime rate and added to their work load. But hell, as he often remarked when his wife complained to his long hours: it kept him in work, didn't it?

One of the young officers poked his head around his office door.

'I think we may have got something on that hospital query, Sir.'

Forster sat up straighter in his seat at once as the sheet of paper was handed to him. He relaxed his grim expression, only to find it replaced immediately as he read the brief report from the General Hospital.

'Looks like this might be our man, Locke,' he said. 'On Sunday night a middle-aged bloke was fished out of the river, half-dead, but just about breathing when they got him into the hospital. He'd been badly beaten up with bruising all over his body, due to a likely kicking. Both eyes were black and his mouth was so cut and swollen he couldn't speak much, except to mumble that his name was Mickey Mouse and to forbid the doctors to call the police. They need to keep him fairly well sedated, because of the severe injuries.'

'Then let's go,' Locke replied. 'With any luck we might still get home at a decent hour tonight.'

'After what you've just heard, is that all you can think of?' Forster snapped.

'Sorry, Sir. It's just that I'm getting a bit fed up with Pargeter leading us such a dance.'

'Well, from the sound of this report, I doubt that he'll be doing much dancing for a while,' Forster said.

He was right about that. Enquiring for a patient by the name of Mickey Mouse didn't endear Forster to the smirking nurse at the hospital either. It was only when he produced his ID card that the smile faded.

'Mr Mouse will be here for a week or so yet, and even if he does wake up, he won't talk to you. We haven't been able to get any information from him, except for the name he gave us, and the fact that he didn't want the police informed,' she added pointedly

'Regardless of all that, we need to see him

at once,' Forster said.

'I'm sorry, but if you'll excuse me, Sir, I'll see if one the doctors is available to speak to you,' she said defensively, clearly wanting to escape.

'Never mind all that time-wasting. I'll take the responsibility *Now*, please, nurse,' he barked, giving her his freezing glare.

He wasn't used to having his commands ignored. After a moment the nurse gave in and nodded, and then took them stiffly to a side ward where a heavily bandaged patient was in a semi-comatose state, before she went scuttling off to find a doctor.

'Well, well, so this is Mickey Mouse,' Forster said softly. 'I think he's a long way from the Magic Kingdom, don't you, Locke?'

He leaned over the patient and spoke close to his ear.

'I know you can hear me, Pargeter, so don't think you're safe in here. You've got a lot of questions to answer.'

There was no response for a moment and then Pargeter opened one bruised and swollen eye to scowl as best he could. It gave him the look of a gargoyle.

'Get lost, copper.'

Forster put on a hurt expression. 'Now is that any way to speak to someone who's got your best interests at heart?'

Pargeter winced as he attempted to laugh.

'You lot have only got one effing thought on your mind, and that's to get people banged up.'

'All we want to know right now is who did this to you,' Forster went on.

Pargeter clamped his lips together painfully.

'Was it the two goons at the churchyard?' Locke put in.

This time Pargeter's eyes opened a fraction wider.

'What two goons? Get out and leave me alone.'

He fumbled for the bell at the side of the bed, but not before Forster leaned over him again.

'I mean the two strangers that Rosie Redman saw at your sister's funeral, who got you so worried that you had to put on a show at the pub for the villagers. Were they the ones who followed you home and beat you up because of your debts? Are they the loan sharks who are after you?'

'I'll kill that effing Rosie Redman if I hear her name again!'

Pargeter's voice had become a mixture of a gasp, a shout and a sob before he sank back into his pillows, his eyes closing.

The next minute a furious doctor arrived

and ordered the officers out.

'Don't panic, we're going,' Forster told him. 'We've got enough for now, but we'll be back. We need to speak to this man again on a serious matter. And for your information, his name is Edgar Pargeter, and any resemblance to Mickey Mouse is only in his dreams.'

Whether Edgar could hear him now or not, Forster neither knew nor cared. What was certain was that there was a lot more going on between him, his debtors and whatever had happened at the doll factory than had at first been imagined, and Forster intended to get to the bottom of it.

15

Charlie arranged to come down for the weekend again, and he called for her at home on Friday evening before they went to the pub. Rosie told him that at this rate they should be giving him a discount. It was early in the evening and they virtually had the pub to themselves until the regulars came in later. At the sound of her mobile, Rosie fished it out of her bag and she was still smiling as she answered it.

'*Keep your nose out of my business,*' she heard a thickened voice say.

'Who was that?' Charlie said sharply, seeing her bright expression change to one of alarm.

She couldn't speak for a moment. 'I don't know. I couldn't recognise it. The voice was sort of muffled.'

'Well, what did he say? If it *was* a man.'

Rosie shivered. 'I think it was. It was hard to say. Yes, I'm sure of it. Whoever it was, it was a threat. He told me to keep my nose out of his business.'

'*Edgar Pargeter*. The bastard,' he added savagely.

Rosie shook her head slowly. 'I really

couldn't be sure that it was him. It just didn't sound like him.'

Charlie was holding her hands tightly now, feeling them tremble.

'Well, whoever it was, you've been threatened and you should report it.'

'I'm not reporting it to Damien.' She spoke more forcefully as the initial shock of the call began to fade. 'He already thinks I'm too interfering, and I'm not giving him the ammunition to make him think I'm a neurotic female as well.'

'I didn't mean him. I mean the DI who's involved with the Pargeter case. You have to report it, Rosie,' he repeated seriously.

She was suddenly angry. 'I don't see why I should let Edgar Pargeter ruin our weekend, if that's who it was. But if it wasn't him, who else could it have been? I haven't upset anybody else, as far as I know.'

'Well, only the two thugs you saw at the funeral for mentioning them to the police, and the ex-boyfriend for trying to do his job, and probably the two Bristol cops as well,' he said more indulgently. 'That's enough of a list, I'd say.'

'So you really think I should let them know about this?' she said.

'I think everybody should report a threatening phone call. Give them a bit more paperwork to do. It keeps them off the streets,' Charlie told her in an effort to lighten the mood when he was feeling anything but complacent. Because if Rosie didn't report it, he knew damn well he would.

'All right, but not here,' she said at last, seeing the sudden interest the landlady was taking in the two of them. 'Let's go up to your room.'

'That's the best offer I've had all night,' he said with a grin.

* * *

DI Forster was looking forward to the weekend and a round of golf if the ground wasn't too sticky after all the rain they'd had earlier in the week. Locke was having a laugh with some of the duty personnel, and already preparing to leave the building. Forster was about to pack it all in on Friday evening when the phone rang on his desk.

For a minute he was tempted to ignore it, but it might be something important, and habit was too ingrained in him to do so. He picked it up with an impatient sigh and just said a short 'Hello', in the hope of not needing to answer any more official calls tonight.

'I've got something to report,' said a

hesitant female voice he didn't recognise immediately.

'Please hold on a minute while I pass you on to somebody to take down the details,' he said with relief.

'No, wait! Don't fob me off like that. I don't want to speak to anybody else. I need to speak to you. That is Detective Inspector Forster, isn't it? It's me, Rosie Redman.'

God Almighty! He groaned, wondering what damn fool idea she'd got in her head now. *Amateurs . . .*

'Unless you've got something significant to say, can you make it quick, Miss Redman?' he said, already seeing his golfing weekend slipping away.

'How significant is it to report that somebody has warned me to keep my nose out of his business?'

There was a small pause when she could almost hear him digesting her words. Then he spoke more sharply.

'What kind of warning was it? A letter, text message, email or what?'

'Nothing so elaborate. Just a common or garden phone call, that's what,' she said, starting to feel resentful of his impatience.

'Well, did you know the caller, and did you do a 1471 to get his number?'

Rosie held on to her temper. 'Inspector

Forster, I wasn't born yesterday. I don't know who it was, though Charlie thought it had to be Edgar Pargeter. And of course we tried 1471, but they didn't have the caller's number.'

'When did this happen, Miss Redman?' He ignored the irritating fact that the reporter would have to be with her.

'About half an hour ago.'

'Right. Leave it with us, Miss Redman, and we'll deal with it.'

'How are you going to do that if you don't know who it was likely to be?'

But by then he had hung up and she was left looking in frustration and annoyance at her phone.

She turned to Charlie. 'Well, I suppose he was marginally interested.'

'Of course he was. Nobody leaves a message like that without a reason, and I'd say you should be extra careful from now on, Rosie. Somebody doesn't like you, and there's only one person I can think of who would call especially to warn you off.'

'I'm not doing anything to harm Edgar! I'm just looking out for Edith's interests, that's all.'

Charlie tried not to sound too alarmist. 'I'd say you've done quite a bit to harm Edgar with all your suspicions about him, and he's got a lot to lose if any of it is proved true.'

Rosie shivered. She had never really taken to Edgar Pargeter, but she knew how much he had always seemed to care for his sisters, and that counted for a lot. All the same, she had never considered herself to be in any real danger, but the phone call had definitely unnerved her, and Charlie wasn't actually helping now. She wished they could all go back to several weeks ago, before anything had happened. When the factory was still across the fields from Bately, and Edith was still chattering about the latest romance book she was reading. But you couldn't ever go back and change the past . . . and besides, if none of this had happened, she wouldn't have met Charlie, so there was a bonus to it all.

Even as she thought it, she felt her eyes prickle, knowing that meeting Charlie was also at the expense of losing Edith.

'What are you thinking now?' he said.

'I'm trying not to think at all, and I'm switching off my phone.'

'Good. Then now that you've done your duty and reported it, I think we should go back down to the bar and socialise, and forget all about mysterious phone calls that probably mean nothing.'

But she knew he didn't believe that, and neither did she.

★ ★ ★

'We'd better get over to the General and see that lunatic Pargeter again, and see if he knows anything about this phone call to the Redman girl,' Forster snapped, after passing on the latest information to Sergeant Locke.

Locke was also less than pleased at having his evening disrupted. 'She's probably getting paranoid about the bloke now — and I've got a date tonight, Sir.'

Forster rolled his eyes. 'Well, whoever it is, she'll just have to wait, won't she? I'm not exactly thrilled at spending any more time with Mickey Mouse either, but that's life.'

Locke groaned, knowing he couldn't get out of it when Forster got that steely look on his face. He might scoff at what he considered to be Rosie Redman weaving fairytales, but the Pargeter bloke was not high on anybody's list as a charmer. There was definitely something dodgy about him, and the sooner they could get this case sorted, the better.

They drove to the hospital and went straight to the reception and spoke to a girl they hadn't seen before. As ever on a Friday night, the hospital was busy with drunks and minor accidents, even this early in the evening, and Forster told her they were here to see Edgar Pargeter, refusing to be so undignified as to ask for Mickey Mouse.

'Oh, you mean the river patient,' the girl said blankly after a moment. 'I'll have to call for somebody to speak to you about him, if you'll wait a minute.'

'Don't bother, we know the way,' Forster said.

'Here, hang on a minute!' the girl called out indignantly, but by then they were striding along the corridors in the direction of the side ward where they had last seen Pargeter. They went straight inside, hoping to surprise him.

They surprised somebody all right, but it wasn't Edgar Pargeter. The elderly woman in the bed he had occupied took one look at the two strapping, dark-suited men bursting in, and began screaming as loudly as she could while she fumbled for the bell at the side of her bed.

As Forster was still trying to apologise, his face an angry and embarrassed red, several nurses came rushing in.

'What do you think you're doing?' one of them gasped, clearly outraged, while the other one tried to placate the woman as best she could.

'I'm sorry,' Forster snapped, whipping out his ID card and thrusting it at her. 'We need to speak to Mr Pargeter, the patient we interviewed in here a few days ago. Has he been moved elsewhere?'

The nurse glowered at him, totally unimpressed by the sight of the ID card.

'Mr Pargeter discharged himself yesterday, and very foolishly too, if I may say so. He was in no fit state to do so, and now if you'll excuse me I need to see to my patient, and I'll thank you, Detective Inspector Forster, for not barging into my wards unannounced in future.'

Without waiting to hear any more, the police officers turned and went out, with Locke muttering that he wouldn't want to cross that one in a hurry.

Forster spoke furiously.

'She was right, of course, and we should have checked first. But from the sight of him when we last saw him, nobody would have expected Pargeter to discharge himself.'

'So where is he now?' Locke said, the likelihood of his date that evening disappearing fast.

'Well, presumably at his flat. We'll get back there and check it out. I've got an uneasy feeling about this now.'

'If he was the one who made the threatening call to the Redman girl, I doubt that he could have tried to get back to

Bately-sub-Mendip in the state he was in, could he?'

Forster frowned. 'That's something I'd rather not consider, but having given her a verbal warning, my guess is he'll wait for her reaction before he does anything else. But who knows what anyone will do if they're driven to it?' he added grimly. 'But we can't waste time speculating. A wounded animal always crawls back home to lick his wounds, so we'll try there before anything else.'

A short while later when they had driven across the city, they each felt a sense of relief as they saw the light from the window of Pargeter's flat.

'So he made it home. What now?' Locke said, still hoping to salvage something of this wasted evening.

'We go and ask him about the phone call to the Redman girl. He won't be expecting it, and he won't be expecting us either, so it's shock tactics, Locke.'

They went up the stairs at the rear of the building, and hammered on the door of the flat. After a few minutes there were shuffling movements inside, and then they heard Pargeter's harsh voice.

'Go away. Whoever you are, I'm ill and I'm not seeing anybody.'

'It's DI Forster and Sergeant Locke, Mr

Pargeter. Open the door, please, unless you want your neighbours overhearing what we've got to say.'

He didn't reply immediately, and then they heard bolts being drawn back and a chain being removed. For a man who frequently handled large quantities of money in business hours, Pargeter obviously took no chances in his flat either.

'Good God, man, what the devil did you think you were doing, discharging yourself from hospital?' Forster said at once, trying to ignore the sight of him for the moment.

But not for long. The smell of whiskey was evident. Edgar's face was still swollen and etched with pain, the area around his bruised eyes was still rainbow-hued, and he held his ribs when he walked.

'What's it to you?' he growled, sinking gingerly into an armchair.

'You're in no fit state to be fending for yourself right now, that's what it is to me, and anybody with any sense would have stayed in hospital,' Forster said sharply. 'But apart from your obvious injuries, I take it your brain's still in working order.'

'What's that supposed to mean?'

He took a quick slurp from the large glass of whiskey by his side, which was probably not the best sustenance in the circumstances.

The bottle was already half empty. Apart from that and a half-eaten sandwich on a plate, a quick look around the room showed that nothing had been disturbed since the officers' last visit here.

Locke consulted his notebook. 'Did you make a threatening phone call to Miss Rosie Redman earlier this evening?'

Pargeter's eyes narrowed as best they could. 'Christ Almighty, is that bitch still trying to make trouble for me?'

'Answer the question please, Sir,' Forster said evenly.

'Do I look in any fit state to bother making threatening phone calls?' he tried to shout. 'It's as much as I can do open my mouth to take a drink and force any food down without having to answer your damn fool questions as well.'

'Do I take it that you're denying it then?' Forster stated.

Edgar scowled, and the word gargoyle came to Forster's mind.

'Of course I do. The less I have to do with that little tart the better. Now go away and leave me alone.'

'Don't you think you should still be receiving hospital treatment, Sir?' Locke put in, seeing the difficulty with his breathing.

'No, I effing well don't. I'm perfectly

capable of sorting myself out, without those effing nurses fussing over me all the time.'

'That kind of language won't do your cause any favours, Mr Pargeter,' Forster said coldly.

'So unless you want to hear some more, get out!'

Forster tried another tactic. Rosie Redman's accusation wasn't the only thing that needed investigation. 'After the damage that was done to your sister's cottage after the funeral, Sir, for which you have our utmost sympathy, has anything been disturbed here while you were in hospital?'

Edgar flinched and took another swig of whiskey.

'God knows. I'm in no mood to start inspecting the place, but since you ask, it doesn't look like it, does it?'

'And how about your business premises?' Forster persisted. 'Have you managed to go down there to take a look?'

'Only to put up a notice to say that business will be closed for a while owing to illness,' he growled. 'Look, all this talk is killing me, so that's all you're getting out of me.'

Forster nodded towards Locke, who went down the stairs leading to the bookie's premises below. They had been ransacked. In particular the cash drawer had been wrenched open, and the safe door was hanging on its hinges, the contents removed. Reporting it to his boss upstairs, it was obvious that Pargeter must have seen all this, but he hadn't seen fit to make a complaint, which was suspicious in itself.

'Is it likely that your premises were ransacked by the same person or persons who vandalised your sister's cottage, Sir?' Forster said.

'How the hell do I know! I'm not an effing clairvoyant! Look, I need to get to bed. My head's bursting.'

'Just a few minutes more, Sir. Would you mind telling me how much money your sister left you? And the insurance money you are expecting for the loss of the factory?'

'That's my business,' Pargeter snapped.

'I'm afraid it may very well be our business as well, especially if you're in any financial difficulty, and are perhaps being blackmailed. You do know that under English law, insurance money cannot be paid out on a property where a suspected crime has been committed.'

He stared at Pargeter blandly, already well aware of the vast amounts of debts and unpaid bills the man owed. Edgar gave a harsh laugh, even though he had gone visibly paler beneath the rainbow hues of his face.

'I'm not answering anything else without my solicitor present.' His words were getting slurred now, and he staggered to his feet. 'You know the way out.'

'We only want to help, Sir. Has anyone been threatening you?' Forster persisted, fully aware of the messages they had heard on the man's answering machine. There was no longer any light flashing, so either he had listened to the messages or simply switched it off.

'*No!* Why the hell would they?'

'Just one more thing, then, Mr Pargeter, and we won't bother you again tonight,' Forster said. 'Do you know a man called Denny?'

At the question, Pargeter's face took on a strange, greyish hue and he seemed to be struggling with his speech.

Forster spoke quickly. 'All right, I can see you've had enough, so we'll leave it for now, Sir. Would you like me to call a doctor for you? It really was very unwise of you to discharge yourself from the hospital.'

'*No!* No bloody doctors!' he croaked.

As he blundered off towards the bedroom, it was clear they were getting nothing more out of him tonight, and the two officers let themselves out of the flat. If Pargeter had anything more devious in mind, then unless

he was superhuman he wasn't going anywhere for a while yet. Forster was also certain
from his reaction that he had known Denny,
and probably also far more about the whole
factory fire business than he let them believe.
And if that accounted for his sister's death
also, the bastard could be looking at a murder
charge.

★ ★ ★

As the evening wore on and the Bately pub
became its usual sociable place, filled with
people she knew, Rosie's nerves were still
taking a while to settle down. Friday was pay
day for many of the locals, and the pub was
always a hubbub of noise, but the usual
minutiae of village life had taken second place
now, and much of the chatter was centred
around the flurry of activity at Edith's
cottage.

The brother had obviously organised it
quickly, since there was a team of people
from outside the village clearing out the
damaged furniture, and cleaners and decora-
tors working on the paint-spattered walls.

'It was all a bit damn hasty, if you ask me,
though it had to be done, o' course, and it
was obvious he didn't want none of us locals
getting involved,' Bert Smith remarked with a

sniff, parking himself on a chair beside Rosie and Charlie. 'Don't see why he couldn't have put a bit of money our way though, instead of hiring outsiders to do the job.'

'I expect he wanted to keep everything as neutral as possible, Bert,' Charlie said. 'I understand that Miss Pargeter was a very private person, and perhaps her brother didn't want too many people who knew her dealing with her possessions. It might have been upsetting for them too, I imagine,' he added as an afterthought, remembering how Rosie and her aunt had been brought in to sort out some of her belongings.

'Well, it's still a pretty feeble excuse for taking the livelihood away from local folk,' Rosie said, agreeing with Bert.

'It's not as though the poor old dab had much to hide from anybody,' Bert went on, warming to it now, and banging his empty pint jug on the table, to which Charlie responded with a grin.

'Look, can we talk about something else?' Rosie said desperately. 'There's no point in going over and over what can't be changed. It's up to Edgar Pargeter to do as he thinks best, and we just have to live with it.'

Since there was little chance of avoiding all the cottage talk now, she realised she was still feeling agitated about the gutteral phone call she had received earlier. She still couldn't be sure that it was Edgar, but who else could it have been, and who else thought she was interfering in a private matter?

She wished she had never felt obliged to report it as Charlie had urged her to do, even though she knew in her heart it had to be done. But if DI Forster went to check it out with Edgar he would have to bring her name into it. That would really stir things up. She really didn't know why Edgar had always seemed to dislike her so much, when she had never shown anything but kindness to his two sisters. It was almost as if he was jealous of their affection for Rosie. In any case, she was damn sure she was never going to be flavour of the month as far as he was concerned now.

'Do you want to go home, Rosie?' Charlie said, his face coming into focus as she gazed vacantly ahead, her mind too full of unwelcome possibilities.

'No. I think I want another drink,' she said forcefully. She looked directly at Bert, now well into his next pint. Where did he put it all, she marvelled? He must have an ever-open tank.

'What did you really think of Edgar Pargeter, Bert?' she asked him.

'Didn't care for him. Slimy devil if you ask me.'

'But he really cared for his sisters,' she persisted. 'He wanted to look after them, didn't he? And they thought the world of him.'

'*Rosie!*'

She ignored Charlie's warning as Bert sniggered.

'I reckon it was to his advantage to care for 'em. Stands to reason, dunnit? They were so much older than him, so when they copped it, he'd be sure to come into money.' His rheumy eyes widened a little, as if something he had never really considered before suddenly struck him. 'Blimey, you don't think he had a hand in finishing off poor old Edith, do you? And Edna too?'

Charlie took control. 'You should be careful about spreading any rumours like that, Bert.'

'Well, I daresay I ain't the only one. There's plenty of gossip going on around here, especially with the brother not even bothering to come down and see how the house repairs are getting on. You'd think he'd take an interest, seeing as how he wants to sell it so fast, wouldn't you?'

He snorted, clearly still sore at the way he himself had been snubbed by Edgar after his offers to help the Pargeter sisters with all their odd jobs.

Rosie couldn't help feeling sorry for his obvious hurt. He was hardly one of the TV buffs who could turn a slum into a swish residence in the space of an hour, ha ha, and who believed that! But he was a good worker, and many local people relied on him for odd jobs, especially the older ones who enjoyed his endless supply of gossip as well.

'They're still at it, I take it?' she asked, as his face became glum. 'The cleaning firm, I mean?

'Oh ah. From early morning till night, and making a devil of a racket for everybody living near by.'

Charlie cleared his throat meaningly. If they didn't get off this subject, Bert was going to be complaining about the cleaners at the cottage all evening. But at least it took Rosie's mind off the phone call she'd had earlier, which alarmed him more than he let on to her. If it was Edgar Pargeter — and who else could it be? — then he could be an even nastier piece of work than they had first thought.

He saw her face lighten as Norman Youde and Frank Grey, one of his buddies, came into the pub. She waved them over, with the added relief that Bert went on his way to gossip with somebody else.

'Thank goodness,' Rosie said. 'I thought we'd never get rid of him.'

Norman laughed. 'So that's the only reason you wanted to talk to us.'

She could be embarrassed, or bluff it out. And she had known him long enough to do the latter.

'Of course. Don't I see enough of you all day?' she said airily, knowing he would take no offence.

'True enough. We'll go and get our pints and be back to join you.'

Rosie relaxed. Frank Grey had travelled extensively in the Far East, and once she got him on the subject she knew they'd be fine for the next hour.

But her attention wandered long before then. She couldn't get the phone call out of her mind, and if it really was Edgar, which she had to believe now, she didn't like the way he had sounded at all. He sounded so sinister . . . so *evil* . . .

'Are you feeling all right, Rosie?' she heard Charlie say a while later, and she realised she had been staring into space.

'I'm a bit tired, to be honest, and I've been promising myself an early night all week and haven't had it yet,' she improvised. 'I'm sorry, Charlie.'

'Don't be daft. We've got the rest of the

weekend.' He looked at their companions. 'I'll run Rosie home so keep my pint warm until I get back, OK?'

He knew very well what was troubling her, and by the time he had taken her home and gone back to join the others he hoped he had talked some sense into her and made some plans for the following day once her morning stint at work was over. A drive to the coast and lunch at a country hotel sounded pretty good to him.

Rosie promised to do as he said and try to put it all out of her mind. She didn't go straight to bed, which might make her auntie wonder if she was sickening for something, but instead she watched some inane game show on TV with her until she said she couldn't take any more.

Once in her bedroom she tried to get it all into perspective. Edgar had nothing on her, except to call her a busybody, and there were plenty of those around Bately-sub-Mendip. Gossip was rife in any case, so why pick on her! She tried to convince herself she was worrying over nothing, and she had just got into bed and switched her mobile on again, when it rang almost at once. She smiled, guessing that it would be Charlie wishing her a good night's sleep, and she answered cheerily.

And then her heart leapt and began to race erratically as she heard the same thickened voice she had heard earlier that evening.

'*I warned you, bitch.*'

16

Sick with panic, Rosie switched off her mobile with scrabbling hands. If she couldn't listen to the words, they didn't exist, despite the fact that they wouldn't stop drumming in her head. This was more than just a warning. It was a definite threat. She was scared and she was sweating, and her mind was in turmoil. She should tell her aunt and uncle, but she didn't want to worry them. She could call Charlie again, but what good would that do tonight? She probably wouldn't make any sense, anyway, and tomorrow would be soon enough.

She took some deep breaths, trying to calm down. DI Forster would think her a crazy woman again if she called him at this time of night. Maybe she should call Damien. After all, it was a police matter when somebody was threatened, and he was the nearest. But then he'd come tearing round here, wanting to know every detail and demanding to know what was going on, and why she hadn't contacted him before.

She dismissed the idea, although at some stage it probably wouldn't be such a bad idea to let him know that she was convinced that it was Edgar Pargeter who was making these calls. Maybe it would stop him thinking she was such a dunderhead — and she needed somebody local to be on her side.

There were so many *maybes* . . . and in the end she buried her head beneath the bedclothes and tried to make her mind a complete blank, even though she knew she was never going to sleep tonight.

★ ★ ★

But she must have slept at some stage because she awoke with a thumping head, and a sense of fury replacing the panic she had felt last night. How *dare* he treat her like this! Trying to frighten her off as if she was some silly little girl dabbling in his affairs. She kept that thought in mind while she ate as much breakfast as she could manage, avoiding her aunt's questions as to why she had such dark shadows beneath her eyes and if she was going down with something.

'Nothing like that, Auntie,' she said as cheerfully as she could. 'I probably had one too many glasses of wine last night, that's all. I'll be as right as rain when I've had some coffee.'

'You looked all right when you came

home,' Laura said, not altogether convinced. 'Perhaps you shouldn't go in to work today.'

'I have to. Saturday morning's always busy.'

Sometimes it was and sometimes it wasn't. But keeping busy was always the best thing in any circumstances. And besides, she was spending the rest of the day with Charlie. She bit into her toast more forcefully, as if she hadn't a care in the world.

But once into the village, she rang Norman to tell him she'd be a little late, and went straight to see Damien before she could change her mind. The thought of having another person besides herself and Charlie sharing her anxiety was a weird kind of comfort.

'Good God, to what do I owe this pleasure?' Damien said at once.

Rosie sat down heavily on the chair across the desk from him.

'There's no need to be sarcastic. I've come to give you some information.'

She saw his heavy sigh, and knew he'd be expecting some more crackpot theories about how and why Edith Pargeter died, and her thoughts about the wicked brother. Well, she had a few of those all right, but she was determined to keep calm and merely give him the facts.

Wasn't there some old American TV

programme where the detective spoke out of the corner of his mouth and used those very words?

'Give me the facts, Ma'am. Just give me the facts.'

'What is it, Rosie? I do have work to do,' Damien went on impatiently.

'Yesterday I reported an anonymous phone call to DI Forster in Bristol. I couldn't swear who it was, because the voice was thick and muffled, although Charlie was sure it was Edgar Pargeter.'

For a minute she thought he was going to explode at the sound of Charlie Walters' name, but he merely tightened his mouth.

'Go on,' he said.

'I hope DI Forster took me seriously, although I don't know if he did anything about it. But then last night, just as I was getting into bed, the same person rang me again, and this time it was an even more sinister threat. And before you ask, the number was withheld, but I *know* it was Edgar. And I'm *scared*, Damien.'

To her horror her eyes filled with tears, blinding her as her throat thickened and her voice cracked. This wasn't what she had intended. It wasn't what she wanted. She hated to appear so vulnerable. She didn't know why she had come here at all, expecting understanding from an ex-boyfriend who thought she was crazy . . .

The next minute she felt Damien's arm around her, and he was thrusting a box of tissues at her.

'Come on, kid,' he said in an oddly gruff voice. 'Take it slowly, and tell me exactly what happened. What did the caller actually say?'

'He said — ' she swallowed hard. 'First of all he said 'Keep your nose out of my business'. That was early in the evening. And then, much later as I told you, he said 'I warned you, bitch'. Are those the words of a sane person?'

Damien went back behind his desk and scribbled down some notes.

'How long was it between these phone calls, Rosie?'

'I don't know. About four or five hours, I suppose. We were in the pub when the first one came, and I phoned DI Forster about it straight away. I switched my phone off after that, and didn't switch it on again until I got home and went to bed. I thought it might have been, well, somebody else, not him again,' she ended with a sob.

She hoped Damien would ignore the obvious implication that she would have thought it was Charlie Walters calling her to check that she was all right.

'So if, as you believe, it was Edgar Pargeter making these calls, it would have given DI Forster time to check on the first one before you got the second one,' he said.

Rosie looked at him blankly. Of course it would. Where was her so-called detective mind now? Why hadn't she thought of that? But ever since the second phone call, she hadn't been thinking rationally at all.

'Have you informed DI Forster of this second call?'

She shook her head. 'I haven't told anybody but you so far. I guess I just wanted somebody local to know, somebody close at hand that I could trust, just in case anything happened. Anything bad,' she said finally.

'Well, thank you for that vote of confidence,' Damien said briefly. 'It's good to know that you still think of me as a trusted friend, Rosie.'

'There's no reason why I shouldn't, is there? We've known one another too long to be at loggerheads.'

'True. So I'll file this report and send it through to DI Forster. He has to know about it, of course.'

'I know, and at least I won't have to hear his impatient sighs coming down the phone line,' she added.

Damien stood up again, signalling that it

was time for her to leave.

'Try not to brood on it, Rosie, and if anything else happens, come straight to me, all right?'

She finally managed a smile. 'I promise,' she said.

* * *

It was just as she had told herself. It was good to have somebody local on her side. She went to work feeling considerably lighter than she had before. The morning passed quickly, the way Saturday mornings usually did, and before she knew it, Charlie had poked his head in the door.

'I want to go home and change once I've finished here,' she said, 'and you can pick me up half an hour after we close, OK?'

'Sounds good to me,' he said, and she realised that as yet he had no idea of the turmoil she had been going through since the second phone call last night, nor that she had gone straight to Damien instead of confiding in him.

How was he going to take that when they had become so close? But that was the least of her worries, and temperamental boy-friends were best left between the pages of romantic novels.

But by the time she had changed into jeans and t-shirt and jacket, the nerves were catching up with her again. There had been no more phone calls, but what would happen when DI Forster got Damien's report? If he went storming round to Edgar's flat, would there be even more abuse coming her way? Or would he just think she was a ridiculously neurotic female?

The hell of it was, she had somehow become caught up in this whole affair that had started with the doll factory being burnt down and an unknown man trapped to his death inside it. And then the discovery of poor Edith Pargeter's drowned body that had shaken the village to the core. None of it had been fully resolved as yet, but now, because of what Edgar Pargeter was doing, it seemed to Rosie that she was suddenly the victim, the one who was in danger through no fault of her own.

'You're very quiet today,' Charlie said as they drove through the village and out on the open road. 'What's up? If you're still worrying over that phone call, try to put it to the back of your mind, Rosie. He can't harm you here.'

'There was another one,' she said abruptly.

'What? When?'

'Last night as I was getting into bed. I

didn't want to call you at the time, since there seemed no sense in both of us worrying.'

By the time she finished speaking he had already pulled over to the side of the country road and turned off the engine. His voice was harsh.

'Tell me exactly what he said.'

'He said 'I warned you, bitch'. Just that. At least, that was all I heard before I switched off the phone.'

She was shaking by just reliving the moment, and having to repeat it for the second time that day. Charlie had grabbed both her hands, and he felt how cold they were.

'You should have called me, no matter how late it was. Have you reported it to Forster yet?'

She shook her head. 'I went to see Damien before work this morning. I thought it was best to let him know, being a local man, in case anything unusual should happen. He's an old friend, Charlie, and he was going to send a report to DI Forster later today.'

She didn't know why she should sound so defensive, and it was probably her imagination that the atmosphere had gone a few degrees colder, but she wasn't imagining the fact that Charlie had let go of her hands. Oh God, whoever said women had priority on being possessive?

'You probably did the sensible thing,' he said at last. 'So why don't we put it all out of our minds and just have a good day? Does Minehead sound all right to you?'

Rosie wasn't sure if he was hurt or defensive or just being bloody-minded and pretending that it didn't matter that much to him at all.

'Sounds great,' she muttered.

'Good,' he said, starting up the engine again. 'And when I get back to town tomorrow night I'll take a look around Pargeter's place. I wouldn't mind having a few choice words with him myself.'

She felt a flood of relief that he did care, as she had always known that he did. But if Pargeter was a more violent man than he had appeared to be when his sisters were alive, she wouldn't want to risk him getting hurt.

'I'm not sure that's such a good idea. Leave it to the police, Charlie.'

'We'll see. Don't worry, I don't fancy being the next murder victim on Edgar's list. Now shut up, woman, and enjoy the view.'

He was smiling as he said it, teasing her, and he squeezed her hand before returning it to the steering-wheel. She gave a small shiver all the same. Putting it into those words . . . *being the next murder victim on Edgar's list* . . . had made the possibility all too horribly real. But she could tell that Charlie was determined not to let the day be spoiled, and so was she. They spent a carefree couple of hours on a windswept Minehead beach and racing back shrieking with laughter from the waves; eating fish and chips in a beach-side café; and then going to the cinema and holding hands in the back row like a couple of teenagers.

It was late in the evening when they returned to Bately. Rosie invited him into the house for coffee, where her aunt and uncle were watching television.

'Well, today's certainly done you good,' Bernard said heartily. 'I'm told you looked really peaky this morning.'

'We've had a lovely day,' Rosie replied without any more explanation.

'Good,' said Laura. 'And you'll come for Sunday lunch tomorrow, won't you, Charlie?'

He agreed at once, and Rosie couldn't help thinking that it was all going rather well. If you could ignore the bad happenings of the past few weeks, and in particular those of Friday evening, then life was looking good.

★ ★ ★

Charlie drove around the city on Monday morning as soon as he could get out of the office, feeling far less complacent than he had let on to Rosie. As he approached Pargeter's betting shop, he couldn't miss the large notice on the door, announcing that the shop was temporarily closed due to illness. Upstairs, the curtains of the flat were still drawn across, even though it was nearing midday. He felt a new alarm, wondering if the bastard had decamped somewhere near Bately-sub-Mendip, which might put Rosie in real danger. Charlie had long ago decided that Pargeter must be twisted, if all Rosie's theories were true. And he, for one, totally believed that they were.

But a quick glance through the letterbox of the betting shop revealed the piles of letters and flyers and other junk mail on the floor. Many of the letters were in ominous brown envelopes. It was impossible to see anything else in the room, as discretion for the business Edgar was in, kept it as private as possible.

'You won't get no luck there today, mate,' he heard a voice say behind him. 'The place has been locked up for days, so if you're wanting to collect any winnings, you'll have to wait, like the rest of us.'

'Do you know what's wrong?' Charlie said, declining to give any more information to the unshaven bloke lounging by the wall.

The man shrugged. 'Couldn't say. Pargeter

was always a close one, and since that business with his sister and the fire and all, he's gone a bit queer in the head, if you ask me. Either that or she left him a packet of money and he's gone off to Barbados with it,' he said, sniggering at his own joke.

'Thanks,' said Charlie.

He got back into his car before the man could launch into some other imaginary plan that Edgar might have had. The fact was, the shop was shut, and Edgar didn't appear to be here, and that was alarming enough. He drove straight round to the police station and demanded to see DI Forster.

'What's it about?' a bored constable asked.

'Just tell him it's Charlie Walters from the *West Gazette*, and I'm sure he'll see me,' Charlie snapped.

He was more confident than he sounded, knowing there was no love lost between him and the senior officer.

'I thought you looked a bit familiar,' the constable said with barely perceptible interest. 'Wait here.'

Charlie wasn't in any mood for waiting around, but it was a good ten minutes before he was ushered into a room where DI Forster sat behind a desk. Like a middle-aged potentate on a throne, came to mind . . .

'What do you want, Walters?' he was

greeted. 'If you've come to tell me about the phone calls Miss Redman's been receiving, I know all about them, and the matter's being dealt with.'

Forster leaned back in his chair, hands behind his head in a manner that infuriated Charlie. He was hard-pressed to keep his temper, but common sense told him he would get nowhere with Forster if he started lashing out.

'Good. That saves me wasting my breath. I've just been round to the betting shop and it's closed up. There's a pile of mail inside, and the upstairs curtains are drawn. So where is Pargeter? And if he's not in his flat, don't you think you should be taking these threats to Miss Redman more seriously than you seem to be doing?'

The next minute the chair came crashing down and Forster glowered across the desk at him, his eyes murderous.

'Don't tell me how to do my job, Walters. Why should I know where Edgar Pargeter has been recently, and where he is now?'

'You damn well should know if you're still following this case,' Charlie said, too enraged to care what he said now. 'And before you tell me it's none of my business, I'm here on Miss Redman's behalf, and she certainly has a right to know, since she's been threatened.'

Forster spoke shortly. 'All right. Pargeter was badly beaten up and fished out of the river near the General Hospital. He was detained for a few days, and then he discharged himself, very much against medical advice. As for where he is now, when I saw him on Friday night, he was in no fit state to be going anywhere. He could hardly drag himself around his flat, and for such a vain man, my guess is he's simply shut himself away, rather than let anyone see the state of his pretty face. Now get out of my office.'

'You saw him on Friday night?' Charlie persisted. 'Was that after Rosie reported the first phone call?'

The implication was obvious to him, if not to Forster. If it was so, then Pargeter would have been incensed that she had reported him, and that was why he had made the second call.

'Mr Walters,' Forster said with exaggerated patience. 'I assure you we are still conducting this entire case with great seriousness, and I can also assure you that Edgar Pargeter is going nowhere at the present time.'

Charlie knew he would get nothing more out of him, but at least he was relieved to hear that Pargeter was as incapacitated as Forster said. He had no reason to doubt it, and he phoned Rosie as soon as he could, glad to put her mind at rest.

★   ★   ★

Edgar Pargeter had dragged himself out of bed by mid-morning, bemoaning the business he was losing because of present circumstances. Even so early in the day, he was well tanked up on whiskey and painkillers, despite knowing that the combination could be lethal. But he needed something to get him through the day. Enforced isolation didn't suit him. He needed to see people, even though he wouldn't want people to see him now. He positioned himself on a chair by the window of his flat. He was hidden behind his curtains, but they were flimsy enough to enable him to see the comings and goings in the street below.

He didn't recognise the car that parked on the other side of the street, but he recognised the bugger who got out of it all right. It was that effing reporter who seemed to have taken Rosie Redman under his wing, and was probably knocking her off at every opportunity. He felt his blood begin to boil at the thought, not with lust, since such emotions were not a part of Edgar Pargeter's persona, but with outrage that his carefully thought-out plans were all falling apart. And this smart-assed bugger, through his association with the Redman girl, to put it politely, was part of the problem and was as good as stalking him.

He leaned forward, careful not to disturb the curtains, and guessed that Walters was trying to see inside the shop. Well, hard luck to that, because it was an unspoken rule in his profession, that outsiders didn't see the punters who came to place their bets, nor what went on inside. He didn't miss the sound of the letterbox though, just as he'd heard it earlier that day when probably yet more bills came thudding through, so he guessed that the bugger was taking stock.

Then he heard the voice of one of his regulars, and felt a sense of relief that what he said was enough to send the reporter on his way. He had a bit of a chortle at the thought of going to Barbados to spend Edith's money, but the chortle turned to a sob as he wondered when or if he was ever going to get any of it. Then the sob changed to a scowl that hurt his bloody face as he heard old Toby say that he thought Edgar had gone a bit queer in the head lately.

Effing queer in the head, for Christ's sake! Who wouldn't go a bit queer in the head after all that had gone on since the fire, and how everything had gone wrong? He felt the beat of his heartbeats jangle and jump. Years ago, when he was just a child, there had been talk among his doctors that there was something missing in his head. Some medical term that he didn't understand, and his parents had hidden it from him. He only knew it had something to do with his being a very late baby, born to elderly parents and that he'd been starved of oxygen at his difficult birth. It was why his sisters, so much older than himself, had made such an extra special pet of him all his life. He was their special baby, and when their parents had died, they had cosseted him even more.

But there was nothing wrong with him! How could there be, when he had made such a success of his business? That he'd been in and out of school, playing truant more often that he'd attended, and not interested in girls when the rest of his classmates had mocked him unmercifully at the time, had nothing to do with anything. His thoughts were becoming muddled with the effort of remembering — or rather, trying *not* to remember some of those times.

But the images kept swimming up in front of him, like ghostly reminders that wouldn't go away. There was one hateful incident in particular when some of the older boys had caught him in a school toilet, taunting him and chanting at him for his small dick. They'd called it a bloody *miniature,* and no use to anyone. Then they'd sat on him and tied it up with a red ribbon so tightly that he'd had to beg for mercy until he'd peed himself and they'd all run off in disgust, and a teacher had found him and sorted him out to his intense humiliation.

Well, he'd shown them all now. Wherever they were, he was the one who ran a good business and a factory and had two sisters who pampered him and still thought of him as their baby . . . As the words filled his head he found himself whimpering as a burst of lucidity entered his mind, knowing it was all gone. All of it was gone. Edna was gone. Edith was gone. The cottage was in no state to be sold as quickly as he needed — and would anybody even want it now, considering its history? He'd never even thought of that. The factory was gone. Even those bloody grinning dolls were gone.

He dashed the feeble tears from his eyes, since they stung his bruises so much. There had to be something he could salvage from it all. Edith in particular wouldn't want him to be suffering like this. Edith loved her baby brother.

He hauled himself away from the window and punched out some numbers on his phone. It was time those bloody insurance agents paid out, and then he could put everything right and get back to where he belonged: the successful businessman who counted for somebody in this town. His accountant should see to it on his behalf. It was his job to look after him.

'Harry?' he barked, even though it was an effort to speak at all. 'Have you sorted out those bloody insurance agents for me yet? It's time they paid out on the factory.'

The voice at the other end was frigid.

'I'm sorry, Edgar, but it's going to take a while. They still need to investigate the cause of the fire, and until they can be sure it was an accident, they won't do anything. You know that.'

'Of course it was an accident. What else could it have been?'

'Come on, man. We both know there are plenty of causes for a place to catch fire. I'm not saying there was anything untoward in this one, but these people have to be sure, and the fact that there was a death involved complicates the investigation even more,' he pointed out tactfully, as if Edgar wasn't well aware of it.

'Well, see if you can gee them up. It's what I pay you for.'

'As a matter of fact, I was going to talk to

you about that, Edgar. You haven't replied to the last two letters I sent you, and there's a considerable bill outstanding.'

Edgar slammed down the phone. It probably wasn't the best thing to do in the circumstances, but since it seemed as though the whole world was against him, what did upsetting one more person matter a damn?

Without warning, he felt as though his bowels were turning to water, and he had to rush to the bathroom before he disgraced himself. At least, in his mind he was rushing, when in fact he was crawling, moving in slow-motion and holding on to every bit of furniture to get him there, since his ribs felt as though they were on fire with all the tension he'd been trying to suppress. He reached the bathroom in time and sat down thankfully on the toilet, but then a foul-tasting bile threatened to choke him, and he spewed his guts all over the bathroom floor.

The effort of puking had savagely hurt his ribs, and once he managed to recover a little and had got his breath back, he stared at the filthy mess in horror and disgust. Unmanly sobs surged out of him, wondering how the hell he could clean it up, and feeling unutterably alone as he had never felt alone before. Where was Edith, who would have taken such loving care of him in her sweet little cottage at the first sign of a cold? Where was Edna, with her soothing hands and blackcurrant cordial to put him right? Why did nobody in the world care what happened to him any more?

He was so dizzy with pain and self-pity that once he managed to haul himself off the lavatory he simply threw a bath towel over the disgusting mess on the floor and told himself he'd see to it later. Memories of Edith's gentle voice kept wavering in and out of his consciousness. Edith and her effing romances. One of her favourites that had been made into a film, and there was a line she always quoted whenever she was cooing at him and telling him not to bother his handsome head about anything, and that she would see to it later.

Gone with the wind. That was the name of the film. And the line she always said so softly . . .

'Don't worry, Edgar, my dear. I'll see to it all. We'll think about it tomorrow. After all, tomorrow is another day.'

He heard himself give a strangled laugh that sounded more like an animal in pain. Which he was. But she was right, Tomorrow was another day, and the mess on the floor wasn't going to go away if he left it exactly where it was. Maybe the angels would even come and clear it up, he thought in a kind of stupor.

His head was throbbing fit to burst, and he desperately needed his bed and to sink into sweet oblivion for a couple of hours, or as long as the whiskey and painkillers would let him. Tomorrow was another day, and so was next week, or as soon as he could get himself decently back to normal and do what he had to do. He couldn't even think what that was for the moment. Somewhere in the back of his mind he knew it had something to do with a girl who was blighting his life, and that she was going to get her comeuppance before he could achieve any real peace of mind.

But he couldn't be bothered with any of it right now. After all, tomorrow was another day.

17

Rosie was forced to accept that Edgar Pargeter wouldn't be going anywhere for the time being if he was feeling as ill as it seemed, and she prayed that once he recovered he would have come to his senses and realise how bad it looked for him to keep harassing her. He would know that she had alerted the police, and perhaps it was that, combined with the beating that had put him in hospital, that had made him so vindictive towards her. In her mind it was a bitter irony that he had survived drowning, the way poor Edith hadn't.

He would surely leave her alone now, not wanting any more suspicions heaped on him. Though you never knew what thoughts went through a madman's head, and after all that had happened she was quite convinced that he must be deranged. What sane man would harm his own sister?

She reminded herself that he hadn't actually killed Edith. Nor Edna, as far as anybody knew. But she was sure he had certainly been instrumental in starting off the whole process that had led to Edith's death, and nothing would make her changed her mind about that, short of a murderer coming forward to confess to everything. And she wouldn't put it past Edgar Pargeter to pay somebody to do just that!

As her thoughts chuntered on, she listened to herself with something like horror. When did her feelings towards Edgar turn to such outright dislike, almost approaching hatred? It hadn't been a sudden thing. It had been more insidious than that, like the drip drip of a tap that was simply annoying until it turned into a hammering that couldn't be ignored. But she would be well advised to ignore it now, or she'd be the one going out of her mind with fear.

★ ★ ★

Edgar was still hobbling about in his flat and taking no interest in anything but seething over the troublesome Rosie Redman. He'd had no further communication from the police so he felt lulled into a false sense of peace, so that he could just concentrate on getting himself fit again. Since he hadn't been able to get out of doors since discharging himself from hospital he was reduced now to eating whatever staples, packet and frozen meals he had in his cupboard and freezer, and these were getting in short supply. The last of the milk was off and he'd long run out of bread, but there were crisps and biscuits and black coffee and frozen chips, so he wasn't going to starve just yet.

A week after the police's last visit the smell of burning alerted him late one evening. It was coming from below, and he felt an acute sense of panic. If he didn't deal with it, he'd lose everything, including himself . . .

He had enough nous to grab a damp towel, and he struggled down the stairs to the shop as best he could. A burning packet of newspapers had been pushed through the letterbox and was quickly catching fire to the growing pile of mail inside. Well, bloody good riddance to all the bills it was devouring, was his first savage thought, but then he was thinking more of himself, as he smothered the fire with the damp towel, his hands and body shaking all over. If he'd been asleep, or out for the count on whiskey . . .

He had no doubt that it was the loan sharks who had done this. It was one more warning to add to all the others. Who knew what was going to come next? With sheer terror now, Edgar knew he had to get away from here as soon as possible. There was no way he could pay off even a fraction of his debts until something came through from

Edith's Will, the sale of the cottage, and the insurance on the factory, and it didn't look as though there was a snowball's chance in hell of getting any of it any time soon. He'd be dead before then.

In a cold sweat now, he swept up the unburnt letters in the damp towel. If this ever happened again, at least there'd be nothing for the fire to get hold of. He flung them away from him on the sofa in his flat and sank down on it, trembling all over. How the hell had everything gone so wrong?

His phone was ringing and he let it ring, knowing the answering machine would kick in. He hated the thing with its flashing, demanding light, but since Edna and Edith could never hold with new-fangled mobile phone numbers, he'd kept the old phone and the answering machine for their benefit. There was no need for it now, and he should chuck it in the nearest bin.

When the voice began to speak, he knew the menacing tones at once.

'We know you're there, Pargeter, and you've had your last warning. There won't be another.'

His gut clenched and he wanted to puke. He should call the police, but what would they do? Effing nothing, that's what. He wasn't high on their list of good guys at the moment, if he ever was.

One of the letters on the sofa caught his attention. It was bulkier than the others and stamped on the outside of the envelope was the name of the building and contractors' firm he'd hired to work on the cottage. He ripped it open with a kind of masochistic anticipation. Seconds later a wild, maniacal laughter left his lips, followed by uncontrollable sobbing as he tore the bill to shreds, and let the keys to the cottage slip to the floor.

He sat in the dark for a long time with his thoughts whirling before any semblance of sense came back to him. If he stayed here he knew what would happen. The loan sharks would never leave him alone now, and if they thought they were never going to get their money they would get their revenge in the only way they knew how. He'd already had too many tastes of that. They were a so — called legitimate business: it was only their methods that smacked of the Mafia.

Again, for one crazy moment he was tempted to call the police and report it all, and demand that he be given protection. He knew who the bastards were, and it wouldn't take much to put the police on to them. But those people always had answers for everything, and however shady their methods they presumably kept books to explain away their business dealings. The extent of his debts would come out, leaving him open to more suspicions about the factory fire and the death of that Denny bloke, and his sister . . . the tightness in his chest was gripping him like a vice now, and he abandoned the idea as quickly as it had come, fearful that he was heading for a heart attack.

He wished to God the pain would stop giving him so much grief so that he could get out of here and disappear for good where nobody would find him. But he couldn't do any of it until he got his strength back. Dosed up with whiskey and painkillers, just a few more days, that was all he needed . . .

He finally crawled into bed, burrowing down into the bedclothes in the same way he'd done as a child, fearing that the monsters of the night were going to come and get him. Hearing the soothing voices of his sisters, telling him not to worry, and that they would always be there to look after him. He could hear them now if he tried hard enough. Or even if he didn't try at all. They were always there in his head, reminding him that they loved him and would take care of him.

He wanted to shriek at them to go away and leave him alone. He wasn't afraid of ghoulies and ghosties, however loving they were! He was a man now and he didn't need them. But the choking shame in his throat that he couldn't suppress told him that he was far less than a man. He was a failure, A non-person. Even as the hateful word crept into his head, he felt the hot dampness in the bed and knew that he'd peed himself.

Oh God, oh God, oh *God* . . . how many times had Edna and Edith come to him at such times and told him not to be ashamed and that it happened to all children and that they would soon wash him and change him and make him clean and dry again? And he would feel their female hands over his privates, dabbing and drying, their voices cooing like a couple of effing doves as they tucked him back into bed again. Was that the reason he'd never been able to think of a woman in the way that normal men did? Because of their moon faces inspecting him, their calloused hands, pin-pricked with all the sewing, tenderly fondling him and keeping him as their baby?

Inside himself he was raging now, even though nothing came out except the hateful whimpering. But unless he was going to lie all night in his own piss, he knew he had to get up and do the business for himself. He'd never sleep anyway. Who could, with the threat of ruin, and worse, coming ever nearer?

Charlie phoned Rosie every evening now. He was careful not to let her know how much he worried about her, but in his business he'd come across a lot of twisted men, and Edgar Pargeter was up there with the worst of them. Once such people became obsessed about something or someone, they never let it go, and he knew that Pargeter was obsessed about Rosie's interference. She had thwarted him at every turn, throwing suspicion on him even if it was impossible to prove, and he wasn't going to forget it. Political correctness had rid the world of the words 'funny farm' and a good thing too, but in Charlie's opinion it was the only place where Pargeter needed to be.

'I've got a job to finish on the paper on Friday evening,' he told Rosie during the week, 'but I'll get down to Bately as early as I can. You don't finish until seven anyway, do you?'

'That's all right, Charlie. You don't need to mollycoddle me, you know.'

'I'm not. I just want to see you. That's all right, isn't it?'

She gave a forced laugh. 'Of course it is. But don't think I don't know that you've got another motive as well.'

'Well, somebody's got to look after you.'

'Everything's settling down here now, and although it's sad, I know life has to go on. The people working on Edith's cottage have moved out, and it's all quiet around there again. In fact, it's awful how quickly people seem to forget, and it's as if she never lived in Bately at all. I still miss her coming in to the library on Fridays to change her books. She loved her weekly quota of romance, even if it was only between the pages of a book.'

'Stop it, Rosie. You're letting this become an obsession, and you need to get out more,' he added, trying to lighten her mood. 'We should go dancing sometime. I've got two left feet, but it'll do you good. How about it?'

She laughed more naturally now. 'I'm not sure I could cope with that. But it sounds like a good idea.'

'Well, keep that thought in mind, and I'll call you again tomorrow.'

She wasn't all right, and she knew it. He uncle kept telling her she should take a holiday and get right away from Bately, since she had taken recent events so badly. But she'd already had her holiday for this year and she couldn't leave Norman in the lurch. Besides, if she went away, she wouldn't see Charlie, and he had become too much a part of her life now, to imagine it without him.

Edith Pargeter's cottage in Butcher's Lane was in a quiet backwater of Bately-sub-Mendip. Most outsiders would consider the entire village to be a quiet backwater, except for recent happenings, but there was a strong community spirit for all that, and a general respect for the memory of the poor lady who had died such a horrible death. Butcher's Lane had only a scattering of cottages, and now that the builders and other workers had gone, the few residents were thankful to be left in peace. There wasn't even a For Sale notice outside the place yet.

'I reckon that in due course Edgar Pargeter will inform an outside estate agent to get the sale moving,' Norman Youde remarked to Rosie on a particularly damp morning when the library was idle and most folk were staying indoors. 'I doubt that we'll see the likes of him down here again, and good riddance to him too.'

'You've changed your tune, haven't you?' she said, bringing them both a mug of tea. 'I thought you rather admired the way he looked after his sisters, or at least you never thought badly of him.'

'Well, that was then and this is now,' he said enigmatically. 'Anyway, you once thought he was all right, didn't you?'

She shivered. 'My parents brought me up to always believe the good in everybody unless it was proved differently.'

Now why had she said that? She hadn't thought of such a thing for years, but it was true. Her parents had gone to Africa to be missionaries when she was only eleven years old. Trusting people was part of their creed, but it was a bittersweet memory now. She had felt abandoned by them then, and she felt that same loss of abandonment now. She took a deep breath, shaking off the feeling of melancholy.

'I think I need a tonic,' she told Norman, echoing one of her uncle's favourite cure-alls. 'Charlie suggests we go dancing, and it would probably do me more good than a dose of medicine.'

'Attagirl,' Norman chuckled. 'I can just see you twirling the light fantastic dressed in feathers and boas.'

'Blimey, Norman, what century are you in?' she said with a grin. 'I think I've got too much up top to be a flapper!'

'And very nice it is too,' he said cheekily.

She laughed, knowing him too well to take offence at his nonsense. He had cheered her up, though, and she was determined to spend no more time worrying about things she couldn't control. Edgar Pargeter was miles away, and probably too busy feeling sorry for himself, getting himself fit again and counting out what money was coming to him, to bother about her any more. It was the best thought she had had for weeks.

★   ★   ★

Edgar would hardly call himself a wheeler and dealer, but he had always fancied himself as a bit of a Baldrick. With nothing else to do in his enforced idleness but wait for his bruises and pains to subside, he had plenty of time to think and scheme, and he now had a cunning plan. There had to be an end to all his troubles, and there was only one way to begin the process, as far as he could see. There was always a solution to any problem, and if you had a problem, you had to get rid of the cause. And his problem was Rosie Redman.

He ignored the two twittering female voices in his head that were condemning him so roundly. In a frenzied kind of acceptance, he had got used to them always being there now, always clamouring at him with their wisdom and advice, and trying to mould him to their ways. But they weren't going to change his mind over this. He was the man, not them!

And a man had to do what a man had to do . . .

He chuckled, rather partial to the way these corny old phrases kept running through his head. Who ever said there was anything wrong with cliches and the like? If they said just what you wanted to say, then to hell with the purists who looked down their long thin noses at them!

But his cunning plan had to be put into operation carefully. He shouldn't rush it, even though there was a certain amount of urgency if a bomb wasn't going to be the next thing on his doorstep. Action might be slow, but thought was quick, and he knew exactly what he had to do. It was devious and clever, and he congratulated himself on the way it was going to work out. And nobody would even know he had ever had a hand in it, just like . . .

He refused to let his mind go over the past. The future was what mattered now, and if he didn't do as he planned, there might not be one for him at all.

Late on Wednesday night, he let himself out of the flat quietly, and walked stealthily through the streets of the city, glad of their rowdiness as the pubs spilled out their drunks as he reached the nearest taxi rank. There was no way he'd have driven his car, alerting folk to the fact that he was no longer in his flat. He carried a small bag, which was enough for his needs. Even so, his sides had already begun to ache, and he was glad to sink inside one of the taxis and bark out a destination.

'You sure you want to go all that way?' the cabbie said dubiously. 'It'll cost you.'

'That's no problem,' Edgar snapped. 'Do you want the fare or not? There's plenty of other taxis around.'

'OK, mate! Frome it is then. Not much a town to go visiting at this time of night, though, I'd have said.'

'I didn't ask for your opinion. Just drive,' Edgar growled.

He sat back, trying to ignore the jolting of the taxi and closed his eyes for the journey, until at last he felt the car come to a stop.

'Here you are, Sir. Middle of town, such as it is. Have a good evening.'

Edgar ignored the sarcasm and thrust some money into his hand as he got out carefully. It was raining again. It had to be bloody raining, he thought, but that was the least of his troubles. He watched as the tail lights of the taxi disappeared from sight, and then he walked carefully around until he saw a late night corner store where he bought some milk and bread and a few meagre provisions.

He didn't expect the small town to be

thriving with taxis, but you could guarantee that there would always be one or two hanging about for late night revellers outside the pubs, and he found one easily enough.

'I want to go to Underwood,' he said to the driver. 'Do you know it? The outskirts will be fine.'

The man nodded. He was thankfully not a talkative sort, and Edgar sank into the back seat with a sharp wince of pain, wondering if this was such a good idea after all. But it had to be done. Feverish with intent now, this was the start of his cunning plan and Baldrick would be proud of him. His brain wasn't so warped that he couldn't work things out, and the hamlet of Underwood was near enough to Bately that he could cut across the fields and there would be none the wiser about his presence there.

In his pocket he had the keys of Edith's cottage — *his* cottage now, he reminded himself, and he could be holed up there until the next stage of his plan was ready to be put into operation.

★   ★   ★

Rosie was eagerly looking forward to Friday evening and seeing Charlie again. In a burst of generosity and sensing high romance,

Norman had insisted that she should take Saturday morning off, so that she could get titivated, as he called it, in preparation for Saturday night. By now she and Charley had arranged to go dancing at a new nightspot in Bristol then, and it was a pretty fair guess that they would end up at Charlie's flat for the night.

She felt a delicious shiver of anticipation. As Edith might have said:

When you find the right one, nothing else matters, and you should just do as your heart dictates.

Well, either Edith would have said it, or it was a line straight out of one of her Barbara Cartlands.

Whatever it was, it definitely felt right, and Rosie knew Edith would have been enchanted to know that she had fallen in love at last. It was poignant to think that but for what had happened to Edith, she would never have met Charlie at all. And how was *that* for a plot for one of her romances? Or was it more of a crime novel?

Rosie ignored the unwelcome thought as Friday became seemingly interminable. It had been raining all week, and the library, like everywhere else in the village, was sticky and humid. But at last it was seven o'clock, and they could close the doors on the last customer, and the weekend could begin.

''Night, Norman,' she called out.

''Night 'night, sweetie. Enjoy yourself, and don't do anything I wouldn't do!' he said archly.

She laughed, blowing him a kiss, and hurried to the alley alongside the library where she always parked her car. She never bothered to lock it, and she slid inside thankfully out of the rain and the ever-darkening sky, putting her bag and her mobile on the seat beside her as always. If Charlie should ring, to check that she had left work, she wanted it handy. The car smelled really stuffy, with an undefinable smell she couldn't readily identify, and she reminded herself to get it serviced asap.

She had driven away from the library and was halfway through the lanes towards home, when she fancied she could hear a kind of shuffling, and she told herself she must be imagining things. The next moment she gave a small shriek as she felt something cold and hard at the back of her neck.

'Keep driving, bitch, and don't stop until I tell you to.'

She gave a loud gasp, and sick with fear, she glanced into the driving mirror and saw the ugly face of Edgar Pargeter close behind her. She could feel his breath on her neck as

347

well. It was heavy and disgusting with the stale smell of cigar smoke.

'What do you want?' she croaked. 'What are you doing here?'

The hard metal was thrust harder into her neck. 'Shut up and just drive, and don't stop until you get to the quarry.'

'Why would I want to go there?' she stuttered, her heart thumping so hard she could hardly speak.

The rain was lashing down now, and she put her windscreen wipers on at full speed. They clicked rhythmically against the glass. With a presence of mind she hardly knew she possessed in the circumstances, and praying that Pargeter wouldn't notice above the noise outside, she scrabbled for her mobile phone and pressed Damien's speed-dial number. *Please pick up, but don't answer*; she begged silently and she began to talk loudly and frantically in the hope that he would be more on the ball than he sometimes appeared.

'I know who you are, Mr Pargeter, and there's no way I'm driving you to the quarry tonight.'

'You'll do as I say, bitch, or you know what's coming to you,' he snarled, with another shove at her neck with the hard object.

'What are you planning to do then? Kill

me, the way you killed that man in the factory — and Edith — and Edna too, I wouldn't wonder!' she said shrilly.

For God's sake, Damien, get the message. Keep quiet and record everything . . .

Pargeter gave a hooting laugh, but there was a horrible sense of satisfaction in his voice as he answered.

'A clever little tart, aren't you? But since you won't be in any position to tell anyone once we get to the quarry, I'll admit it. Not that I intended to kill Denny. That was a mistake. Nor was he meant to set the factory on fire, the effing fool. He was just meant to frighten Edith so that she'd agree to sell the factory and then I could pay off my debts. She wasn't meant to die either, but it served a purpose all the same.'

Was there actually a choke in his throat at those words?

'What about Edna?' Rosie's mouth was so dry she almost whispered now.

'Edna was always too much of a meddler. It was easy enough to put her pills out of reach and lace her coffee with a strong stimulant. It's surprisingly easy to kill someone,' he jeered, speaking very close to her ear now and trying to peer out of the window at the same time. 'But that's enough talking. Get a move on and let's get this over with.'

'You'll never get away with it,' she yelled as loudly as she could, and trying to suppress the terrified sobs welling up in her throat. 'My family will be expecting me home, and they'll check with my boss when I don't arrive.'

'Well, ain't that just too bad?' Pargeter said mockingly. 'It'll be too late by the time they find you — if they ever do. It's a nice bit of poetic justice for a book person that you'll end up the same way that Edith did, seeing as how you were always so fond of her.'

The roads in the village had petered out long ago and they were driving over rough tracks now, and the darkness of the moors loomed ahead, leading towards the quarry that was filled with deep, impenetrable water. Once anything was thrown in there, it was unlikely that it would ever be found again. Was this going to be her fate, Rosie thought in terror? Was there no way she could save herself?

She became aware of a new sound, and her heart leapt as she recognised Damien's urgent voice coming through her mobile phone.

Before she could scream at him, or hear what he was saying, Pargeter had suddenly lunged across the seats, causing her to swerve the car alarmingly, and for a moment she was tempted to crash it and risk killing them both.

But she didn't want to die, she thought, terror-stricken. She had too much to live for, and after that one moment of madness she held on tight to the steering wheel and righted the car. At the same time as Pargeter reached forward and grabbed her phone, she wrenched open the driving-side door and began running, as far away from him as she could. He leapt out behind her, stamping her mobile into the mud. It didn't matter. Damien would have got the message and heard everything, and even if she died tonight, Pargeter would get what he deserved.

She had no idea where they were, nor how near to the quarry itself, and she was momentarily winded as she tripped over a stump, blinded by rain, and still trying to quell her sobs so that he wouldn't hear. Then she screamed as she heard the blast of a gunshot, giving her position away. She tried to stay as silent as possible, listening to his cursing as his lumbering footsteps squelched in the muddy terrain. She remembered that he had recently been ill and wouldn't be anything like surefooted in the darkness and unfamiliar surroundings, and that gave her a sliver of hope.

Maybe he would even go over the edge and

into the quarry himself, and everything would be solved. But she didn't want that to happen, she thought savagely. She wanted him brought to justice for his crimes.

'You can't get away, bitch.'

She suddenly heard his voice, softer and nearer, and she almost squirmed into the mud and filth, willing herself to be as inconspicuous as possible. And then he was on top of her, falling over her, and yelling out with the pain of his injured ribs as he did so. But he had also dropped the gun, and scrabbling wildly, Rosie managed to kick it away, and they both heard the heavy plop as it fell into the quarry. Only then did she realise how very near to the edge they both were.

He was a short, heavily-built man, and despite his injuries, much stronger than her. Insanity was also giving him extra strength, and he would certainly be able to do what he had set out to do, and Rosie had no doubt now, that he was definitely insane.

Even as she struggled to get away from him, in a total panic, she heard the sound of a car somewhere in the near distance, accompanied by the scream of a police siren. It was coming closer and closer . . . *Thank God* . . .

With one burst of superhuman strength,

she somehow managed to wriggle out of Pargeter's slippery grasp and was running away from him, away from the quarry, gasping and sobbing, as fast as her shaking legs would move.

The next minute Damien's car had arrived, and as the doors flew open it seemed as if it was full of men, racing towards her.

'Never mind me! Find Pargeter. Don't let him get away!' she screamed.

She collapsed without being able to say another word, and when she came round she was sitting in the back of her own car with Charlie's arms around her. Right then she couldn't think how or why he was there. It was enough that he was holding her tight, despite the disgusting state she was in.

'Did they get him?' she asked hoarsely.

His voice was a mixture of shock and relief. 'Yes, thanks to you, Rosie. My God, what an ordeal you've had. But thanks to your ingenuity in leaving your mobile on speed-dial to Damien, he heard every word. The bastard won't get away with it now, and he'll have an extra count of attempted murder to add to all the rest of his crimes.'

'But how did you get here?' she said, a mite more sensible now. 'And who were all those men in Damien's car? For a minute I thought it was the arrival of the Keystone Cops.'

She tried to make a joke of it, but the joke caught on a sob.

'Damien got into his car as soon as he got the gist of your message, and I was just arriving at the pub when he grabbed me and a couple of others and told us what was happening on the way up here. Thank God he did. If anything had happened to you — '

He didn't finish the sentence, but he didn't need to. He merely wrapped her closer in his arms and she could feel his heartbeats as rapid as her own. She made a great effort to speak normally, her mind gradually filling with the enormous relief that Edgar Pargeter was no longer any threat to her, and never would be again. She took a shuddering breath, her voice husky with emotion.

'I must be making a hell of a mess of your clothes, and I stink to high heaven from all this mud. I need to go home and take a shower and wash his stink off me, and you probably need one too by now. My aunt and uncle will want to know what's happened, and my car will need to be fumigated, and maybe even finger-printed, but then please come back to the house for supper, and we can start the weekend properly.'

Charlie gave a half smile, well aware that she was talking too fast as usual with the release of tension, but full of admiration for the girl he was so crazy about.

'Exactly what I was thinking, and I think you should get a medal too.'

'What for?'

'For sticking to your beliefs, doing something the police didn't manage, and getting a confession out of Edgar Pargeter, even if you nearly got yourself killed in the process. You always said you'd make a good detective, didn't you?'

'I don't even want to think about that right now,' she said with a shudder, trying desperately to get her mind on to other things. 'Did you say something about dancing tomorrow night or did I dream it?'

'You didn't dream it, and we'll do it. I'm definitely not going to risk losing you again. Meanwhile, you're in no fit state to drive, so I'll take over, and no arguments, Miss Redman.'

'I never argue,' she said with a tremulous smile. 'I always did like a man who knew when to take control.'

We do hope that you have enjoyed reading this large print book.

Did you know that all of our titles are available for purchase?

We publish a wide range of high quality large print books including:
Romances, Mysteries, Classics
General Fiction
Non Fiction and Westerns

Special interest titles available in large print are:
The Little Oxford Dictionary
Music Book
Song Book
Hymn Book
Service Book

Also available from us courtesy of Oxford University Press:
Young Readers' Dictionary
(large print edition)
Young Readers' Thesaurus
(large print edition)

For further information or a free brochure, please contact us at:
Ulverscroft Large Print Books Ltd.,
The Green, Bradgate Road, Anstey,
Leicester, LE7 7FU, England.
Tel: (00 44) **0116 236 4325**
Fax: (00 44) **0116 234 0205**

Other titles published by
The House of Ulverscroft:

UNFORGETTABLE

Jean Saunders

Gracie Brown's dream is to become an acclaimed seamstress, but because of her background, she believes that success is an unattainable goal. Then, at the opening of the new Palais, she meets Charlie, a dashing saxophone player. Dancing in his arms, she begins to believe that dreams can come true. But a disastrous fire at the Palais breaks the spell and drives the couple apart. Gracie wonders if she will ever see Charlie again. But he is never to forget the girl he danced with at the Palais, and he pauses on his way to stardom to trace the girl he only knew briefly, but had loved from the first . . .

A PERFECT MARRIAGE

Jean Saunders

Robert Jarvis dies from a heart attack, leaving his wife Margaret a widow at forty-two. Family and friends rally round, but their attentions only serve to stifle her, and with increasing suspicions that her marriage had not been as perfect as it had appeared to be, Margaret longs to get away from it all. Six months later she revisits Guernsey, the scene of her honeymoon twenty-five years earlier. There she meets and becomes attracted to the confident Philip Lefarge, but after a night of torrid passion, Margaret is filled with guilt and indecision . . .

DEADLY SUSPICIONS

Jean Saunders

The discovery of a mutilated hand had closed the investigation into the disappearance of sixteen-year-old Steven Leng. Now, ten years later, the victim's mother is still determined to find out what really happened to her son. She contacts private investigator Alexandra Best, who discovers more about the incident in the woods that originally sparked off the mystery. Alex becomes convinced that Steven was murdered and her investigations lead her to the Followers, a religious group that appeared to fascinate Steven. Alex treads a dangerous trail that finally leads to a dramatic denouement.

WITH THIS RING

Jean Saunders

Tania Paget bitterly resented Frenchman Claude Girard, who had survived an appalling mountaineering accident, while her brother, James, had not. Then, astonishingly, Claude asked for her co-operation on a book about the two men's mountaineering exploits. Tania finally agreed, but it meant living in the Girard family chateau in the Pyrenees for six months. As she got to know Claude, Tania began to understand the male fascination with mountains. When Claude's own life was in danger, she discovered the truth about love as well.

GOLDEN DESTINY

Jean Saunders

Beautiful Alexandra Truscott sailed from England to join her diplomat father in India. On the long voyage she was captivated by Fraser Mackinnon, and in a sumptuous Calcutta palace discovered the depths of the handsome Scotsman's passion. Then the violence of a native rebellion shattered their gentle idyll and swept them apart. Disguised as a local, Alexandra must search through battle-fields to find Fraser — and their love.

AVENGING THE DEAD

Guy Fraser

1863. Superintendent Henry Jarrett, chief
of the detective department at Glasgow
Central, begins to investigate a forgery
scandal, involving the Union Bank . . . but
then the murders begin. Each killing is
claimed by a mysterious letter-writer
calling himself the Scythe, who declares
himself to be a righter of wrongs. The
writer is seemingly in possession of facts
known only to the detectives. Jarrett is
troubled — the lady in his life seems far
too interested in a dashing sea captain —
and the most recent murder is not
accompanied by the usual letter. Now it
seems that Jarrett has two killers to
contend with . . .